# SAVING RUNT

## COSMOS' GATEWAY BOOK 7

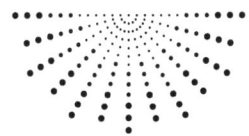

### S.E. SMITH

# ACKNOWLEDGMENTS

*I would like to thank my husband Steve for believing in me and being proud enough of me to give me the courage to follow my dream. I would also like to give a special thank you to my sister and best friend, Linda, who not only encouraged me to write, but who also read the manuscript. Also to my other friends who believe in me: Julie, Jackie, Christel, Sally, Jolanda, Lisa, Laurelle, Debbie, and Narelle. The girls that keep me going!*

*And a special thanks to Paul Heitsch, David Brenin, Samantha Cook, Suzanne Elise Freeman, and PJ Ochlan—the awesome voices behind my audiobooks!*
*—S.E. Smith*

SAVING RUNT: COSMOS' GATEWAY BOOK 7
Copyright © 2019 by Susan E. Smith
First E-Book Published July 2019
Cover Design by Melody Simmons
ALL RIGHTS RESERVED: This literary work may not be reproduced or transmitted in any form or by any means, including electronic or photographic reproduction, in whole or in part, without express written permission from the author.

All characters, places, and events in this book are fictitious or have been used fictitiously, and are not to be construed as real. Any resemblance to actual persons living or dead, actual events, locales, or organizations are strictly coincidental.

Summary: Living in the shadows of the hackers' world, Amelia 'Runt' Thomas plays a cat-and-mouse game with the most ruthless criminals in the world, until a new player enters the game and changes everything - Derik 'Tag Krell Manok, an alien warrior from another world who sees in Runt the bond mate he's been looking for all his life.

ISBN: 9781076118233 (kdp Paperback)
ISBN: 9781944125301 (eBook)

{1. Science Fiction Romance—Aliens. 2. Paranormal Romance. 3. Urban Fantasy. 4. Action/Adventure Romance. 5. Contemporary Fantasy}

Published by Montana Publishing.
www.montanapublishinghouse.com

# CONTENTS

| | |
|---|---|
| *Synopsis* | vii |
| *Cast of Characters* | ix |
| Prologue | 1 |
| Chapter 1 | 13 |
| Chapter 2 | 19 |
| Chapter 3 | 28 |
| Chapter 4 | 38 |
| Chapter 5 | 43 |
| Chapter 6 | 47 |
| Chapter 7 | 57 |
| Chapter 8 | 64 |
| Chapter 9 | 70 |
| Chapter 10 | 77 |
| Chapter 11 | 85 |
| Chapter 12 | 90 |
| Chapter 13 | 97 |
| Chapter 14 | 104 |
| Chapter 15 | 116 |
| Chapter 16 | 121 |
| Chapter 17 | 127 |
| Chapter 18 | 139 |
| Chapter 19 | 145 |
| Chapter 20 | 151 |
| Chapter 21 | 157 |
| Chapter 22 | 163 |
| Chapter 23 | 170 |
| Chapter 24 | 177 |
| Chapter 25 | 187 |
| Chapter 26 | 193 |
| Chapter 27 | 203 |
| Chapter 28 | 213 |
| Chapter 29 | 221 |

| | |
|---|---|
| Epilogue | 233 |
| *Additional Books* | 240 |
| *About the Author* | 245 |

# SYNOPSIS

Amelia 'Runt' Thomas' life revolves around a dangerous game of cat and mouse with the most ruthless criminals in the world. She follows two codes: the code of hackers and her personal code of honor to bring down anyone who thinks they're untouchable. She was on target until one fateful night when the touch of a strange man sends an unexpected shock wave through her. Now, the faint whispers in her head are growing louder and more annoying, distracting her from her mission.

Derik 'Tag Krell Manok's search for the mysterious woman who changed his life nearly two years before is finally over. As a Prime warrior from another world, he knew the moment he touched Amelia that she was his bond mate—but she disappeared before he could whisk her away to safety. He is determined not to let that happen again, but he also knows that he needs to proceed with caution because Amelia is unlike any woman he has ever known before.

As their connection grows, so does Derik's fear that he will be unable to keep Amelia safe from a man who is just as determined to find her and use her amazing talents for his own devious purposes. Find out what happens when an alien warrior, a determined AI named RITA, and a few other surprising twists come together to save a special woman named Runt!

Internationally acclaimed S.E. Smith has been awarded USA Today Bestseller 14 times! Now she's returning with another science fiction world that will come alive in your hands. This story's a slow burn romance for the ages with the perfect ratio of humor and drama. There's never been a thriller like it!

## CAST OF CHARACTERS

**Characters' Relationships:**
Teriff 'Tag Krell Manok, Leader of Baade - **mated to** Tresa: four sons, J'kar, Borj, Mak, and Derik and one daughter, Terra
Angus and Tilly Bell, humans—**married**: three daughters, Hannah, Tansy, and Tink

**Ruling family of Baade:**
J'kar 'Tag Krell Manok **mated to** Jasmine 'Tinker' Bell: twin daughters, Wendy and Tessa
Borj 'Tag Krell Manok **mated to** Hannah Bell: twin boy & girl, Sky and Ocean
Mak 'Tag Krell Manok **mated to** Tansy Bell: twin daughters, Sonya and Mackenzie
Terra 'Tag Krell Manok **mated to** Cosmos Raines
Derik 'Tag Krell Manok **mated to** Amelia Thomas aka Runt

**Mentioned Members of Cosmos' Security Team:**
Avery Lennox
Trudy Wilson

Rose Caine
Maria Garcia
Amelia 'Runt' Thomas

**Prime Warriors of Baade:**
Core Ta'Duran **mated to** Avery Lennox
Merrick Ta'Duran, Eastern Clan Leader, **mated to** Addie Banks
Hendrik, Northern Clan Leader, **mated to** Trudy Wilson
Brawn, Leader of the Desert Clan
Rav, Leader of the Southern Clan
Brock, J'kar's Chief of Security **mated to** Helene Baskov
Lan, J'kar's Chief Engineer **mated to** Natasha Baskov
RITA (Earth) **zapped by** FRED
RITA2 (Baade) **zapped by** DAR: two children: Darian and Rena.

**Juangans:**
**General Tusk:** Juangan Commander/father of Colonel Tusk
**Colonel Tusk:** son of General Tusk

**Humans**:
Karl Markham: Assassin/Mercenary/older half-brother to Weston Wright—deceased
Weston Wright: Assassin/Mercenary/half-brother to Karl Markham—deceased
Afon Dolinski aka Aaron Dolan: Former right-hand man to Boris Avilov
Boris Avilov: Russian Mafia boss—deceased
Richmond Albertson: US Secretary of State
Askew Thomas: President of the United States
Rex: CRI's pilot
Howard Swarovsky: DiMaggio's Hacker
Robert: Avery's driver
Karl Biggie: Thug for Ramon DiMaggio
Ramon DiMaggio: Small-time crime boss in Washington, D.C.

Marcelo Moretti: Chief of Security to Afon Dolinski aka Aaron Dolan
Bert: Undercover CRI agent
Lou 'Left-hand' Thomas: Amelia 'Runt' Thomas' father
Anne Davis-Thomas: Amelia 'Runt' Thomas' mother

# PROLOGUE

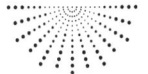

**Two years ago:**
**Washington, D.C. area near the old Navy yard:**

Amelia 'Runt' Thomas felt her black knit cap snag on a jagged piece of wire as she slipped through the opening someone had cut in the tall chain link fence. She paused on the other side and pulled her cap back down over her ears, then tucked her gloved hands into her pockets in an effort to keep them warm.

A black backpack with all her worldly possessions was strapped firmly to her back. She took a moment to appreciate the dark silhouette of the buildings against the backdrop of the Capitol and its famous river. These abandoned warehouses along the Potomac River had been her home on and off for the last few months. It seemed a safe enough spot to stay for long periods of time, but eventually she always left for a while. The few people that she'd talked to on the streets had warned her that it was unwise to remain in one place for too long, and she'd taken that lesson to heart. It was dangerous to get too comfortable.

She wasn't the only one who lived in the forgotten part of the Capital. Sections of the former Navy yard were being revitalized, but this one still remained on the city's 'What-to-do-with-it' list. Personally, Runt didn't mind if it stayed on the list for a bit longer.

A lot of the perpetually homeless stayed in the buildings on occasion, especially during the winter. They each had claimed their own sections—at least until someone bigger and meaner moved in. Overall, most of them were pretty harmless and preferred to live their lives with only the occasional interaction with the rest of the world.

She liked the fact that they were all different. Some lived on the streets because they couldn't stand being confined in small places. Others were there because they were too broke to afford a place to live. Those reasons came from the few who had volunteered why they didn't have anywhere else to go. She never asked because it was none of her business. Besides, if she started asking, someone might decide to question her, and she wouldn't answer.

At sixteen, she'd been on the streets for almost two years. It didn't bother her like most people would think it should. She was her own boss and she liked it that way.

She reached up and adjusted the strap on her shoulder while she waited for a car to drive past her. She remained still so that she wouldn't be noticeable. Her hand tightened on the strap when the car slowed. She breathed a sigh of relief when it turned and headed away from her.

Life could be hard on the streets, but only if you needed a lot to live on. She didn't—need material stuff, that is.

*Well, except for my laptop. I can't live without that,* she thought with wry amusement.

She'd started life poor, so she had never known what it was like to have a lot of stuff anyway. Thanks to her father, even that life had been taken away from her. Money and greed created monsters, and she had met her fair share of them at an early age.

She didn't like to think about how easy it was to lose everything she cared about because of someone else. She hated to brood about the things she couldn't change, so she tried not to. It was a waste of time and energy. Besides, she was doing just fine on her own.

Scanning the area one more time to make sure she was alone, Runt began walking at an unhurried pace until she was engulfed in the shadows cast by the buildings. She had learned a lot in the years since her father was murdered. She had no regrets about that either. Sometimes she wondered if the counselors had been right—that there was something wrong with her.

*Asses,* she thought dispassionately.

The only thing wrong with her was that she was smart—too smart for her father, and too dangerous for her mother. One school psychologist suggested that she was a savant—one of those strange and unusual people who had an ability that was out of this world. All her father saw in her was a way to make money, and he didn't care how he did it.

Her mother had been different. Her mom understood and accepted her for who she was—a little girl who could see zeros and ones and understand what they were saying as if it was her native language. Her mom had tried to protect her from her father's exploitation, but between playing the numbers, creating illegal software, and hacking into accounts, the crimes had grown more quickly than Runt did.

She had always been petite. Her mother was barely in her third trimester when she gave birth. Her father had drunkenly bragged one night about how he had beaten the baby out of her in record time—and that it was hard to believe that fiasco had turned out to be a good thing because Amelia was so smart.

Runt paused and leaned back against the cold corrugated steel of the warehouse. She remained still as another lone car drove down the road. It turned at the corner. Whoever was inside was probably looking for drugs or a hooker.

She watched the lights disappear, but didn't move. There was no need to hurry to the small, secluded section of Warehouse B11. The night was hers, just like it was every night. Instead, she let the vivid memories come. There was no use fighting them, she'd discovered that during her first year on the streets. If she tried, they would only turn into nightmares when she fell asleep.

"Let the memories come, then store them back in their box," she whispered to herself.

*He didn't pull the trigger, but he was responsible,* she thought angrily for the thousandth time.

She didn't know if she'd ever be able to move on. Her worst moments were like a mental tattoo by now. Every time the memories came out of nowhere and she thought about it all again, they branded her more deeply.

Her father was murdered by the same type of criminals who had killed her mom. Her mother's death was meant to be a warning. They thought they could terrify Runt into being controllable. Unfortunately for them, the bastards had killed the wrong parent.

They actually thought she gave a damn about what happened to the brutal man who had made Runt and her mother's life hell. If they had killed *him* and kept her mother alive, well, things would have been different—at least until she made enough money to live in a place where no one could touch them, where no one could use them ever again.

Amelia looked up when a procession of headlights flashed by her and the cars stopped at the gate. She stealthily moved closer, hiding behind a dumpster that lay on its side.

She crouched and peered through a hole in the rusted-out container. A line of luxury SUVs and a limousine pulled through the gate. The doors of a nearby warehouse opened to reveal several heavily armed men who must have been waiting for the motorcade.

The limo pulled straight into the warehouse, while the SUVs stopped at the entrance. Three men jumped out of the first SUV. She pursed her lips with disdain when she saw their expensive suits and their weapons. They didn't look like government men, so they had to be the AHWs—the Assholes of the World.

Her mom had once told her that maybe the reason she was given her gift was to fight against those that hurt other people but were untouchable themselves. Amelia had found a way to touch them.

Money meant everything to these people. Even family was never truly sacred, each member merely a pawn for the one in charge—and when they were no longer useful, dependable, or loyal, they were discarded like refuse. Friends were a myth. People like this had no friends. She had learned that lesson the hard way.

What was sad was money was relative to the individual. She'd seen people with less than a dollar in their pocket treat people better than those that had millions.

She actually couldn't remember how long she'd been stealing from people like this. In time, Amelia Thomas had disappeared, replaced by the hack known as Runt. Her mom had been right. Her purpose in life was to bring down the AHWs, and she did it with a skill that matched the most sophisticated members of the technological world.

*Only better*, she thought with satisfaction.

She silently rose to her feet and began working her way toward the group of cars. In order to discover who they were, she needed to be closer.

She heard angry voices as she crept closer to the warehouse. Looking along the wall of the building, she found a broken window where she could peek through the opening. Several old steel drums and a few wooden pallets were under the window. She worked her way to them and climbed up as silently as she could. Fortunately, whoever was talking now was pissed off enough to conceal the small amount of noise that she made.

Gripping the side of the window frame, she watched as a large group of men spread out around the limo that had pulled inside. Her eyes widened in surprise when she saw a man, then a beautiful woman in an evening gown exit the vehicle followed by a second man whose nose was dripping blood. The smug expression on the woman's face told Runt who had caused it.

She tightened her grip on the window frame and pulled herself up a little so she could see better. She was just about to open the window more when someone grabbed her roughly from behind and yanked her backwards. A startled cry slipped from her before she could smother it. She twisted as she fell, landing heavily on her side in an effort to protect her laptop.

"Looks like we have a wharf rat sneaking around in the dark, Manny," the man who grabbed her chuckled.

"Shoot him, Rick. We don't have time for this," Manny instructed.

"Fuck off," Runt growled.

She thrust her leg out toward the man named Rick, and her booted foot connected with his groin. She was already in motion before his pain registered and the loud curse burst from his lips. She rolled to her feet and had taken only a couple of steps when she was wrenched to a stop. Struggling to break free, she shrugged off the straps of her backpack.

The sudden release caused the man who had a grip on her backpack to fall back a few steps. Unfortunately, Rick recovered more quickly than she'd expected. Pain exploded through the side of her face when he punched her in the jaw. The blow knocked her off her feet. One of the men, she wasn't sure which one, kicked her in the ribs.

She rolled to put some distance between herself and their powerful kicks, and hissed when the ground shook from an explosion inside the warehouse. It was enough to distract the two men—but only for a second. She made it to her knees before she looked up and saw Rick pointing his handgun at her head.

"Asshole," she sneered.

Runt looked down the barrel and braced herself for certain death. She had no sooner spoken than Rick was lifted off of his feet and flung into the barrels that she had been standing on earlier. Manny turned his gun on whoever had appeared. She winced when she heard the distinctive snap of bone breaking followed by a tortured cry.

Runt scrambled to her feet and pressed her back against the cold metal wall. The sounds of screams and gunfire coming from inside drowned out what was happening out here. It sounded like a war was going on inside the warehouse.

Horror gripped her when the man who had saved her from certain death twisted around with Rick's body dangling in front of him like a limp doll, just as Manny fired several shots. Rick jerked as each one pierced his body.

Runt waited for her savior to collapse. She was sure that the bullets must have gone all the way through Rick's body. Shock immobilized her when the man tossed Rick's body aside like it was a store mannequin.

She switched her focus from him to the other gunman. Manny's gun had jammed, and he was reaching for another one. In a fraction of a second, her rescuer had stripped Manny of his weapon; then he placed his hands on each side of Manny's head, and with a great deal of force, he wrenched it to the side. Runt heard the sickening snap despite the loud chaos going on inside the building behind her.

Fear flooded Runt when the man in black turned toward her, pulling a sword from his waist as he did so. In the flickering light through the window, she could see his features. His silver eyes glowed, and his mouth....

She swallowed. He looked like the alien vampires from a comic series that she liked to read. The guy looked young, not much older than she was, but that was where their similarities ended.

The primal response of fight or flight kicked in, and since she honestly didn't have a death wish, she decided to flee. Surging forward, she grabbed her backpack and took off. The low, animalistic snarl behind her added wings to her feet, and she ran as if the hounds of hell were nipping at her heels.

Turning the corner, she reached out and yanked down a pile of metal bars that were leaning against the building. The loud clanging of metal on concrete drowned out any other sounds—or it did until the guy following her had to navigate through them.

She raced across the parking lot to the next warehouse. This building had holes that she could escape into, and were small enough that he would never fit. There were also places under the warehouses that only she and the rats knew about. The joy of being smaller than the average person was that she could go where most people would never dream of entering.

Runt sensed he was gaining on her. The large bay door was ajar, stretched as far as the chain across it would allow. Adrenaline flooded through her. Holding her backpack in one hand, she turned sideways and ducked under the chain. She slipped cleanly through the narrow opening, only to mutter a curse when her knit cap caught on the chain and came off.

Twisting around, she snatched the cap seconds before the man reached the door. She pulled the cap back over her head and stumbled back, looking at him with wide, defiant eyes. He stared back at her through the opening.

"You cannot escape me," he vowed.

Runt snorted. She had heard that before—a lot of times. So far, she had proved all the AHWs wrong. She watched as he gripped the doors. The chain was thick. There was no way he could get through unless he either broke the chain or broke the door. Since neither was likely, she took a few seconds to catch her breath and study him.

His lips were slightly parted; and up close, she could see that his canines were longer than normal. Either this guy was into the whole Goth thing and had implants done, or he thought dressing like a vampire gave him supernatural powers. She decided it must be one or the other because her first thought had been too far out there —literally!

She shook her head. Enough was enough. This guy had just killed two people.

*Well, technically he only killed one, but that was one more than I needed to witness,* she decided.

It was time to disappear. It wouldn't take long for this guy to figure out another way into the building. The bay doors with the chain across them might stop him, but there were at least a dozen other ways in—if you didn't mind kicking in a door or climbing through a window.

Keeping a wary eye on him, she slowly backed away from the door. Once she was several yards away from him, she turned and began to run again. She was halfway to the far side of the room when a loud screech of metal on metal caused her to look over her shoulder. Her eyes widened in stunned disbelief when she saw his sword slice through the thick links. He smiled menacingly at her as he pushed one of the heavy metal doors aside.

He twirled the long blade in his hand. Muttering a soft curse under her breath, Runt turned and fled toward the far side of the warehouse. His roar echoed through the large, vacant area behind her. A long stream of curses that she had learned from her father swept through her mind as the chase began again.

Runt considered all the different spots in this warehouse and throughout the yard where she could hide. There was a gaping hole in the back office wall that she could slip through. The lower wall was made of concrete and had a hole in it where a safe used to be until it was pulled out.

She hit the door with her shoulder. The metal door swung wildly inward before it hit the wall and slammed shut again. She lunged and slid across the top of the metal desk, landing on the other side. A gaping hole about three feet wide led to the outside.

Dropping to her knees, she pushed her backpack through the opening and frantically began crawling through. A startled yelp escaped her when her pursuer grabbed her ankle and yanked. She felt his warm fingers even through her socks and jeans. Rolling in the narrow space, she kicked the man as hard as she could.

He smothered an oath of pain and released her ankle to hold his nose. She scooted through the opening, and had just parted her lips to tell the bastard where he could go when she saw a glint of silver hanging on a thin piece of electrical wire sticking out of the rough concrete she had just passed over. Pulling off her glove, she reached up to her neck and desperately searched for the necklace she had been wearing. It was gone. She couldn't leave it—the necklace was the last gift her mother had given her. The locket held a picture of Runt and her mom inside.

She darted forward and grabbed the fine chain, but before she could pull back again, his strong fingers shackled her sleeve-covered wrist and pulled her forward. She braced her free hand against the wall and struggled to break free.

"Let me go!" she angrily hissed.

Instead, he tightened his hold on her wrist, and she locked gazes with him, momentarily mesmerized by the up-close view of the guy's molten silver eyes.

"You are a female!" he stated, clearly shocked.

For a moment, they stared at each other through the hole in the wall. She tugged on her arm. He loosened his fingers just enough to slide them along the coarse material of her coat and touch her bare palm. A startled cry slipped from her lips.

It felt like he had zapped her with static electricity! He must have felt it as well because he yanked his hand back. She scrambled back out of his reach but continued to gaze at him in shock.

"What are you?" she asked, the words coming out more curious than afraid.

He glanced down at his palm before he looked back at her with eyes that glowed with silver flames. He smiled at her, and she could see the tips of his sharp teeth. This wasn't some guy dressed up as his favorite fictional character, this guy was real—and he wasn't human.

"I am Derik 'Tag Krell Manok, and you, little human, are my bond mate," he stated.

His quiet, accented voice was warm and reverent and sent a shiver of warning through her that pissed her off. She narrowed her eyes, and her lips tightened into a flat, disapproving line at his claim and his possessive tone. She pulled her backpack closer and rose to one knee, then stood up and began backing away.

She abruptly stopped when he turned his hand over and she clearly saw something delicate dangling from his fingers. She looked down at her own hand. The necklace her mother had given her was gone. In its place was a tingling symbol in the center of her palm that had not been there before. Briefly closing her eyes, she realized that she must have dropped the necklace into his hand when he shocked her.

Fury poured through her at the loss. There was no way she could retrieve it without being caught. Turning on her heel, she did what her mom had taught her to do when she was in danger—she fled into the darkness.

'Retreating is not defeat, Amelia. As long as you are alive you can fight another day. Hope will keep you going.'

Her memory of her mother's gentle voice soothed her mind. She would fight alright. The sound of sirens was getting louder, which told her that the explosions had been reported and the police were almost there. By tomorrow, she would know who to target—and she hoped one of the guys she hit hardest would have silver eyes with flames in them.

*Derik 'Tag Krell Manok. You are so going down,* she thought as she slipped through the chain link fence and disappeared into the dark bowels of the city.

Derik kicked open the warehouse door and ran outside. He paused and looked both ways before he took off in the same direction that the female had disappeared. He rounded the corner and stopped again. He scanned the area for any signs of movement.

A faint breeze caressed his hot skin, and he lifted his head to sniff the air, hoping to catch a scent that would give him a direction to follow. Turning in a semi-circle, he raised his hands to his head in frustration before he dropped them to his side. There was nothing but the distant sounds of the battle raging in the other warehouse.

He curled his fingers into a fist. It had taken him several minutes to find a door that wasn't blocked with debris.

He looked toward the fence that ran the length of the warehouses, and strode toward a jagged gap someone had cut through the wire. When he was close enough to touch the metal barrier, he noticed a dark shape lying on the ground near the opening. Kneeling, he picked up the fingerless black knit glove. The woman had been wearing gloves like this.

Lifting the glove to his nose, he sniffed it. A surge of warmth flooded him—it was her scent. He curled his fingers possessively around the glove, looked up, and scanned the area again. He now had two items that belonged to her.

Derik hesitated a moment longer at the gap in the fence. She had escaped into the city. His gaze swept the area before he looked down and studied his tingling palm again.

A sense of wonder swept through him when he saw the distinctive mark that had not been there earlier. Rising to his feet, he curled his fingers into his palm. He was torn between duty to his people and his need to find the female who was his bond mate.

The primitive need to find and protect his mate was stronger. He gripped the wire and was just pulling it back when the sound of more sirens filled the air. A fervent curse slipped from his lips. He released the wire and stepped away from the steel barrier. He would be no good to his mate if he was captured by her people.

"I will find you, little warrior. You cannot hide from me forever—no matter how hard you fight," he murmured as he turned back, reaching up to rub his bruised lip where she had kicked him.

# CHAPTER ONE

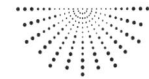

**Present Day:**
**Cosmos Raines Industries (CRI)**
**Houston, Texas**

*R*unt stared moodily out the window at the lights below. She was in the apartment that Avery had given her when she first arrived to work at CRI. The spacious elegance within Cosmos Raines' Tower still didn't feel comfortable to her, but the busy energy of the city below was soothing.

She wrapped her arms around her waist as she stared down at the city that never seemed to sleep. A sudden tickle made her feel like she was going to sneeze. Lifting her arm, she absentmindedly rubbed her nose against her sleeve. Her mind churned with random thoughts as she contemplated what she was about to do.

"Amelia…," RITA's gentle voice murmured.

"Yes, RITA," Runt quietly responded.

"What's wrong, love? You've been staring out at the city for almost an hour," RITA reflected.

Runt's lips twitched at RITA's concern. The slight wafting of air told her that RITA had manifested a somewhat corporeal form. She turned her head and looked at the holographic image.

"Are you watching me again? You're getting better at moving things," Runt commented.

RITA wiggled her nose. "Yes, but that does not answer my question," RITA pointed out.

Runt turned to gaze out the window again. She was silent for a few seconds, unsure whether she wanted to share what she was thinking and feeling—even with RITA. She tightened her arms around her waist.

"Nothing's wrong. I'm just thinking," she finally replied.

"About Derik?" RITA teasingly inquired.

Runt grimaced in distaste. She was *not* going to admit that she had been thinking about Derik 'Tag Krell Manok! A shiver of unease ran through her. That was usually a sign that it was time to disappear. Of course, it wasn't like this was the first time she'd thought about leaving. It was just the first time that she knew she was actually going to do it.

The problem was doing it without RITA knowing. Cosmos Raines' AI system, RITA, which stood for Really Intelligent Technical Assistant, was as close to family as Runt could get. It was that connection that made her reluctant to hurt RITA, even if she was only a computer program.

*She's more than binary code,* Runt thought, observing the soft concern in RITA's glowing eyes.

"I wish...," she started to say before she shook her head and looked down at the floor.

"What do you wish, Amelia?" RITA asked.

Runt shook her head again. "I'm going to go out for a bit. Now that Avery has been found and we know that Markham and Wright are dead, I don't need to be here as much," she stated, dropping her arms to her sides. She turned and grabbed her backpack from the floor near the chair and pulled it onto her back.

"Amelia...," RITA started to protest.

Runt turned and looked at the holographic figure of the woman she had come to love. The AI glided forward and lifted a nearly transparent hand to caress her cheek. Runt pulled back when RITA's fingers passed through her flesh. Sorrow and a sense of loneliness enveloped Runt. It had been so long since she'd been touched by another human that she had almost forgotten what it felt like. The last hug had been from her mother.

"Oh, sweetheart," RITA said with regret.

Runt shook her head. "I'll be back later," she lied.

She turned away and headed for the door to her apartment. This was not her world. She belonged in the hackers' underground, out on the streets where people talked and the shadows listened. She had a place among those who knew about the darkness—not in a castle in the sky.

**Baade: Prime Home World**
**Prime Palace**

"Derik," Tresa called, drawing his attention.

He had seen his mother enter out of his peripheral vision, but couldn't halt what he was doing. He struck several flying disks before he lowered his arms and stepped back. He reached for the controller at his waist, but before he could pull it out and end the program, another attack disk shot toward him.

Turning in a blur of speed, he twisted and kicked. The disk shattered under the force of his blow. Tiny particles fell to the floor.

He lowered his leg and wiped the sweat from his brow. His scowl of annoyance softened when he saw the expression of concern on his mother's face. A rueful smile tugged at his lips. He knew he had been difficult to live with lately.

"Mother," he said with a slight, respectful bow of his head.

She picked up a towel and handed it to him. As he used it to wipe the sweat from his face, he surreptitiously regarded her serene face and recognized her expression. As the youngest sibling, he'd had plenty of practice observing his mother as the beacon that guided everyone, including his father. Baade might be considered a patriarchal civilization, but he knew better when it came to his family. His father might be the face of the Prime—but it was his mother who was their heart.

"I see that you have been improving. Brock is not going to be happy that you keep destroying his new training equipment," she observed, walking over to toe one of the shattered disks.

Derik's lips twitched. "He already warned me that he asked Lan to change the code to the equipment room. He said I was far worse than my brothers when it came to destroying his inventions," he admitted.

He watched his mother turn and assess him with an expression of curiosity. After a few seconds, he looked away. How was it that just her look could make him feel like he was an adolescent again?

"Come sit with me a moment," she said, crossing over to a bench near the training room window.

He frowned and slowly walked over to where she had gracefully lowered herself. He sat down next to her, and they both stared out at the garden. It had become dark outside since he'd first entered. He hadn't realized that he had been training for so long.

"Tell me about her," his mother quietly requested.

He parted his lips in denial at first before he closed his mouth and leaned forward, resting his elbows on his knees. He rolled the towel between his hands and thought about the woman who had haunted his every waking moment for the last two years.

"RITA2 told me that she was born Amelia Thomas, but she goes by the name Runt," he began in a low tone.

"Runt. That is an especially unusual name for a woman. I have not heard that one used before in any of the vidcoms I've watched," Tresa commented.

He sat up and leaned back against the back of the bench. A slight smile curved his lips. He'd thought the same thing—at first.

"My mate is an unusual woman. Runt is her hacker name. She is very skilled at their computer language," he explained.

"She works with Cosmos?" Tresa asked.

Derik nodded. "Yes. Under Cosmos' protection, Amelia uses her skills to fight against those that harm innocent people. RITA2 said that Amelia has angered many powerful people on her world, and if she were left on her own, her life would be in danger. Part of the reason she was brought into Cosmos' team was precisely so that they could protect her. She... doesn't like to accept anyone's help," he added.

He turned his hand over and looked down at the intricate mark in the center of his palm. The mark had grown more defined in the last few weeks—and his driving need to find the woman who had escaped him two years before had increased. It was time for them to meet again.

Still looking out into the garden, Tresa casually remarked, "RITA2 told me she is young... and very independent for her age. You have that in common."

He turned in his seat and looked suspiciously at his mother. It had been a long time since he'd met Runt, and since that time he hadn't wanted to talk about the bond mate he'd let slip through his fingers... so of course his mother would have looked for more information on her own. He wondered how much she knew.

Over the last two years, he had done everything he could to learn more about Amelia. He had also spent a great deal of time keeping himself busy while he waited for them both to grow a little older. His mother was right—Amelia had been young when they met—sixteen, according to RITA2.

He looked down at his hand again. He was barely two years older than Amelia. Was he capable of being a good protector? His brothers had been older than he when they found their mates. He knew nothing about being a good mate except from what he had read and watched on the assorted vidcoms that were available.

"She is my bond mate. I... can feel the need growing inside me to claim her, but... what if she doesn't want me? What if she thinks I am unsuitable because I don't...," his voice faded and he looked at his mother with a frustrated expression.

Tresa softly laughed and shook her head. Derik scowled at her when she reached over and patted his leg.

"You are far too much like your father to worry about whether she will want you… or about whether you'll be able to handle the responsibilities that come with being a good mate," she said.

Derik felt his cheeks heat and knew it wasn't from his workout. He looked out the window. This was not a conversation that he really wanted to have with his mother. For that matter, he wasn't sure it was a conversation that he wanted to have with anyone.

They both turned when the door opened. His father walked into the room, glanced around, and walked up to them as they slowly stood. Derik frowned in confusion when his father's gaze locked on him.

"Derik, get cleaned up and meet me in the council room in twenty minutes," Teriff ordered.

"Yes, sir," Derik immediately responded.

"What is it, Teriff?" his mother demanded.

Derik paused when he saw a flicker of unease cross his father's face. It took him a moment to realize they were having a silent exchange. Derik's frown deepened when his mother reached for his arm.

"What has happened?" he asked, turning to look at his mother's worried face before turning back to his father.

"A member of Cosmos' team has disappeared. They fear one of the men from a previous confrontation may be responsible. Cosmos has asked for our assistance," Teriff replied.

"Who…?" Derik demanded, stepping around the bench as his stomach tightened with dread.

"A woman named Amelia Thomas," his father told him.

## CHAPTER TWO

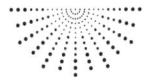

Two guards stood at attention outside of the council room doors. The guard on the right stepped forward and opened a door as Derik approached. He nodded to the man as he passed him; then stopped inside the room to survey those in attendance. He was surprised to see the council members standing in front of the dais where they normally sat. Of course, this was a new council with less formal ways than the previous group.

He saw his older brothers and father quietly talking with Lan and Brock. Both men worked under his brother J'kar as his Head of Security and Chief Engineer. Brock shot him a pointed look, and then glanced down at his feet. Derik's eyes followed Brock's, and he grimaced when he saw the box filled with broken attack disks. It would appear Brock knew about the latest casualties to his weapons supply. The Chief Engineer must have discovered them while he was getting cleaned up.

"Brock," Derik greeted.

"Derik. I'm changing the locks again. I don't care whose family you belong to," Brock stated with a dark scowl.

Derik deliberately put aside his impatience to get to Earth and chuckled. "Bypassing it will just give me another challenge," he retorted with a self-satisfied grin that was only a little stiff. The meeting would begin momentarily, he told himself. Any moment now.

Lan laughed. "You might as well give up, Brock. I've seen what the young Lord can do," he informed his friend with a playful slap to his shoulder.

Brock turned his scowl on Lan. "Only because you helped train him using *me* as a target," he growled.

"Let's get this meeting in session," Teriff ordered, looking in Derik's direction.

Derik nodded tightly, fighting to control his surge of anticipation and rage. He was one moment closer to seeing Amelia again, and something horrible could have happened to her in the meantime. Something horrible could have been happening to her every moment since she'd been missing.

Every second seemed an eternity, but acting on his emotions would likely slow down the proceedings rather than speed them up. He followed his father, brothers, and the other members of the council as they took their seats around the large oval table and sat down.

"I call the meeting to order," Teriff said. "This is a closed session of the council. I've asked Brock, Lan, and Derik to attend. Does the council approve my invitation?" Teriff formally asked, glancing around at the men sitting at the table.

Derik listened as each council member stated their approval. He took the seat next to his brother Borj. Out of all of the 'Tag Krell Manok brothers, Borj was the calmest—as long as no one messed with his bond mate, Hannah.

Hannah was human, like all of his brothers' bond mates. Each woman was captivating in an absolutely unique way—though the women were sisters, so of course there were similarities. Tink was the most like her mother, Tilly. Tink was a talented auto mechanic who could work on practically any type of engine or power generator while her mother was a programmer and mechanical engineer. Hannah was like their father, Angus, the thoughtful writer, except

Hannah preferred photographs over words. Tansy was—well, Tansy was like RITA, the powerful, mischievous AI who had made a partial clone of herself called RITA2 to stay in the Prime computer systems and wreak havoc there in her charming way. RITA was originally created by Tilly, Tink… and Cosmos. Derik frowned when he noticed that Cosmos was missing from the large group of attendees.

"Cosmos will be monitoring what is going on through RITA2," Teriff announced, answering his unspoken question.

"Hello, everyone," RITA2 suddenly greeted.

A grumble of sighs ran through the unmated males sitting at the table. Despite the severity of the matter at hand, Derik couldn't help being amused. RITA2 knew how to make an appearance!

The AI was dressed in a long, slender gray skirt with a light blue blouse tucked in at her waist. A wide black belt made her waist look small and her breasts—well, large. Derik suspected that they were slightly larger than the last time he'd seen them, and wondered if RITA2 had been playing with her programming again.

Her dark red hair was fashioned into an elegant bun, and she wore a pair of oversized silver-rimmed glasses. She walked around the table and flashed an amused grin at one of the clan leaders who almost fell out of his seat trying to turn and look at her.

"Keep your eyes on my mate's *face*, Brawn," DAR's deep voice warned as his holographic form suddenly appeared next to the offender.

Derik snorted when he heard DAR's snarky comment to the leader of the Desert Clan. When RITA2 had first arrived, she'd had an unexpected effect on their Defense Armament Response system, which previously had… less personality. DAR didn't change his appearance nearly as often as RITA2 did, though. He looked the same as when he'd materialized with a body for the first time, much to RITA2's delight.

Brawn shrugged, grinned, and sat back in his seat as the men around the table chuckled. "A warrior can look, DAR," Brawn quipped.

DAR folded his arms across his chest and began to glow brighter. "Not if he wishes to keep his eyes in his head," the male AI retorted.

"Turn down the power, love. I can feel the surge," RITA2 cautioned.

Derik wanted to roll his eyes. Everyone could feel the surge. Not only were the lights flickering, but the hairs on his arms were standing straight up. His father stood up and drew everyone's attention back to the matter at hand—at least until they saw the ghostly forms of two children sitting in Teriff's vacated seat. The sound of curses filled the room, and several men rose and moved away from the table.

"What is it now?" his father growled in exasperation.

"Behind you…." Brock choked out, pointing his finger at the chair.

"Oh dear. DAR, love, can you take the children?" RITA2 asked.

"Children? What…? RITA2! DAR! This is…," Teriff snarled as he scooted to the side and cast a glare between the AI and her replications. "Do Cosmos and Terra know about this?"

"Yes," DAR replied.

Teriff ran his hand over his face and sighed. "I'm getting too old for this," he muttered.

Derik snorted. His father was still in the prime of his life, and from the twinkle in his eye, he was enjoying this as much as the other men who were now peering closely at the two children as they crawled across the table. Derik would have been just as intrigued if it weren't for the fact that his mate was missing, and he needed to find her.

"Father… the meeting," he said, speaking above the other men.

"Yes, DAR, if you please…," Teriff said with a wave of his hand at the two children who shimmered with excitement.

"Of course. Darian, Rena," DAR said.

"You've named them?" Teriff asked in astonishment.

"Of course we've named them! They're our kids, after all," RITA2 retorted.

Derik watched as DAR and the two AI children dematerialized. He looked around. RITA2 had vanished as well. A second later, he discovered why.

"I'm afraid my ability to retain a three-dimensional corporeal form is still limited. I'll have to give my presentation this way," RITA2 spoke up with a sigh. "The little ones are draining me as they feed from my code."

"Yes, well, we'll see what can be done," Teriff responded in an uncomfortable voice. "I've called a meeting because I need to send Derik to Earth to find a woman named Runt."

"Why Derik? Surely a more experienced warrior would be better—no offense, my Lord," Rav, the Leader of the Southern Clan, protested.

"The woman is his bond mate. He has the mark to prove it. That connection will help him locate her," Teriff growled.

"In that case, I'll go with him," Hendrik announced, slapping his hand down on the table before rising to his feet and rubbing his hands together. "I have plenty of tracking experience and can watch over the young lord since I've been on the planet before. When do we leave?"

"What makes you think you should be the one to go?" Brawn demanded. "I think I should go with him. I have just as much experience with tracking, and I think it is about time I had a chance to explore the world."

"Hendrik only wants to go because he thinks the injured human who was in Medical a few weeks ago is his bond mate," Rav insisted. "If anyone should go, it should be me. I was the one who spoke first, and I can focus on protecting Derik without distractions because I don't have a bond mate."

"You want to try to entice Trudy! I know the human woman is my bond mate. I felt the connection between us. All I need is a chance to touch her. Once the mark appears, you will see that I am right!" Hendrik retorted.

"This connection you felt—are you sure it wasn't all in your head? If I remember correctly, she banned you from the medical ward!" Rav retorted.

"Actually, RITA2 banned all the warriors from the medical ward," Brawn pointed out.

"The female is mine," Hendrik scowled, rising to his feet and leaning on the table. The muscles in Hendrik's arms bulged as he curled his fingers into fists.

"Enough or I'll ban the lot of you and send you back to your regions!" Teriff roared.

"Brawn's right. All the warriors were too much for poor Trudy to deal with in the aftermath of what happened at Addie's parents' lake house. I was afraid she was going to start shooting all of *you* if you didn't leave her alone," RITA2 replied. "Teriff is also correct about Derik's ability to connect with Amelia. It will certainly be useful, because though RITA was certain that she would be able to keep track of her, unfortunately, either Amelia has discovered a way to go completely off the grid or something has happened to her to prevent her from going online. Afon Dolinski's body has not yet been located. Until it is, I believe he is still a threat. Remember, he worked for Avilov, the crime boss who killed Cosmos' father and endangered Tansy. Dolinski isn't the only one who has a reason to hunt down Amelia. There are also several minor criminals that have never forgiven her father. I'm worried about her. She's never been silent this long before, and DAR and I could really use her help at the moment. It feels like my code is about to replicate again."

"Goddess forbid that we end up with more miniature versions of you running around the palace," Teriff muttered, and the other warriors around the table chuckled.

"That settles it," Derik said, rising to his feet. "My bond mate is in danger and RITA2 needs her help. I will journey alone to Earth. Cosmos and Terra are there—as well as Avery and Core. They can help me if I need assistance."

"I still think I should go," Rav grumbled under his breath. "I wouldn't mind seeing if Trudy is my bond mate."

"That's it, I'm going to beat the shit out of you," Hendrik snarled.

Rav grinned. "I was hoping you'd try," he retorted.

Derik stepped back as the two men lunged across the table at each other. In seconds, the warriors were in a good old-fashioned free-for-all. Derik stepped back again when Brock and Lan shrugged, grinned, and joined in. Only his father stood to the side—well, except when Brawn got in his way.

Derik watched with appreciation as his father grabbed the equally tall man and tossed him over the table as if he were a toy, not even breaking his stride as he did it. Teriff jerked his head toward the door of the chambers, and Derik followed him.

"This reminds me of the early days, except we used swords along with our fists. Your mother banned them from the chambers after there were complaints about blood staining the floors. She told us that if we wanted to kill each other, we'd have to do it outside because it wasn't fair to those who were assigned to clean up the mess afterwards. Your mother has always brought dignity and grace to the palace. I should have let her know back then how much I appreciated it," his father said as they exited the chamber room.

"I don't understand the purpose of getting their permission. Why the delay? I could have found my mate by now," Derik impatiently growled with a wave of his hand.

Teriff reached out and gripped his upper arm. Derik's frustration was rising to the boiling point, and he knew his father was aware of it as well. He took a deep breath and forced his mind and body to calm.

"We are still affected by all the arguments that came before this. Those tensions have not disappeared, and they have consequences. The old Council was reluctant to allow any of our people to journey through the Gateway until strict security procedures were in place. Even then, two of the members voted against continuing the use of the Gateway—at least not without changes that would have been very harmful for the humans. In fact, Derik, several of the former Council members wanted war. The torture of Merrick and the human men's abuse of their own women—it did not sit well with them. Observing Cosmos' love for your sister and Angus' love for Tilly and their daughters kept the rest of the members from joining those calling for war. I knew it was time for a younger group to be on the Council. I just forgot what it was like when I was their age. Even so, this was the best road we could have traveled to get to this point. The discovery that human women can successfully mate with our people was important to share with all the clans. They needed to have a voice in the matter," Teriff explained.

"Once there is hope, it is impossible to stifle it again," he murmured.

Teriff nodded. "Yes. I know you have been to Earth before, so you are familiar with the humans. This mission is what Cosmos and Avery would call a covert mission—they do not want their government to know about you," he said as they walked down the long corridor.

"Why not? I thought the agreement was that Cosmos would notify his leader about our presence," Derik replied with a frown.

Teriff grimaced, and when Derik followed his gaze, he realized that they were no longer alone. RITA2 had returned, this time wearing a pair of jeans and a light green blouse. Her hair was pulled into a high ponytail, and the glasses she'd been wearing earlier were replaced with sunglasses. She flashed him a smile.

"Governments around the world have been trying for years to recruit Amelia. She has outsmarted all of them, including ours, and upset more than a few powerful people around the world. For her own safety, Amelia has always been one of our most important secrets, and quite recently, we have had dangerous altercations initiated by high-ranking US government officials. We need to be very careful about who is able to find our Amelia," RITA2 explained.

Derik stopped in front of the control room for the Gateway and looked at RITA2. "So not only are Afon Dolinski and many other criminals searching for my mate, so are the human governments?" he demanded.

"Mm, and everyone at Cosmos Raines Industries," RITA2 agreed. "Amelia really is very good at hiding."

"She better be," Derik bit out between clenched teeth.

"Find her and bring her back," his father ordered.

"Yes, please," RITA2 eagerly agreed.

"I will," Derik promised.

"If you need help, send word. Your brothers and I will be there," Teriff added in a gruff voice.

He nodded and proceeded through the doorway. Inside, one of

Lan's security detail stepped forward with a black bag. Derik opened it and scanned the contents. Clothing, weapons, and a portable Gateway device were inside. Resealing the bag, he slung it over his shoulder.

"The Gateway has been programmed for Cosmos Raines' living quarters per RITA2's instructions," the warrior informed him.

"Excellent. Initiate the Gateway," he ordered.

"Yes, sir," the warrior replied with a nod to his comrade.

In seconds, a shimmering door appeared where the wall had been moments before. On the other side, he could see his sister, Terra, and Cosmos waiting for him. His stomach tightened with anticipation as he stepped through the Gateway. He was going to find his bond mate, and this time, he wouldn't let her go.

CHAPTER THREE

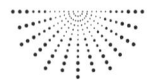

**CRI Headquarters:**
**Houston, Texas**

"When and where was she last seen?" Derik asked.

"Two weeks ago outside of Washington, D.C.," Avery replied, stepping into the room and answering his question before Cosmos could.

Derik turned around and watched as the Head of Security for CRI stepped into the room followed by a large Prime warrior he recognized. He nodded his head in greeting to Core before he returned his attention to Avery.

"Have you found something new?" Cosmos asked.

"Perhaps. I would have known sooner if Runt had used a credit card or at least an online registration, but I thought she might return to her old stomping grounds in Washington, D.C.." Avery flashed Cosmos a triumphant smile. "Surveillance cameras picked her up at the train station. You have no idea how glad I am for RITA's ability to process so many facial recognition images in a short amount of time," she said.

She tossed a folder down on the table. Several grainy images slid out. Derik picked them up, and scanned the images as he flipped through them. He paused on the last one. A small, amused smile curved his lips. In this one she was looking straight into the camera—with her tongue sticking out.

"Do you have a team on the ground?" Cosmos asked.

Avery nodded. "Bert went to Runt's favorite haunts. He hasn't seen her yet. He will notify me the moment he does, and he'll try to make contact with her," she said.

"I should have come sooner," Derik muttered, his voice filled with frustration.

Terra walked over to him and looked worriedly into his eyes. His expression softened when he saw her rub her extended stomach. After more than two years of trying, she and Cosmos were finally expecting their first child.

"You couldn't, Derik, not without severe consequences. Even Core and I were only permitted to be here because we promised to remain within the CRI complex," Terra quietly reminded him.

"A lot could have happened to my mate in two weeks," he quietly responded.

"I've met Amelia. She is very resourceful," Terra teased before she grew serious. "I'm glad that you are finally here, though. Amelia…"

"What is it?" Derik demanded, looking from Terra to Cosmos.

"Runt was determined to find Afon Dolinski," Cosmos replied in a grim tone.

Derik picked up the file on the coffee table and opened it to the pages inside. They were written in English. He'd been studying Amelia's native language over the past two years, and as he scanned the documents, he was able to understand the gist of the report. It appeared that someone named DiMaggio had something that Amelia wanted.

"I'll brief you on what Amelia found out before she left," RITA said, suddenly appearing in the room with FRED, the Prime's AI protocol computer for dealing with dignitaries from other worlds, and now RITA's constant companion.

"Is the plane ready?" Avery asked.

RITA nodded. "Of course. Everything is taken care of. Rex has the flight plans, and Robert will be at Derik's disposal once they arrive in Washington," she said.

"We will go with you," Core stated with a roll of his shoulders.

"I think Derik should go alone; or Amelia will be reluctant to come back," Terra said.

Derik blinked in surprise. The last person he'd expected to defend his desire to go after Amelia alone was his sister. From the stunned silence in the room, he wasn't the only one taken aback.

"I don't think...," Avery started to protest before she pursed her lips together when Terra shook her head.

"This is between Derik and Amelia. It is his right to go to his bond mate—alone," she insisted.

"I hate to say this—but Terra's right," Cosmos stated. "Derik is the only one who has a chance of finding Runt without scaring her off. The longer she is gone, the greater the chance that she will be in jeopardy. She must be found."

"Okay—well, there go my security plans again," Avery muttered under her breath.

"No worries, Avery. FRED and I will be near Derik should he need some assistance, won't we, darling?" RITA said, turning to the male hologram standing next to her.

"As long as he carries the new communication device Terra and Cosmos created," FRED replied.

"I will carry your communication device. Now—where is this plane?" Derik demanded.

～

Four hours later, Derik sat in the front passenger seat of a black SUV. He blindly stared out the tinted windows, his mind not on the pedestrians or the unusual buildings. He had seen enough of this world and others to avoid being distracted by the differences from Baade.

*Go away!* demanded the annoyed feminine voice of Amelia 'Runt' Thomas in his head.

He smiled. Their connection had grown stronger. A wave of warmth filled him, and he absently stroked the mark on the palm of his left hand. He could sense her reaction to the caress—she was *not* pleased.

*Tell me your location,* he silently ordered.

*No,* was her swift reply.

*Amelia... I will find you one way or another. If you tell me where you are, it will make life less complicated,* Derik suggested.

*Life is always complicated, get used to it. And my name is Runt, alien. And you are annoying me! I'll only tell you this once more—Get lost!* she replied.

*I am not going away, at least not without you. It is time for you to accept your future with me. I will take care of you from now on,* he stated.

Silence greeted his comment before he heard a sound that he didn't recognize at first—her snort of laughter. The sound ricocheted through his head. His surprise changed to chagrin when he received a visual image of her rolling on the floor laughing at him.

He replayed what he'd said and groaned. He probably shouldn't have been so... 'bossy' as Tilly and RITA would say. If he had learned anything from watching his brothers with their mates, it was to be careful about trying to boss them around. They were far more likely to do the opposite.

"Are you okay?" Robert asked, glancing at him before returning his attention to the road. "You're not going to be sick, are you?"

"No." He sighed. "I think I have made my first of what will be many mistakes," he confessed.

*Big time! Go home, alien,* Runt ordered.

*Amelia—Runt, please....*

Derik took a frustrated breath when he felt a wall rise between them. She had shut him out. He ran his hand across his forehead; then rubbed his chin.

*That went worse than I expected,* he thought with a long sigh.

"There's a trash can on the floorboard behind my seat if you need it. It's a lot easier than cleaning the carpet. You can never get the smell of vomit out completely," Robert offered.

Derik frowned, trying to follow what Robert was saying. He shook his head and looked moodily out at the increasing traffic. It would be dark in a couple of hours. It looked like the mission to bring his mate back to his world would take a little longer than he'd hoped.

"I am not feeling sick. Where are you taking me?" he asked.

RITA piped in from the SUV's audio system. "Avery thought it would be a good idea if we met up with Bert. Amelia befriended him when we were looking for her a couple of years ago, and she kept in touch with him even after she went to Houston. He contacted Avery a few minutes ago to say he thought he might know her location. Hello, Robert," RITA added. "How is your cholesterol doing?"

"Hello, RITA, as if you don't already know. I've cut out the fried foods and lost ten pounds," Robert chuckled.

"Good for you, love. Derik, Bert will meet you outside the old warehouses along the river. Cosmos purchased the buildings and has been converting them to studio apartments. The area is still under construction. Robert, be a sweetheart and drop him at the corner up ahead," RITA instructed.

"Yes, ma'am," Robert chuckled.

Derik watched as Robert pulled up to the curb. Robert touched his arm and indicated he should wait for the car behind them to pass. A white car with blue and red lights mounted on top and red and blue markings on the side of it drove by before turning at the end of the street.

"There's no sense in asking for trouble from the local police. If you can, avoid anyone in a car like that or in a uniform. I know that Avery would deeply appreciate it. Bert will look like a homeless man, but don't let that fool you. He's five foot ten and weighs one hundred and ninety pounds," Robert started to explain.

"Here is a picture of him, Derik," RITA said.

Derik looked at the image that appeared on the built-in screen in the dash of the SUV. The weathered face of a dark-skinned man with a salt and pepper beard stared at him. The man's eyes were dark brown and twinkled with mischief. He was wearing a worn gray knit cap and a black wool coat that looked like it was two sizes too large for his lean frame.

"This man knows where Runt is?" Derik demanded, looking at Robert.

"Bert knows this city like the back of his wrinkled hand. If you need to find someone in Washington, D.C., he's the one you go to," Robert promised.

"He'll meet you by the gate—and Derik, make sure you keep the communicator Terra gave you with you at all times. It is the only way FRED and I can take on a corporeal form here without causing a major blackout," RITA warned him.

"I have it," Derik replied.

He pulled the door handle and stepped out. Reaching into his coat pocket, he pulled out the pair of dark glasses that Avery had handed to him before he left Houston, and slipped them on to conceal his unusual eyes. He scanned the area before he walked over to the metal barrier that surrounded the warehouses. Ten-foot high, colorful images depicted what the area would look like when the construction was completed and hid most of the view of the warehouses. He could hear the sounds of construction coming from the other side of the fence.

He continued along the fence to a wide gate. Peering through a gap, he saw men working. The area looked a lot different than it had two years ago. He turned around when he heard the faint sound of footsteps approaching.

"You Derik?" the grizzled older man asked.

Derik gave a brief nod. "You are the one called Bert," he replied.

Bert's lips twitched, and he chuckled. "Yeah. Runt said to watch out for you—that you aren't quite right up here," the man replied, tapping his temple.

"You have talked to her?" he asked, ignoring Bert's obvious enjoyment of Runt's description of him.

Bert nodded. "Yeah. She asked that I meet up with you. I heard you're an alien from another world and needed to have your hand held so you don't end up like the last one," he replied.

Derik blinked. "She said all of that?" he asked in an incredulous tone.

Bert's deep laughter was muted by the wind. "Naw, Avery told me about the alien part. Runt just told me that you were a pain in the ass. That little girl says a lot without saying much, if you know what I mean. So, I'm guessing they are both right. You don't look like an alien from another world. You look more like one of them actors from Men in Black or the Matrix," he said with a critical look at Derik's black silk shirt, black jeans, and black overcoat.

"Cosmos said I should look more human. Where is my—where is Runt?" Derik asked.

Bert looked him up and down. "Come on. Runt asked me to dinner, and when that girl asks for something, you better do it. Just so that you know, I'm a little protective of that little lady, if you know what I mean," he said with a grim look.

Derik didn't know what Bert meant, but he nodded anyway and started walking beside the cheerful man. He shoved his hands into his black overcoat.

"Avery says you're from an alien world. I always thought there had to be life out there. I think a few live here, too. There are just too many weird people for us all to be from the same gene pool, if you know what I mean," Bert continued.

Derik listened as the man rambled on about the different people he thought came from another planet. Derik could have told them that they didn't, but Bert seemed to be lost in his own world. They walked down the street for almost a mile before they cut across the four-lane road to the other side.

He was about to question Bert when he saw the bowed head of a young woman. She was sitting at a table outside the restaurant. She slowly raised her head, and a pair of defiant brown eyes stared back at him.

*You're blocking traffic,* she informed him.

Derik blinked and stepped to the side as a group of young people walked by him. He clenched his hands when she tore her gaze away from his and looked at Bert. She suppressed a grin of amusement.

"I thought I told you to lose him, Bert," she stated.

"I thought you said *not* to lose him," Bert chuckled. "What did you order?"

"Three rice bowls and two of the tacos with steak and chicken," Runt replied. "They wouldn't let me order the beer."

"I'll get it. You want one, Derik? I assume you are old enough to drink, if you know what I mean," Bert said with a wink.

"Yes, I like human liquor," Derik replied.

"I'll be right back," Bert cheerfully said.

Derik watched Bert disappear through the clear doors. He looked down at his mate. Now that he was standing in front of her, he didn't know what to say.

"I do not think I understand what he means when he asks me if I know what he means," he confessed.

Her lips twitched before she pursed them together. She waved a hand at the chair across from her. He pulled the chair out and sat down, watching as she placed one of the covered bowls in front of him. She held out a packet of utensils wrapped in paper, and he automatically reached for it. They both froze when their fingers touched.

"Amelia...," Derik started to say in a raw voice.

She jerked her hand back and shook her head. "Runt.... I told you that my name is Runt," she replied in a low voice.

"Here you go!" Bert said, placing the tray holding four plastic cups filled with the amber liquid in front of Derik before he sat down next to Runt. "I bought us each two beers. The lines get pretty crazy starting about now. I love the food they have at this place."

*Why did you come?* she silently demanded.

*You know why,* he replied, unwrapping his utensils and removing the top from the food.

She shot him a heated look before she looked at Bert. "Where's DiMaggio?" she asked.

Bert froze, his fork halfway to his mouth, and looked at Derik before he turned his gaze back to Runt. Bert unhappily lowered the fork to his bowl.

"You should let it go, Runt," Bert quietly said.

Runt's eyes narrowed before she shrugged. "Okay," she responded.

Derik examined Bert's uneasy expression at Runt's reply, and asked, "Who is DiMaggio?"

Bert opened his mouth to respond, but closed it just as quickly when Runt glared at him. Derik's confusion turned to irritation. How was he supposed to know how to do the right thing if he didn't know what was going on?

*Maybe the right thing is to mind your own business,* she suggested.

*Everything about you is now my business. You felt our connection the night we met. It has only grown stronger. We would not even be able to communicate like this if we were not meant to be with each other,* he argued.

"I don't care!" she hissed out loud.

"About DiMaggio?" Bert asked. "That's good. Going after the man won't do anything but bring you heartache."

"We are bond mates," he argued, ignoring Bert. "You wear my mark just as I wear yours."

"I'll stick my hand in acid before I'll ever be anyone's mate. Better yet, you should stick your hand in it. That's the noble thing to do, isn't it?" she retorted.

"Trying to remove the mark will not change anything! Our bond is deeper than a mark; it is a chemical reaction that proves we are compatible! The symbol merely shows that we are a match if anyone dares contest it," he furiously replied.

"I *don't* have chemical reactions unless it is a bad case of indigestion, and you are right up there with the worst I've ever had!" she snapped back before she rose to her feet. "Go home, alien. You aren't wanted here."

Derik held himself still as Amelia 'Runt' Thomas grabbed her empty cup, turned, and walked over to the clear glass doors. She pulled the door open and disappeared inside. His gaze followed her as she crossed the crowded interior of the restaurant.

"Okay, you both lost me, but I'm pretty sure you weren't talking about DiMaggio," Bert murmured, turning in his seat to face Derik again.

Derik looked down at the rice bowl in front of him and shook his head. He stabbed the fork into a piece of meat and reached for one of the cups of beer. He drained the contents before he picked up the other one, and he looked into the restaurant again. Runt was waiting to refill her drink from a machine.

"No. It is… complicated," he finally replied.

Bert chuckled and nodded his head. "Women in general are complicated. Women like Runt—well, I don't know if there is a how-to manual big enough on how to deal with someone like her. I do have to say, I don't think I've ever heard her say so much before. What did you do to piss her off?" Bert asked.

"I'm not sure," he confessed with a rueful look at Bert. "Who is DiMaggio?"

All traces of humor disappeared from Bert's face, and the older man leaned forward, resting his arms on each side of his bowl. Curious about the change in the man, Derik leaned forward as well.

"DiMaggio had started out as a small time crook three decades ago, but soon took over this part of the city and held onto it ever since. I worked the beat near the river during that time…," Bert quietly began to share.

## CHAPTER FOUR

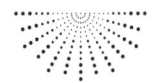

Runt adjusted her backpack and took a sip of the cold water that she was carrying as she strolled along the sidewalk. The sun had sunk below the horizon and the streetlights were coming on one by one to cast the world in an eerie tug-of-war between artificial light and shadows.

It had taken a little bit of maneuvering, but she had managed to slip out the restaurant's back exit without Bert or Derik seeing her. It helped that the restaurant was so busy—and that Bert was filling Derik's ear with some wild tale. Bert loved having a captive audience.

Runt sighed. She knew Bert was on Cosmos' payroll. At first, she was hurt that he had deceived her. She'd thought he was one of the many homeless who lived by the code of the streets, but an intensive background search on him had shown he was a highly decorated former member of the Metropolitan Police Department, and he wasn't homeless. *Score one for my super cautious nature and my insane invasions of privacy,* she thought with a wry smirk.

Still, there was something about Bert that drew her to him. He had the same calming effect on her that her mom had when she was alive. Of course, the last thing she needed was another parental figure in her life! Between Cosmos, Avery, and RITA, she had enough replacements without adding more.

"I also don't need a creepy alien who thinks I'm his!" she muttered to herself.

*What in the hell do you think you are doing?*

Runt snorted when she sensed the frustration and outrage in Derik's silent demand. The guy was really too easy to fluster. She smirked at the thought of what she could do next. If she was really good at annoying him, maybe he would finally give up and go back to wherever he came from.

*Not without you,* he growled in response.

*Game on, alien,* she retorted.

*What does that mean? What kind of games?* he demanded.

She raised one eyebrow in disbelief. Derik didn't look like he was much older than she was, and he didn't know what 'game on' meant? She would have thought even an alien teenager could figure out that one.

*It means 'yes, without me, and if you want to try, go ahead. You're gonna lose',* she dryly replied.

*Stay where you are. I will come to you,* he ordered.

*Whatever,* she replied.

She kept on walking. The shadows grew as the streetlights started to be spaced further apart. The only things lighting this stretch of cracked sidewalk were the plethora of neon signs and the muted lights from the windows nearly covered with advertisements.

She reached out as she passed a trash can and dropped her empty cup on top of a mound of trash, then shoved her cold hands into her coat pockets, scanning the area as a sudden sense of unease rose inside her.

She stared at a man across the street who was leaning against the brick wall, talking on a cellphone. The tip of his glowing cigarette stood out in the darkness, and the faint light from the store cast an eerie shadow on his acne-scarred face. A thin spiral of smoke rose when he exhaled and straightened.

She pursed her lips when he met her gaze, his eyes filled with animosity and recognition. Karl Biggie—ex-con and right-hand man to Ramon DiMaggio, one of the men responsible for her mother's death.

*Well, if nothing else, I've found what I was looking for,* she thought with distaste.

*What? What were you looking for?* Derik demanded in her mind.

Runt frowned. She'd forgotten about her alien. Well, not *her* alien —but *the* alien, she hastily corrected with a grimace.

*I like your first thought better,* he chuckled.

An unexpected sensation of warmth filled her, and she gritted her teeth. Runt forced herself to shrug off the feeling. She would not be distracted from her mission. That was the reason she had left both men back at the restaurant. She'd quickly decided that if Bert wouldn't tell her where DiMaggio was currently residing, she'd find someone who did know. After all, she reasoned, it shouldn't be that difficult to find one of DiMaggio's goons in the area and simply follow him back to wherever his boss was hiding.

It was just her luck that Karl was the one she'd run into. There was no love lost between the two of them. Karl was one of the few who would recognize her.

Karl tossed his cigarette down on the ground and stepped on it. Runt pulled her hands out of her pockets and gripped the straps of her backpack. He crossed the road, heading in her direction. She lifted her chin when he slowed and stepped onto the sidewalk in front of her.

"It's been a long time, Runt," Karl commented.

She shrugged. "Yeah," she agreed.

"The boss has been looking for you. He wants to see you," Karl said.

She rolled her eyes. Of course DiMaggio would want to see her. He would probably like to see the five million dollars that had disappeared from his bank account, too, but she had given it to a dozen charities across the country a long time ago.

"I bet. Sorry, not interested," she muttered.

Karl's eyes narrowed. "I'm not asking," he sneered.

Runt raised her eyebrow. It amused her to see a flash of irritation sweep across Karl's face. There was really too much foot traffic about for Karl to do anything without being noticed. Not to mention the fact that she had stopped in front of the CCV cameras outside of Wong's Family Foods.

"And I'm not going," she replied with a glance up at the camera. "Say cheese, asshole."

She watched Karl lift his hands and curl his fingers as if he would love to wrap them around her neck. He opened his mouth just as a sleek BMW sedan pulled up behind him. The doors swung open in unison and three men in dark suits stepped out.

At first, she thought the men might be some of Cosmos' people until she saw the smirk on Karl's face. She turned to run, but she was quickly surrounded. Strong fingers gripped her upper arm in a bruising hold. Fury swept through her.

"I'll take care of the video. Take her to Mr. DiMaggio," Karl instructed.

"Asshole," Runt muttered as the man holding her arm pulled her toward the waiting car.

"I'll show you how much of an asshole I can be— later. It's a date," Karl promised with a malicious grin.

Runt kicked, and with great satisfaction, she felt her foot connect with Karl's crotch. Clutching his throbbing balls, the man fell to his knees and began rocking back and forth while uttering a string of strangled curses.

"Just a little something to remember me by until we see each other again," Runt growled.

"Come on," the man holding her arm demanded.

Runt sensed a force of rage and denial barreling toward them, and when she peered over the car's open back door, her gaze collided with Derik's. Before she could try to escape again, her captor pushed her head down and shoved her into the car, following her inside with a growled command to the other two men.

They all drew their guns as the driver swiftly pulled away from the curb and accelerated. The man next to her rolled down the window as they drew near Bert and Derik. Panic engulfed Runt when she saw him aim his gun.

Twisting in the seat, she grabbed the man's hair and pulled as hard as she could. Pain exploded through her cheek when he backhanded her. Behind her, his companion wrapped his arm around her neck and began to squeeze. She didn't let go of her captor's hair until they passed Bert and Derik.

Dark spots danced in front of her eyes. She struggled to remove the arm around her neck, but the man refused to let go. As her mind grew fuzzy, she closed her eyes and mentally reached out to Derik.

*DiMaggio... Bert... knows...,* she forced through her oxygen-deprived brain.

*I will come for you,* Derik responded.

*I... know,* she thought before the world went black.

## CHAPTER FIVE

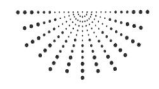

"Hold up," Bert cautioned. Derik ignored him and started to follow the car, but when a man inside the car extended a weapon through the open window, Bert grabbed his arm and jerked him back into a nearby narrow alley, dragging him down to crouch in the dark.

When Derik caught a glimpse of Runt struggling with the man, he looked down at Bert's hand on his arm. His eyes blazed, and his teeth grew noticeably longer and sharper. Bert held fast until the car sped past them, only then reluctantly releasing him.

"She said you would know where they are taking her," he growled, turning toward Bert as his teeth slowly began receding into his gums.

Bert grimaced. "I *have an idea of* where they may have taken her. DiMaggio has been moving around a lot since he lost a huge chunk of change. Some of his creditors didn't believe he'd been hacked. But, listen, we can't go anywhere until you look a little more human, if you know what I mean. The guy that Runt put on the ground is Karl Biggie, DiMaggio's right-hand man. His only job the last two years has been to find Runt. He would know for sure where DiMaggio is hiding," Bert said, slowly rising to his feet.

By the time Bert finished speaking, Derik's teeth and eyes were just as scary as they'd been when his mate was taken. The pain the man felt from Runt's kick would be nothing compared to what Derik would do to him.

"Then we will ask him," Derik replied.

"Seriously, you need to… Oh, to hell with it. Come on, you don't look much weirder than half the teenagers anymore," Bert finally muttered.

Derik followed Bert around the corner and into the store. A young Asian woman stood behind the counter. Her eyes were wide and fearful. She anxiously looked at him and Bert as they entered. He kept his lips pressed firmly together to hide his teeth while Bert talked to her in a low voice.

"Where'd he go?" Bert asked.

"To the back office—please, he has my husband…," she quickly added.

"We'll take care of this," Bert gently promised.

"The man has a gun. He said if I called the police, he would kill him," she warned in a shaky voice.

Bert reached out and patted her trembling hand. "I've got something even better," he reassured her.

Derik saw the woman look at him. Her eyes widened even further when she saw the unnatural swirl of fire in his silver eyes. A glimmer of hope appeared in her expression, and she nodded.

Bert motioned to him before he pointed to a door in the back of the store. Derik replied with a sharp nod. In unison, they threaded their way through narrow aisles, Bert pulled a weapon from his coat pocket, and they silently went through the door to the short hallway on the other side. They pressed their backs against the wall, and behind another door, Derik could hear Karl Biggie ordering the woman's husband to erase the hard drive for the closed-circuit video system.

Derik edged in front of Bert, and kicked the door with such force that it was ripped off the hinges. The door hit Karl, knocking him into a shelf lined with cleaning supplies. Derik stepped into the room, grabbed the flimsy door, and tossed it aside.

Karl's dazed, startled eyes met his, and the man instinctively aimed the gun still tightly clutched in his hand. Derik struck like a cobra and grabbed Karl's wrist. With a quick twist, the sickening sound of snapping bones filled the small office, followed by the thump of Karl's gun as it hit the linoleum floor.

Derik wrapped his fingers around Karl's neck, cutting off the man's scream of pain. He then lifted the man up until his feet dangled several inches off the floor. Karl desperately clawed at his arm. Derik flashed Karl a menacing smile.

"Mr. Wong, why don't you go let your wife know you're okay," Bert said to the frightened store owner. Then he instructed, "Give us a couple of minutes, though, before you call this in, okay?"

"Yeah… Okay," Mr. Wong choked out.

Out of the corner of his eye, Derik saw Bert step to the side so the shop owner could leave, then he returned his full focus to the man he was holding. Karl was no longer struggling to escape. In fact, his eyes were beginning to roll back in his head. Derik realized that the man was about to pass out from lack of oxygen. In disgust, he turned and dropped Karl onto the rolling chair that was in front of the desk.

The chair tilted at an odd angle under Karl's weight. Derik removed a long blade from the sheath at his waist, gripped the arm of the chair to steady it, and placed the sharp point against the pulsing artery in Karl's neck.

"Where did the men take my mate?" he demanded.

"Wha….?" Karl asked, his voice slurred from a mixture of dazed confusion and pain.

"Where have they taken my mate?" Derik growled slowly, the point of his blade drawing blood.

Bert reached out and gripped his arm. "You better let me handle this before you kill him, son," he grimaced.

Derik tightened his grip on the chair arm, leaving deep imprints in the metal; then he straightened and stepped aside. Bert gave him a relieved nod before he stood in front of Karl and slapped the man several times on the cheek.

"The bastard broke my wrist," Karl whimpered.

"Yeah, well, be thankful he didn't rip off your whole arm. Now, where did the others take the girl?" Bert demanded.

Karl looked back and forth between Derik and Bert with a desperate, calculating expression. Derik narrowed his eyes. If the man so much as twitched wrong, he would break a few more of Karl's bones.

"The Digs… They took her to The Digs. DiMaggio wants his money back… with interest," Karl finally replied.

"You better be telling us the truth, Karl. My friend here doesn't take kindly to being lied to," Bert said.

Karl shot them a pain-filled sneer. "I don't need to lie. If you want to die, I'm more than happy to help you into the grave. DiMaggio has enough firepower to kill an army. You don't stand a chance," he choked out.

Derik had heard enough. His fist slammed into Karl's chin with a sickening thud. Karl's head snapped back, then he slumped off the chair and fell in a boneless mass to the floor. Derik turned, looked at Bert's bemused expression, and shrugged.

"The shop owners will not have to worry about him escaping," he stated.

"You think?" Bert dryly retorted as he stepped over Karl.

## CHAPTER SIX

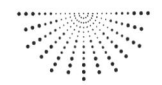

Bert muttered under his breath as they walked along the dark streets. Derik wasn't sure if the old man was doing it to fit with his persona or just liked talking to himself. He grimaced when Bert repeated for the fourth time that they were probably going to die.

"We are not going to die. I will go in and rescue my mate," he said.

Bert scowled at him. "Mate? What are you, part animal? Animals mate. That little girl deserves to be respected. She's either your wife, your girlfriend, or that newfangled term couples call themselves nowadays—significant other. I don't like the word mate; it just don't sound respectful enough for my little girl. I'm old-fashioned in that sense, if you know what I mean. And for your information, yes, we probably are going to die because there is no way I'm going to stand outside while you face DiMaggio and his men alone," he snapped.

Catching Bert's wrist when the old man started to wave his hand, Derik turned and faced the human. He studied Bert's face, expecting to see a fearful expression. Instead, he saw resignation and determination. A small crooked smile curved his lips.

"I am not human, Bert," he quietly reminded the man.

Bert raised an eyebrow. "Does that mean you can't die?" Bert demanded.

Derik shook his head. "No, I can die—I am just not that easy to kill," he grudgingly replied.

"Yeah, well, neither am I, and I've had a lot more years of practice with people shooting at me," Bert stated.

"I'm sure that you are not, though I believe this time it would be best to allow me to go alone. Something tells me that my ma… that Runt would not be happy if something were to happen to you," Derik said.

*No, I would not be. Take your time. I need about another ten minutes, then just create a distraction. I can get myself out of this shit hole.*

Derik blinked in shock when Runt spoke in his mind. He shook his head. How could he forget that she was linked to him?

A soft snort sounded in his mind. *You're an open book, alien,* she replied.

"What is it? Do you have some kind of alien sixth sense about danger or something?" Bert asked with a baffled expression.

Derik realized he had stiffened and was standing with a scowl on his face. He impatiently shook his head and released the man's wrist.

"Runt is communicating with me. She wants us to take our time and cause a distraction," he replied.

"Runt…? How?" Bert stuttered.

A tiny version of RITA appeared suddenly in a soft transparent glow emitted from the communicator on his wrist, and she caroled triumphantly, "She has tapped into DiMaggio's computer system!" RITA's dark red hair was pulled back into a tight bun, and she was dressed all in black, which made her look like she was a floating head. "Thank goodness she connected to the Internet through the new computer Terra and Cosmos designed. Now I can locate her. Do you want me to go to her, Derik?" RITA asked.

"Holy Mother of Mary! What the hell is that?" Bert exclaimed, stumbling back several steps.

Derik could understand Bert's alarm. If he had not known about RITA, he would have been shocked as well.

"Hi Bert, I'm RITA, the most advanced AI on Earth, besides my darling FRED. I work with Cosmos and Avery at CRI. I'm the one who has been chatting with you," RITA introduced herself.

"CRI RITA? You mean you aren't real? Bloody hell! Now, I've got aliens who can hear voices in their head and floating heads that talk. What will Cosmos think of next?" Bert muttered with a shake of his head.

"It is amazing, isn't it? Derik, we should coordinate our approach. Do you want me to connect with Amelia? I can also scope out DiMaggio's security system and might be able to deactivate it through the link Amelia has created," RITA suggested.

"Gather what information you can get covertly and let me know where she is once we get there," he instructed.

*I don't need RITA's help.*

Derik absently held up a hand to indicate his companions should wait as he focused on what his mate was telling him.

*I can get out on my own. DiMaggio is using a system that is heavily encrypted. I needed to be online here to access it. Yeah, the big turd is still pissed about the last time he captured me—I hacked his system and escaped—but I'm fine. I can deactivate the security myself, just not yet. I don't want to alert him to what I'm doing,* Runt stated.

*Forget about his system. You need to get out of there. I'm sending RITA to you. She can find what you need,* he retorted.

*No, she can't. All I need is a distraction once I've got what I want,* she snapped in response.

Silence stretched for several seconds while he counted to ten. He was trying to remember his training. Emotions caused mistakes, and he couldn't afford to make any at the moment. The trouble was, none of his training had prepared him for dealing with a stubborn, opinionated, single-minded human woman who lived by her own rules.

*How do you plan to get out?* he finally asked.

*I've got a plan,* she replied.

Derik waited… and waited… and waited. He groaned and ran his hand down his face. He ignored RITA's amused expression and Bert's perplexed one.

*Are you going to tell me what this plan is, or do you expect me to guess what it is?* he demanded.

*You cause the distraction I need, and I escape,* she stated.

"That's it? That is your plan?" he exclaimed in a low, disbelieving tone.

"Whose plan?" Bert asked in confusion.

"Oh, dear, this doesn't sound good," RITA replied.

"That is *not* a plan—that is…. I don't know what it is called, but that is not a plan," he growled.

*Whatever, gotta go,* she responded.

Just like that, she was gone again. He fought against the barrier she erected, but it didn't give. He raised his fists in the air and took a deep breath. Aggravated, he turned his attention back to RITA and Bert.

"RITA, go to Amelia. Be ready to cause a distraction if I am not close enough when needed. Bert, show me where this Digs is located," Derik instructed.

RITA murmured her assent before she disappeared back into Cyberspace. Bert looked at him for a moment before shaking his head.

"This has got to be the craziest assignment I've ever had," he muttered.

*Stay safe until we get there,* he silently ordered, *and Amelia... we are going to have a serious discussion about some of the decisions that you make.*

*My decisions...? Oh, wait! They are MY decisions, aren't they? Why? Maybe because I am the boss of me,* she sarcastically replied.

*Yes, they are.... You are.... You know what I mean! You should have asked for help. You are no longer alone,* he countered.

*Only because you are always in my head! Do you have any idea how distracting that is?* she retorted.

*I do now,* he muttered.

Her low snort of amused laughter made him grin. His mate was turning out to be everything he had dreamed about over the last two years—and more. He shook his head when Bert raised an eyebrow and shot him a questioning look.

*Whatever. Gotta concentrate now. Don't get Bert killed,* she instructed before she pulled away from him again.

Derik released a softly muttered curse before he gestured to Bert that they should move out. He silently followed Bert as they worked their way deeper into the city. Several blocks later, they turned down a long, dark alley littered with large dumpsters. Bert paused at the end and pointed at a building across the street.

"That's The Digs," Bert said, shoving his hands in the pockets of his coat. "So, what's this plan you were talking about?"

Derik was silent for a moment. "I will go and introduce myself to the human called DiMaggio," he replied.

"That's your plan?" Bert hissed in disbelief.

Derik ignored Bert's muttered comment that he should have retired to Florida when he had the chance. Instead, he stared at the entrance to the building in front of him. There were several men standing out front. He recognized two of them. They had been with the man who had grabbed his mate.

*Runt,* a soft voice corrected him in his mind.

*How do you keep doing that?* he silently demanded.

*Doing what?* Runt replied.

*I should sense your presence in my mind, yet I don't,* he grudgingly admitted.

*I dunno. You're the alien. You should know more about this stuff than I do,* Runt responded.

*I am coming in,* he replied.

*That's your plan? Just... coming in?* she asked.

*You said you needed a distraction, I am giving you a distraction,* he growled in response to her skeptical tone.

*Wow! Getting killed. Now that is a novel idea. Why didn't I think of that?* she sarcastically replied.

"I will not get myself killed," he retorted under his breath.

*Whatever,* she replied with a snort.

Bert shook his head, thinking that Derik was talking to him. "Well, you could've fooled me," he muttered.

∾

**An hour earlier:**

Runt woke with a start. She sat up and looked around, thinking that it was amazing how fast a body could recover once it had oxygen, then her mind turned to the fact that her mission had been a success—of sorts.

She was in an elaborately decorated room, sitting on a luxurious dark brown leather sofa. The floor was covered with rich oak hardwood while several cheap reproductions of Greco-Roman Renaissance paintings from various artists decorated the wall. It didn't take her long to deduce that she had been deposited in DiMaggio's private office.

What surprised her the most was that she was alone. She hadn't expected DiMaggio to make that mistake after what had happened the last time they met. She grimaced when the thought struck her that DiMaggio had either set up a trap or he was getting sloppy in his criminal old age. Whichever was the case, there was something very weird going on.

Curious, she stood and walked over to the door. It had an electronic lock. She tested the handle and sighed when it didn't open.

Turning around, she scanned the room again. There was one window. She walked over and pulled back the curtains covering it. There were bars across the glass on the inside that were secured with another electronic lock. She would need the code to unlock it.

*Obviously DiMaggio does not believe in being in accordance with fire regulations,* she thought dispassionately as she studied the bars.

Releasing the curtains, she turned and began to search the room for hidden cameras, listening devices, and her missing backpack, but had no luck finding anything. DiMaggio had probably handed her stuff over to his tech guy. She would have to remember to get it before she left. Her favorite pair of headphones was inside the bag. The tech guy better not take them, or she would hunt him down and personally hand him his balls. First code of a hacker—okay, maybe not the first, but it should be, was never to mess with another person's headphones.

She walked over to DiMaggio's desk and sat down in the oversized chair. A few framed photos cluttered the right corner. They showed several beautiful women laughing up at the fat old man. She rolled her eyes in disgust.

"Really? I swear some women just need to be bitch-slapped for being so stupid," she muttered under her breath.

She sat back in the plush chair and nodded in approval when it gently rocked. It was nice. Too bad she couldn't take it with her when she decided to leave—not that she would have anywhere to put it, but it was really sweet.

Bending forward, she peered under the desk. There was a panic button to the left. She should try to avoid pressing that, she thought with amusement.

She slid her fingers down and tested each of the drawers. They were locked. Biting her lip, she looked at the door and then shrugged.

*Honestly, if the man didn't want me going through his stuff, he shouldn't have locked me in his office,* she thought.

She pushed back her sleeve until she saw her emergency kit wrapped around her forearm, then slid out a thin, straight piece of metal. One of the main things she'd learned on the streets was always to be prepared for any occasion. After all, you never knew when you might have to pick a lock to escape.

In seconds, the top drawer was open. It didn't take long for her to unlock the rest of the desk drawers after that. She wiggled her nose when she saw the wide variety of gourmet chocolates and other boxed delicacies. There was nothing in any of the drawers except junk food.

"Wow! Somebody has a sweet tooth," she chuckled. She muttered to herself as she slid out of the chair so that she could look under the drawers. "I bet his doctor and dentist love to see him—not! I should cut off his candy suppliers. I bet that would get his attention and he'd really be pissed at me then."

She closed the drawers, climbed back into the office chair, and removed her wide, gothic-style leather bracelet from her wrist. In the center of the bracelet was a large onyx jewel with silver inlays. She smiled as she pressed her finger to the center and pulled her hand away.

A hologram of a screen and keyboard appeared above the center of the jewel. The technology for the micro-computer had come from Baade, the design had come from Cosmos and Terra, but the programming inside this particular model was uniquely hers and RITA's.

She began typing, and a layout of DiMaggio's security system soon appeared. She glanced swiftly through the three-dimensional diagram. Her mind absorbed the encrypted code that appeared on the screen beside the diagram. Soon, she had access through a backdoor in the program.

She was in the middle of her search when she felt the first tingling sensation that she wasn't alone sweep through her. She looked at the door; then scanned the room again. The feeling grew stronger, and she realized it was coming from inside her head, not from her surroundings. The sensation was slightly different from the other times she had connected with the alien. During the past two years, whenever she felt the odd pressure, she usually pushed him into a metal file cabinet in her mind and kept him there.

This time she analyzed the sensation. It was as if she were there with him—seeing the same thing that he was seeing. His thoughts were clear and focused. He wanted to find her. She could feel his determination, but she could also sense something that he was trying to hide. It took her a few seconds to recognize the emotion. Fear—he was afraid—for her. He also wanted RITA to find her.

*I don't need RITA's help. I can get out on my own. DiMaggio is using a system that is heavily encrypted. I needed to be online here to access it. The big turd is still pissed about the last time he captured me—I hacked his system and escaped—but I'm fine. I can deactivate the security, just not yet. I don't want him to know what I'm doing,* she informed him.

She groaned and shook her head. She hadn't planned on reaching out to him, but she just couldn't help herself.

*Forget about his system. You need to get out of there. I'm sending RITA to you. She can find what you need,* Derik ordered.

*No, she can't. All I need is a distraction once I've got what I came for,* she snapped in response.

She absently realized that he hadn't responded to her retort. She grinned when he suddenly 'spoke' to her. He sounded a little annoyed.

Their silent argument made her grin. She couldn't remember the last time she'd ever had this much fun. She also couldn't remember the last time that she had talked so much, even if it was in her head!

*Are you going to tell me what this plan is, or do you expect me to guess what it is?* he pressed.

She bit her lip and thought for a moment. Yes, she had a plan. It involved a lock, a window, and hopefully a fire escape or sturdy pipe attached to the building next to said window, but he didn't have to know that. It would help if DiMaggio and his thugs were a little preoccupied while she was doing all of that.

*You cause the distraction I need and I escape,* she suggested.

She absently listened to his outraged reply with one part of her brain while the other part of her mind focused on her search. She briefly pulled away from him when she found an interesting thread of code that needed her undivided attention.

Following it, she felt a sense of triumph when a file appeared with the name she had been searching for. It wasn't a huge find, more of a nibble, but it was a lead. Her gut feeling had been correct. She had been right to come looking for DiMaggio.

She blinked when Derik's suddenly fervent thoughts pushed through the fragile wall she had built. This had to be a first! What guy even thought about threats like this in real life and was actually serious about carrying them out? It was kind of sexy in a weird, primitive way.

Her expression twisted into wry amusement when he continued his silent rant, and she wondered if he even realized that his thoughts were being loudly broadcasted to her—in 16K UHD!

*I'm coming for you, and when I get my hands on you this time, I'm going to tie you up, throw you over my shoulder, and carry you to my world where I know you will be safe!*

Unable to resist, she sent an image to him of a hairy caveman standing in front of a cave, holding a wooden club. Biting her lip to keep from laughing too loud, she added the caveman picking his nose.

Runt could sense Derik's confusion as he tried to understand the image. She sighed. Aliens! And they were supposed to be the smarter species.

*You're acting like a caveman. A man who's all brawn and no brains,* she explained.

*I don't pick my nose,* he defensively retorted.

*But you don't deny the caveman part?* she asked with amusement.

*I only appear to act like this primitive creature where* you *are concerned. And I am not that hairy,* he teased.

The thought of him without a shirt on brought an unexpected blush to her face. She wiggled in the chair as the warmth spread through her. This was getting a little too personal for her.

*Whatever,* she replied.

This time when she pulled away, she made sure that, instead of building a wall between them, her mental image of Derik was shoved back into the file cabinet that she usually kept him in. The guy was beginning to get under her skin. She didn't like that—*not* one bit!

She had no sooner locked Derik away than RITA's face appeared in the center of the holographic screen in front of her. RITA's disapproving gaze made her wince.

"Amelia, darling, what were you thinking when you disappeared like that—and now you're trying to go after this awful man by yourself! Do you have any idea how worried everyone has been?" RITA chided.

## CHAPTER SEVEN

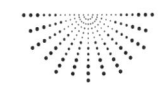

Derik dropped the last man standing between himself and the front door of the building. Bert shook his head and slid his gun back into the pocket of his coat. He looked around before nodding to Derik.

"We can drag them around the corner to get them out of sight. I have some plastic restraints we can put on them," Bert said.

A nearby SUV slowed and pulled up in front. They both turned to face it. Bert started to reach for his weapon again, but relaxed and grinned when Robert stepped out and walked around the front of the vehicle. He paused for a moment to study the pile of bodies.

"Are they dead?" Robert asked with a look of distaste.

"Naw, just knocked out. How'd you know to show up here?" Bert asked.

"RITA suggested that you might need some assistance. It seems she was correct, as usual," Robert dryly replied as he took a pair of black leather gloves from his coat pocket and pulled them on.

"Help me pull the bodies around to the side. You got anything we can use to gag them?" Bert asked with a grin.

"I'll have to look. I don't normally carry such items with me. I guess I'll have to remember to store some in the car for the next time," Robert said.

Derik watched the two men struggle to carry one of DiMaggio's men. At this rate, he would be in and out of the building before they moved even half the pile of unconscious criminals. The thought had no sooner formed in his mind than a car drove by and Robert and Bert suddenly dropped their man back to the ground.

Shaking his head, he bent down, threw one man over his shoulder, and grabbed the arm of another. He strode by Bert and Robert. Both men watched him a moment before looking at each other.

"Show off," Bert muttered.

"Wait until he's our age," Robert replied.

Several minutes later, Derik looked down at the line of unconscious men propped up against the brick building. After Robert and Bert finished tying them up, Derik stepped back and asked, "Are you two sure you can handle this?"

Bert shot him a disgusted look. "Son, Robert and I've been doing this kind of thing since before you were born. You go and distract DiMaggio, while I find Runt and get her to safety. Robert will finish up here and have the car ready for us."

Derik nodded in agreement, turned on his heel, and retraced his steps to the front of the building. He was about to kick in the front doors when they suddenly opened. His booted foot hit the startled man in the stomach. The man flew through the air and landed on his back, slid across the polished marble floor, and disappeared through another set of doors. Behind him, Derik could hear Bert's low curses.

"Any idea where Runt might be?" Bert bit out when they clearly heard yelling on the other side of the door.

RITA suddenly appeared and said, "She's in DiMaggio's office on the third floor. There's a service elevator down the hall and to your left. I've taken control of the security system," she added.

"Don't get yourself killed," Bert muttered to Derik before he turned to his left.

"I won't," he replied with a grim smile as he walked toward the still swinging doors.

"Well, what did you find?" Ramon DiMaggio demanded.

"There... there wasn't.... She wasn't carrying any computer equipment. The backpack had clothes, a pair of shoes, and a really sweet pair of headphones.... Nothing... nothing else, sir."

Ramon bit down on his cigar and stared at the nervous young IT tech he had hired. The kid, Howard Swarovski, was supposed to be the best—according to his resume. The twenty-something young man looked more like a twelve-year-old boy. Of course, Baby-Face James had looked that way until he was in his fifties.

He loudly snapped his fingers. Howard jumped when Gabriel stepped forward, and Ramon motioned for Gabriel to bend down so he could whisper to him.

"Bring the girl to me. I don't care if she is awake or not," he ordered.

"Yes, Boss," Gabriel responded.

He silently returned his gaze to his IT man, and signaled Howard to place Runt's backpack on the table. With another wave of his hand, he dismissed the young man.

"Go check the security systems or whatever I pay you for," he snapped.

"Yes... yes, sir," Howard stuttered.

Ramon watched Howard hurriedly back away—right into two of his henchmen. He released a long sigh when the kid practically fell down the curved steps to the empty dance floor below.

*Parents just don't raise crooks like they used to,* he thought with regret before he focused on the bag in front of him.

Unzipping one compartment at a time, he began pulling out the items inside. Soon, rolled up shirts, a pair of black cargo pants, and a mesh bag of lacy undergarments were lined up on the table in front of him. The guards snickered when Ramon held up the set of sexy black panties and matching bra.

"She has nice taste," Ramon observed, drawing out more chuckles from his men.

He shifted his gaze from the lace he was holding between his fingers to the staircase. He grinned when he saw Runt's eyes flash from his fingers to his face, and she scowled at him.

"Are you adding pervert to your resume? Oh, wait, I saw the pictures on your desk—you've already done that," she said in greeting.

Ramon curled his fingers around the black lace, and with his other hand, he removed the cigar from between his lips. He placed it in the ashtray in front of him. Deep down, he didn't consider himself a bad man—life was about business—though he recognized that he lived by a different set of laws. The laws he followed were set by the wealthy and politically connected. This little urchin couldn't begin to understand, not for quite a few more years, he suspected.

"Ah, Amelia. It has been a while. Where have you been? Tormenting and stealing from other unsuspecting businessmen?" Ramon asked.

She rolled her eyes at him, pulled out the chair across from him, and sat down as if she owned the nightclub herself. He observed her with an analytical clarity, keeping his underlying resentment and nostalgia from showing in his expression. There was something about the defiant, almost bored look in her eyes that reminded him so much of himself as a young man.

"Are you finished fingering my panties?" she asked.

Ramon dropped the lace onto the table. He sat back and moodily gazed at her through half-closed eyes. Indecision coursed through him. On the one hand, Runt fascinated him. On the other, she was a thorn in his side. She was brilliant. He had no doubt about that, but she was also a threat because of her willful and defiant attitude.

He had kept tabs on her since the first time he'd heard about her. Her loser of a father, Lou 'Left-hand' Thomas, had bragged that his kid could hack into any computer in the world, and when Lou had started showing up to gamble with unexplained amounts of cash on hand, Ramon had started to think there might be something to what Lou had been saying.

Unfortunately, Lou not only got greedy—he also thought he held more power than he really did, blithely bragging about his only asset

—Runt. Without her, he was nothing—and the two of them were nothing against Boris Avilov.

No one stole from that Russian oligarch. The mobster had a long reach. The word on the street was that he had an insider in the White House, and it turned out that it had been true—until several of President Askew Thomas' cabinet members resigned or were arrested.

He wasn't sure what had happened to the Vice-President, but the Secretary of State was recently charged with working as an unregistered Foreign Agent—among other things. What fascinated him was the sudden hushed chatter that Avilov and his number one man, Afon Dolinski, had vanished without a trace, leaving a huge hole in the organization that had yet to be filled.

Ramon absently scratched his large belly. He really could use Runt's talents. The small taste he'd had when her father was alive and the changing times made him realize how much of an asset she would be to his organization. He had been trying to move up for years, but with the Russian's connections in the White House, that was damn near impossible. Now that there was a vacuum, he might have a chance—if he had the right information on a few key Washington players. Information that Runt could access.

"I have a proposition for you," he stated.

"No," she immediately responded.

"Girl, didn't you ever learn anything from your father?" Ramon growled.

She reached over and grabbed her undergarments as well as the mesh bag she kept them in. Her gaze never left his, and he knew she was creating the silence to irritate him. He grabbed his cigar off of the ashtray and brought it back to his lips where he clamped down hard on the butt.

"Yeah, never to deal with assholes like him," she finally replied.

He leaned forward and rested his thick arms on the table. "You almost make me wish your father was still alive, Runt," he said in a low tone.

She smirked. "Yeah, well, neither one of us miss the fact that you can't bring back my dear, old dad," she retorted in a voice filled with sarcasm.

Ramon pushed his chair back and stood. He had tried to be nice. Maybe it was time to show the little girl what happens when she plays in the adult world. He wanted his money back. Once he had wrung out of her what she had done with it, she could either work for him or join her worthless father in the cemetery.

"Where's my money?" he demanded.

She carefully folded her undergarments, ran her fingers along the colorful top of the mesh bag, and put all her belongings in her backpack, then she looked up at him thoughtfully… and shrugged. He ripped the stub of the cigar out of his mouth and smashed the smoldering end into the glass ashtray, littering the table with flaming bits of ash.

"Gone," she finally replied. "I gave it to a bunch of different charities. The Humane Society thanks you for your generous donation, by the way," she said sweetly.

"You…," his voice faded as outrage filled him.

Gone! His money was gone. The bitch had given away five million dollars of his money to charities. He opened and closed his mouth like a fish gasping for oxygen. He furiously raised his hand and she warily watched the sudden movement. He would wring every penny, with interest, from her scrawny little neck.

He'd begun to step around the table when he heard a loud crash from the lower section of the building. He signaled to the two men standing behind Runt to find out what was going on. His eyes flickered to her face when she rolled her eyes.

"What is it?" he demanded.

"My signal to leave," she stated, zipping up her backpack and slinging it over her shoulder.

Ramon's retort died on his lips when he heard gunfire followed by hoarse screams. He strode over to the railing, and looked down. In the center of the room, surrounded by four of Ramon's men lying unmoving on the ground, stood a young man dressed all in black. He held a long, glowing blade in one hand and the limp body of another guard in the other.

A shiver of horror ran through Ramon when the man looked up. Even from this distance, he could see unnatural colors swirling in the man's eyes, and... there was something wrong with his mouth.... Were those his *teeth*?

"What the hell is that?" he choked out.

"Vampire. Time to leave," Runt bluntly responded.

He glanced at Runt with a startled expression, but an unearthly snarl made him quickly return his gaze to the threat at hand. The man's expression was possessive, and his focus was locked on Runt.

Ramon quickly reached out and gripped Runt's arm when she started to turn around. The creature below narrowed his eyes and released a savage roar.

"Ouch!" Runt hissed when he tightened his grip on her arm.

"Kill that... that thing!" he barked at his remaining men.

## CHAPTER EIGHT

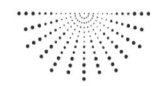

Runt fought to break free of DiMaggio's grip, gritting her teeth at his painful hold around her upper arm. Behind her, she could hear rapid gunfire.

"He's an alien vampire, doofus! You can't kill him," she snapped.

"An alien?" Ramon hissed.

She stumbled when Ramon sharply turned a corner. Because of his girth, he took up more room than he realized. She bounced against the corner. The force of the impact knocked the backpack off her shoulder.

"My stuff!" she protested.

"Leave it!" he snapped.

Runt looked behind her in frustration. She had not planned on DiMaggio bringing her out into the club, but when she'd caught sight of her backpack, she'd thought things might actually work out. It's not like she wasn't familiar with the whole intimidation process. She had seen it dozens of times when she was a kid.

He would try to be nice. She would be rude. He would get mad, but try to reason with her. She would be ruder. He would threaten her. She would roll her eyes and goad him until he got really pissed off and gave her time to 'think'. There was a fine line. If she pushed too hard, she would end up with weighted boots in the bay. If she gave in too quickly, he would know she was playing him for the fool that he was.

The screw-up came in the form of an alien who liked to make grand entrances! If she had been given just a couple of more minutes, she was sure DiMaggio would have sent her—and her backpack— back to his office to seriously think about her future.

*Life would have been a little less adventurous,* she thought as another round of gunfire filled the air—this time closer.

"You are in so much trouble!" she growled.

"I should have killed your scrawny ass when I had the chance the first time," DiMaggio snapped back.

She stumbled when he pushed her into his office. Her eyes widened when she saw the familiar figure standing near the barred window. Bert grinned and winked at her. She hurried over to his side as DiMaggio entered the room behind her. Bert aimed his gun at DiMaggio's head.

"No need to lock the door… it wouldn't do much good anyway. Young Derik can demolish it with one kick," Bert cheerfully stated.

DiMaggio froze, then uttered a long litany of expletives.

"Now, now, there is a young lady in the room," Bert chided. "I wouldn't try to reach for any guns if I were you. I'm a very good shot."

Ramon shot her a nasty look before he lifted both of his hands. He stepped to the side when Bert motioned for him to move away from the door. Runt started toward the door when DiMaggio was far enough away from it.

"What are you doing?" Bert asked.

Runt looked at her friend. "Getting my backpack. My good headphones are in it," she said.

Bert shook his head. "Damn, girl. Can't you hear the gunfire?" he demanded in disbelief.

She rolled her eyes at Bert. "Yes. It is downstairs. My backpack is in the corridor. I paid a lot of money for those headphones," she replied.

"Get them and get your ass back in here. Your alien boyfriend won't be *happy* if you get shot, if you know what I mean," Bert snapped.

Runt grabbed the door handle and pulled—it was locked. She turned her head and glared at DiMaggio when he chuckled maliciously.

"You two ain't going nowhere without me letting you out, girlie," DiMaggio said in a smug tone.

She touched the micro-computer on her wrist. "RITA, can you please unlock the door for me?" Runt requested.

"No problem, love," RITA replied.

She flashed a snarky grin at DiMaggio when the lock clicked, then twisted the knob and pulled the door open far enough to peek out.

"I'll pay you six figures a year to work for me," DiMaggio said urgently behind her.

She looked at him with dark, fathomless eyes. "You don't get it, do you? It isn't about the money. It's never been about the money," she quietly replied before opening the door and walking out.

She took a deep breath and glanced both ways to make sure the area was clear. The sound of gunfire had faded. Hurrying down the hall, she spied the strap of her backpack near the corner. She turned the corner as a figure emerged from the room across from her. She raised her hands to defend herself when he rushed her.

He wrapped his hands around her throat and pushed her back against the wall. She gasped and struggled to break free. It wasn't until she saw the bank of computer equipment glowing through the open doorway that she realized the guy holding her must be DiMaggio's IT guy.

"Let… me… go," she hissed. He wasn't much older than she was, but he was definitely stronger.

The IT guy shook his head. His eyes glittered with fear and anger. She gagged when his hands tightened.

"What is that thing down there? Where is DiMaggio?" he demanded.

"Fu…ck off," she hoarsely replied.

She tried to kick him, but he blocked her. The thumb of his right hand was pressed against her throat, and she could feel a tingling sensation in her body as he slowly cut off her air supply.

This jerk knew more than he let on about self-defense. She had worked long enough with Cosmos and Avery to know the guy was using some kind of pressure point, martial arts maneuver on her.

"Wrong answer, sweetheart," Howard murmured.

Runt turned her head slightly, trying to ease the increased pressure on her neck. Spots started to dance before her eyes. She released her grip on his arm and slid the fingers of her right hand over to the micro-computer on her left wrist, and pressed down on the button.

"RI…TA," she whispered.

The lights in the hallway flickered. Howard loosened his grip on her neck just enough to allow her to breathe again. The hair on her arms rose as the electrical charge built. Next to Howard, she could see RITA's ghostly figure beginning to form as she accessed more power.

"What the…?" Howard choked out in horror.

The building's lights went dark, and Howard's normally deep voice changed to a high-pitched screech when he was suddenly lifted and tossed against the wall behind him. RITA was now life-sized and glowing in all her glory between Runt and the now not-so-brave tech. Long strands of dark red hair swirled around RITA as if she were underwater or caught in a whirlwind. The ghostly AI floated several inches off the floor, which added to the supernatural feel.

"You really shouldn't mess with my little girl," RITA snarled.

Runt dimly registered that the lights were back on, shining with only a small portion of their former brightness, but she couldn't look away from RITA. The AI wore a brilliant light blue gown that sparkled with pinpoints of light. In her hand was a long sword that was pointed at Howard.

Runt slid down the wall until she was squatting next to her backpack. This was a RITA that Runt had never seen before—a furious AI in a futuristic corporeal form. The lights flickered wildly as RITA grew in size until the bulbs began to explode one by one along the entire hallway, sending tiny shards of glass all over the floor.

Runt pressed one of her hands to the floor to hold herself steady, and watched in awe as RITA pulled off a visual effect that would have made a master visual effects designer drool. The enraged AI was also in the running for an Academy award as far as Runt was concerned. She lifted a hand to her hair when she felt it rising up.

"RITA...," she grunted out in warning.

"You dare to lay your filthy hands on my Amelia? I will personally see to it that you NEVER hack another computer system. Every computer you EVER touch will become encrypted, you miserable little excuse for a programmer. I will lock your ATM and you'll have to spend the rest of your life writing checks! I'm talking paper, you sniveling piece of corrupted code! Which I will make bounce so you have additional fees!" RITA snarled.

"Uh, RITA...," Runt said, trying to interject again.

"If you think you'll ever qualify for a loan, forget it! I'll sink your credit score to the deepest recesses of the financial world. You'll be living on the streets, unable to access a single email. Your phones will die and I'll... I'll... I'll delete your music library!" RITA vowed. Faint red emergency lights flickered on in straight lines along the walls.

"Uh, RITA... I think... you might... be pulling a little too much juice," Runt cautioned when she saw flames rising from the bank of computers across the hall.

"FRED! RITA has overloaded the system," Derik's deep voice called out.

"I'm working on it." FRED's voice could be heard before he appeared next to RITA. "Easy, love," he soothed. "Don't let that insignificant piece of virus get to you."

"He threatened Amelia," RITA replied, her voice still quivering with outrage.

"I know, love. I know," FRED responded.

"I'm just *so* mad," RITA sniffed as she began to fade.

"We may have to adjust the adaptive range of our new emotional program. Can't have us 'blowing a gasket'," FRED chortled.

Runt winced when the piercing sound of the fire alarm filled the air. A second later, the sprinklers came on.

She jumped when she felt a hand on her arm. Turning her head, she came face to face with Derik. His silver eyes glowed with the same intensity that RITA's had a moment ago. A shiver ran through her when the cold water raining down on them slid under the collar of her jacket.

"We've got to get out of here," Bert muttered.

Runt looked across the hall where Howard had been pressed against the wall. He was gone. She looked up at Bert in confusion before her eyes scanned the rest of the hallway.

"Where's DiMaggio?" she asked.

"Slimy bastard took me by surprise when the lights began to blow. He tossed me behind his desk and disappeared. You could have stuck me with a fork. I had no idea that someone that big could move so fast." He rubbed his shoulder. "The fire department and police will be here any second. Robert moved the car a block over. We can take the back exit to the alley," Bert added.

"Sounds good. I got what I wanted," she responded.

Derik's strong fingers cupped her elbow, helping her to rise to her feet. Runt blinked in surprise when he held up her backpack with his other hand. His fingers tightened on her arm when she started to turn and follow Bert.

"How badly did he hurt you?" he quietly asked.

"I'm good," she responded.

He narrowed his eyes, his gaze piercing, and suddenly bent his head, pressing a light but possessive kiss to her lips. She sharply inhaled in surprise and her lips trembled from a sudden burst of heat. She shot him a startled, confused look.

"We must go now. I can hear movement downstairs," Derik murmured.

She nodded in agreement, her brow creasing as she worried that Derik would know what she was thinking—and feeling. Determined to hide her troubled thoughts, she pushed them behind a mental wall, pulled away from his strong hands, and hurried after Bert.

CHAPTER NINE

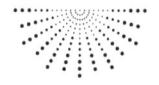

The three of them descended the back staircase, and reached the basement level door just as several firemen opened the door on the first floor. Bert held the door open and motioned for Runt to go ahead.

"There's a service door at the other end that leads into the alley. Take a left and head to the second alley. Robert said he would meet us there," Bert urgently said.

"What about you?" she asked.

"I'll be right behind you. I don't want to use the flashlight on our phones in case the cops or firemen see the light under the door. They might have a few questions that we don't want to answer—especially about Derik and all the bodies lying around. Once I shut this door, you won't be able to see a thing," Bert promised.

"Shut the door, Bert. I can see well enough to get us to the exit. I will guide Amel… Runt while you hold onto my coat," Derik instructed.

Runt looked up when she felt Derik's hand against the small of her back. It smelled musty down here. She shivered from a combination of being wet and the cold. The building was old and obviously had not been brought up to date with the current fire code.

With the power out, there was no emergency lighting in this area. Thankfully, there weren't any sprinklers down here either. Unfortunately, Bert was right. Once he closed the door, the faint red light of the emergency strips disappeared, casting them in total darkness.

"Stand in front of me, and I will guide you around the boxes," Derik murmured near her ear.

"Okay," she replied.

Runt was grateful for the warmth of Derik's hands and his comforting touch through her damp clothing. She could feel the familiar suffocating sense of claustrophobia threatening to swallow her. She tried to breathe through her nose to keep from panting. This was one part of tonight's adventure that she could have done without.

*I am here for you,* Derik promised.

*I... hate cluttered, dark places,* she replied.

*Then I will light your way,* he said.

She covered his hands when they spanned each side of her waist. They moved forward in small steps. He guided her around the boxes that she could not see with her own eyes, until slowly, she began to see what he did. She moved to the left to avoid a bucket. Behind them, she could hear Bert's barely audible curse when his foot caught the plastic pail.

*How can you see in the dark?* she asked.

*According to what I was taught, our ability to see in almost absolute darkness was a necessity for survival when dealing with other species,* he explained.

*So there are other aliens out there—besides you?* she asked.

*Yes—there are many others,* he murmured.

*Oh, that's pretty cool.*

That was the only thing she could think to say. His hands on her waist felt—good. Uneasiness washed through her at her reaction. She could feel the mark on her palm tingling. It took all of her self-control not to rub her hand against the back of his to relieve the feeling.

*It's only because I'm not used to this, that's all. It isn't like I've been touched by a lot of people in my life—especially guys,* she thought—making sure that the wall was a foot thick around her thoughts so that Derik couldn't sense her pleasure at his touch—and her unease.

She breathed a sigh of relief when they reached the door, and she grabbed the handle, unlocked it, and checked for a deadbolt.

*Someone is coming,* Derik warned.

"You might want to get a move on, Runt. I think I hear footsteps," Bert said at the same time as Derik's warning.

"I know," she grumbled.

Yanking on the deadbolt, she pulled it free. With a twist of the handle, she opened the door and peeked out. She could see the flashing lights of emergency vehicles and hear the shouts of first responders as they communicated with each other.

Pulling the door open further, she stooped and climbed the short set of concrete steps. She made sure the alley was clear before she straightened and took off to the left. Behind her, she could hear Bert's heavy breathing as he followed her. She started to look over her shoulder to make sure Derik was there when she felt the faint brush of amusement in her mind.

*Prime warriors don't make much noise when they walk,* he said.

*I'll have to remember that,* she said.

Picking up speed, she turned the corner just as she heard a shout from behind them ordering them to stop. She grimaced and kept going, then grinned with relief when she saw Robert standing by the SUV. He pulled open the back passenger door the second he recognized them.

"Thanks, Robert," she murmured before she climbed onto the seat.

"My pleasure, Miss Thomas. I see that RITA didn't remain contained?" Robert dryly observed.

"A man attacked Amelia. RITA was not pleased," Derik replied.

"Ah… that would explain it," Robert said with a nod.

Robert shut the door after Derik slid in, and hurried around to the driver's side. Bert had already climbed into the front passenger seat. Robert shifted the running vehicle into gear and pulled out onto the street. He made a U-turn, heading away from DiMaggio's building and the police officer who was rounding the corner on foot as they sped away.

"Damn," Bert remarked.

Runt stared at the dark streets around them too. It looked like RITA really had 'blown a gasket'. She wondered how much of the city was down.

Robert chuckled. "I've been instructed to take you to the safe house," he said, glancing at Derik in the rearview mirror.

"That would be good," Derik replied.

The first lights didn't appear for almost six blocks. Runt gently ran her fingers over the micro-computer on her wrist. Her mind swirled with anticipation; her thoughts completely focused on the encrypted file she had downloaded—until she felt warm fingers threading through hers. She turned and looked at Derik. He was talking quietly with Bert and Robert. He wasn't looking at her, but his fingers tightened when she tried to pull away. After a few seconds, she leaned back against the seat and left her hand in his. What did it really matter? They were just holding hands—it's not like they were making out.

*What is making out?* he silently inquired.

Runt could feel her cheeks heat. *Nothing,* she mentally mumbled.

She turned her attention back to the window. Some clouds had rolled in and a light drizzle of rain had begun to fall. She looked up at the elegant townhouse as it came into view. It was one of CRI's safe houses. She had stayed here before, thanks to RITA.

The SUV pulled to the curb. Robert shifted into park and exited the vehicle. A moment later, he opened the back door for her.

"If you need anything, give me a call," Robert instructed.

"Thanks, Robert," Runt quietly said as she slid out of the car. She turned and looked at Bert. "See you around, Bert."

Bert chuckled. "Good luck, Runt."

Runt turned in surprise when Derik followed her. She frowned at him before turning her gaze back to Robert. Robert had already returned to the driver's seat and shut the door. A wave of uncertainty filled her when the SUV pulled away and disappeared down the road.

"I hope you don't…," she started to say, turning her attention back to Derik when she saw him sway.

Under the dim glow of the streetlight, she saw that his hand was pressed to his side. There was a dark stain around his fingers. Her lips parted in dismay and she quickly looked at his face.

"You're hurt!" she exclaimed.

"It is a minor injury," he replied with a grimace.

"Yeah, right," she muttered.

She wrapped her arm around his waist and guided him to the steps. They slowly made their way up the stairs to the front door, the aftermath of so much adrenaline now dragging them both down. She stood in front of the door and waited as the facial recognition scanner did its magic. RITA had programmed her face into it the first time she'd come here.

"Let's go," she said.

She pushed the door open when the lock clicked. They stepped inside, and she used her foot to shut the door behind them. She paused in the foyer, unsure of where to go at first.

"I'm monitoring his vitals as best I can, Amelia. I suggest taking him to the medical room located down the hall and to the left, so I can perform a more thorough scan," RITA suggested.

"Right," she muttered under her breath.

Derik chuckled. "And I thought humans would think we were the strange ones," he commented.

"Shut up, I'm mad at you," Runt scolded.

She guided him down the hallway and turned to the left. Only Cosmos—well, and maybe Avery—would have a hospital room in one of their homes. Derik turned around and sat down on the edge of the bed. She took her backpack from him, placed it on the floor, and began to pull off his coat. He stood so she could pull it out from under him.

She twisted and threw the coat onto a nearby chair, then with an impatient brush of her hand, she pushed his fingers away from the buttons of his shirt and quickly undid them. As soon as she had the last one unfastened, she pushed off his shirt.

"You have no idea how long or how many times I've dreamed of you doing this," he confessed.

"You're delusional. Now, shut up and lay down," she ordered, refusing to be distracted. "RITA, can you tell how bad it is?"

"Scanning," RITA replied. "Hold still, please."

Runt wiggled her nose and peered at the torn flesh of his shoulder. It *looked* like a flesh wound, but she was no doctor. Her gaze moved down to a large bruise on his ribcage before she forced herself to look at the wound that was the most troublesome. Her stomach churned when she saw the obvious bullet wound in his lower right side. Swallowing down the bile that rose into her throat, she looked into his eyes.

"It isn't as bad as it looks," Derik insisted. "Cosmos and Terra gave me one of their new medical kits. I need to remove the metal first. Once that is done, I can use the medical device to heal my body," he said.

"You can't remove the bullet," Runt exclaimed. "How do you know it didn't hit something vital? If you pull it out, you could bleed to death," she said, her voice breaking on the last word.

"I can remove the bullet," RITA said. "Cosmos set up the medical unit so it could be operated remotely. There were times when it was necessary."

Runt blinked when RITA and FRED appeared across from the bed. Derik squeezed her hand. Gazing into his eyes, she could feel the strange burn of tears in the back of her eyes.

"You aren't going to cause another power outage, are you?" she asked FRED and RITA.

FRED shook his head. "Cosmos installed a special generator in the basement. For a short period, we can do what's necessary," the Prime AI system reassured her.

"Okay, what do you need me to do?" she asked.

"Stay linked to him, sweetheart. It will help him with the pain," RITA instructed.

Runt nodded and looked down. Derik had closed his eyes. His lips were pressed together, and she could see the lines of pain around his mouth. Impulsively, she raised her hand and smoothed one of the lines. He turned his head toward her hand and pressed a kiss to her palm, right on the mark that was now clearly visible.

"FRED will create a neurological block that will act as a sedative. The block will relax Derik but not place him completely under. I'll numb the area around his wound so I can remove the bullet. The numbing agent will contain some of the nanobots that Cosmos and Terra developed. Avery upgraded each of the CRI facilities after she and Core returned, just in case something like this happened. I'll have to inform her that it was another excellent decision," RITA replied.

Runt nodded, distractedly listening to what RITA was saying. She followed FRED with her gaze when the Prime AI hologram moved to the head of the table, and placed his suddenly solid hands on Derik's temples.

The lights flickered as the two AI systems maxed out the power grid. Runt parted her lips in awe when she saw the thin streams of light emanating from FRED's fingers. Derek's body arched for a moment before he relaxed.

She looked down at their entwined fingers, licked her lips, and took in a long, deep breath. Reaching out, she connected her mind to his.

## CHAPTER TEN

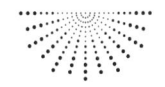

*I will be fine. I have suffered worse injuries than this while training,* he reassured her in a tired voice.

"You must be pretty bad at fighting, then, if you think this is okay," she teased.

*Only when there are more than a dozen men attacking me,* he quipped.

"Only a dozen?" she commented with a roll of her eyes.

She keenly watched as RITA worked on Derik with a surgical skill that could have rivaled the best surgeons in the world. The sound of metal on metal made her wince. She turned her attention back to Derik when he weakly squeezed her hand.

*I cannot feel anything, but thank you for caring,* he faintly murmured in her mind.

*Who said anything about caring? If you're stupid enough to get shot, that's your problem. I was just trying to figure out how I was going to report a dead body without being accused of shooting you,* she silently retorted.

"I love you, too, Amelia," he softly groused out loud.

Runt released an inelegant snort. "Silly alien," she replied.

A strange feeling of loneliness swept through her when he slid deeper into sleep. She lifted her hand to her cheek, and looked down at her fingers in surprise when she realized that they were damp.

Looking up at RITA, she didn't bother to hide the concern in her voice.

"Will he be okay?" she asked.

"Yes. I've removed the bullet. It did not hit any major organs, but it was close. The nanobots are already healing the damage. After a couple of hours, you won't even know that he was in a fight," RITA reassured her.

Runt nodded and returned her gaze to Derik's relaxed face. Releasing his hand, she turned around and reached for the blanket at the end of the bed. She shook it out before she covered him with it.

As she tucked it around his shoulders, she noticed he was wearing a silver chain. She gently pulled on the delicate links, and frowned when she noticed that there was something attached to it.

Sliding her fingers along the chain, she discovered a small oval pendant made of silver. She pulled it closer so she could take a better look at it, and her breath caught in her throat when she turned it over in her hand.

*I know this,* she thought

Trembling, she leaned over him and gently opened the locket. Inside was a picture of her and her mother. This was her locket, the one that she had been forced to leave behind at the warehouse the night they first met.

Tears burned her eyes. He had not only kept the locket, but he was wearing it. She snapped the locket closed and turned the chain until she reached the clasp.

"Amelia," Derik murmured in his sleep.

She froze, her fingers still on the clasp and glanced at his face. He grimaced as he raised his hand to the necklace. She pulled away before their fingers touched and straightened. He wrapped his fingers around the locket and sighed.

"He appears very fond of the silver pendant," FRED observed.

"Yes, he does," Runt softly replied.

After a moment's hesitation, she grabbed the blanket he had pulled free, and tucked it back over his arm and around his shoulder. The light emitting from FRED's fingers had faded, and he had taken several steps back until he was standing next to RITA. Runt noticed that their forms were flickering badly along with the rest of the lights in the room.

RITA shot her an apologetic look. "I'm afraid you'll have to do the rest, love. We've used a considerable amount of energy and need to recharge," she said.

Runt nodded. "Okay," she replied.

"He'll be fine in a couple of hours. Let him sleep while the nanobots finish the repairs," RITA instructed.

"I will," Runt responded.

RITA stepped closer to her. For a brief moment, she could feel the AI's hand brush against her cheek. Runt wrapped her arms around her own waist and lifted her chin.

"Give him a chance, Amelia. When he said he loved you… he meant it," RITA quietly said.

Runt swallowed and shrugged her shoulders. She wasn't going to go down that rabbit hole. How could Derik know if he really loved her? He didn't even *know* her!

She could feel the mark on her hand tingle. Curling her fingers, she lifted the back of her hand to her lips. Things were getting too complicated for her.

She looked at Derik's relaxed face. RITA said that he would sleep for a few hours while his body healed. There was no need to sit and watch him. That would be like watching a pot and waiting for it to boil.

*Okay, maybe not that bad since he is cuter than a pot of water,* she thought before shaking her head at her musings.

She would take advantage of the quiet time to go through the file she had downloaded. Decision made, she bent over and picked up her backpack off the floor. She looked at Derik one last time before she quietly exited the room. She walked down the hallway, briefly stopping by the front door to make sure that it was locked and to double check that the alarm system was activated. Satisfied the townhouse was secured, she climbed the stairs to the upper level of the townhouse.

She walked down the hallway before stopping at the closed door to one of the bedrooms. She liked the smaller bedroom that overlooked the backyard. Opening the door, she stepped inside before closing it behind her. She placed her backpack on a chair near the door, then crossed the room, opened the closet, and retrieved the small stash of clothing from the bottom shelf in the corner that she'd left here the last time she had stayed.

She stepped out of the closet and closed the door. Turning on her heel, she headed into the bathroom. Old habits die hard, she thought as she shut the door behind her and locked it. The house was completely secure and Derik was in no shape at the moment to be a threat to her—not that she thought he would be one anyway. It was just if there was a door with a lock on it, she wanted that added layer of protection.

Her nose wrinkled with distaste when she pulled her damp shirt off. It stank of DiMaggio's nasty cigar. She tossed it in the clothes hamper. She would wash her clothes when she was finished.

Her thoughts went to Derik. He was going to need some new clothes. His shirt was ruined. She remembered from her previous visits that Cosmos kept a small supply of clothing for men and women in a variety of sizes in the room downstairs next to where Derik was resting. She suspected that the infirmary was used far more often than she'd have otherwise guessed. Cosmos was just too prepared. Given everything she had seen in the townhouse during her previous visits, he was stocked and ready for a small army.

Runt turned on the shower. Steam immediately began to rise, and she adjusted the temperature before standing under the steady stream of water. She sighed in contentment and bowed her head as the warm water flowed over her.

She reached for the shampoo, closed her eyes, and slowly washed her hair. She repeated the process with the crème rinse before using the body wash to strip the grime and smell of cigar smoke from her skin. She sighed again when the smell of lavender replaced the stink of DiMaggio.

She stood under the showerhead, enjoying the soothing sting of water as it rinsed the soap from her body. The warm water chased away the chill in her bones and released the tension in her muscles, relaxing her. She turned her palm over and gazed down at the mark clearly visible in the center of her palm.

Derik, he was a problem that she didn't understand. He'd come in with guns blazing—well, DiMaggio's men had the guns, Derik just did the blazing. She'd come back to Washington because she had discovered a link between Afon Dolinski and DiMaggio. It wasn't much, and the reference had come from a sketchy source, but it was the only clue that she'd found since Dolinski's disappearance. The problem was she'd been unable to access DiMaggio's server, which had led to tonight's little adventure.

"What am I going to do?" she murmured, staring at the mark.

*Need me, accept me, love me... not in that order, of course,* he replied.

Runt snapped her head up and glared at the wall with unfocused eyes. *What are you doing awake?! RITA said you would sleep for hours,* she growled.

*I felt... your... confusion. Going to sleep now,* he slurred.

*You better! I don't want any dead aliens in the house. I happen to like it here,* she snapped.

His soft chuckle brushed through her mind. She reached up and impatiently wiped the water away from her eyes. Now she was worried about him. What if he tried to get up before whatever FRED had done to him wore off and he fell? Or worse! What if he got up, and opened up his wound before the nanobots finished healing him, and he bled to death?

She smothered an oath and quickly finished rinsing the soap from her body. Twisting the shower lever, she cut short her marvelous respite, and pushed open the glass door. She grabbed the towel from the hook and dried off.

With each article of clothing she pulled on, she imagined Derik lying unconscious on the floor in a pool of blood. She gave up on brushing her hair or pulling on her boots. Combing her fingers through her short strands with one hand, she snatched up her boots with the other as she rushed out of the bathroom. In minutes, she was down the stairs and hurrying toward the infirmary.

Gripping the doorframe, she looked at the floor, then focused on the bed. A wave of relief swept through her when she saw that he was snugly tucked in, leaving her feeling almost weak.

"You *turd*! I should have known better than to be worried," she growled.

Pushing away from the door, she walked over to the bed. She dropped her boots on the floor and looked down at the strange man who had haunted her for the past two years. It was hard to believe that he was from another world. It was hard to believe he was *here*, and not just…

*… an annoying fantasy, a crazy girl's imaginary guy stuffed in a filing cabinet*, she thought with a sardonic amusement.

She sat down on the edge of the bed and studied his features. Her hand rose and she tentatively brushed his hair to the side. The brownish-black strands matched the color of her hair. She rolled a thick swathe of his hair between her fingers.

Up close, it was hard to tell that he was an alien. A few things were different, but nothing that screamed 'run away in horror'. She had seen humans on the street who looked stranger than Derik.

If it wasn't for the fact that she had seen his eyes swirling with color, his teeth elongate like a vampire, and the supernatural way he moved, she would never have noticed that he wasn't human.

Curiously, she touched his lips and gently lifted the top one to look at his teeth. They looked normal now. She knew he could eat regular food, and that he enjoyed drinking beer, so he didn't act like the vampires in the books and movies she had seen.

She released his top lip and ran her thumb along his bottom one. This was the first time that she had ever touched a guy like this. It felt strange and surprisingly… nice.

She decided he was cute—not handsome, but cute. She liked that he wasn't handsome. Handsome men tended to be more arrogant, while cute guys were more loving and not so full of themselves.

His hair was cut in a military style. It was short on the sides and a little longer on top. She touched his jaw. It was strong, and stubbly with a couple of days' growth.

"Not sure if I like that. It might be scratchy," she reflected.

A light blush turned her cheeks a rosy color. She didn't want to think of all the places his whiskers might scratch her. Well, she did want to think of them as long as he didn't *know* that she was fantasizing about where he would put his lips.

Shaking her head at her crazy thoughts, she continued stroking his skin. He felt warm, but she remembered reading in one of Terra's reports that the Prime tended to have a higher body temperature than humans did. She slid her hand down his throat and touched the chain of her necklace.

"You know, this is all very strange. Aliens are only supposed to exist in books, urban legends, or movies, not in real life. You do understand that our creating a Gateway to a distant world opens up a whole can of worms that humans aren't ready for. I know Avery has been telling Cosmos that, but I'm not so sure that he's been listening. Of course, Cosmos would never have found Terra if he had listened, and Avery wouldn't have found Core. This whole 'touching someone and a mark appears' thing is just—wrong. I mean, where's the challenge in finding someone if all you've got to do is touch them and 'wham, bam, thank you, ma'am', you're a match?" She paused. "I guess it would save on buying food and having a bunch of useless conversations," she murmured.

"Is that what humans do?" he questioned.

She started to yank her hand away from the skin above his collarbone, but he was too fast. He encircled her wrist with his fingers and trapped her hand against his warm flesh. Their eyes met and they stared at each other for several seconds—neither blinking nor looking away.

"You have pretty eyes," she commented without thinking.

He chuckled. "Thank you," he said.

Runt felt heat rise to her cheeks again. "Why?" she asked.

His brow creased in confusion, and he frowned. "Why, what?" he prodded.

She ran her fingers along the chain around his neck until she reached the locket her mother had given her. She grasped the silver pendant. Tears burned her eyes.

"Why did you keep my locket? Why are you wearing it? Why… why is this happening to… us?" she hesitantly asked, gazing into his eyes again.

His fingers closed over hers. "The pendant means something to you—thus, it was my responsibility to keep it safe until I could return it to you. I have worn it since the night we met. As to why this is happening to us… I don't know. I'm just thankful that it is," he confessed.

"Even if it means getting shot?" she asked before biting her lip. "I'm glad you didn't lose my necklace. I'd have been pretty miffed at you if you had."

The warmth of his chuckle filled her with pleasure. She tried not to smile, but it was impossible. Her laughter mixed with his.

Her skin tingled when he released his grip on her wrist and slid his hand up her arm until he cupped the back of her neck. She leaned closer when he applied a little pressure, anticipation fluttering in her stomach like butterflies.

"I'm going to kiss you, Amelia," he murmured.

She parted her lips at his words, and looked at his mouth. She swallowed. She had never been kissed—at least not a real one.

"My name is Runt now," she whispered.

He pulled her closer until their lips almost touched. "You'll always be Amelia to me," he replied before he captured her lips.

## CHAPTER ELEVEN

The kiss Derik gave her held all of his pent-up longings from the past two years. She parted her lips, and he deepened the kiss the way he'd learned about in the vidcoms RITA2 had uploaded for him. He threaded his fingers through her short hair, noticing that it was damp.

She tentatively tangled her tongue with his, growing more confident the longer he held her. He felt her hands tenderly cradle his head and a shiver of pleasure ran through him when she pressed her body against him. Their breaths mingled, becoming one. All too soon, she broke the kiss and looked down at him with turbulent eyes.

He reached out with his mind, connecting to the threads of silver he could feel linking them. Their souls were connected and their bond was growing stronger the more time they spent together. He'd heard about the connection between mates, but to experience it….

"Amelia," he whispered against her lips.

She pulled away from him and straightened, her hand sliding down to his bare chest. The blanket had slipped down to his waist and was partially hanging off the side of the bed. She cleared her throat, stood up, and took several steps backward.

"There's… Cosmos has a room full of clothes next door. There are bathrooms upstairs if you want to take a shower. Avery makes sure that each one is stocked with whatever you might need," she said, not looking at him.

He sat up and swung his feet over the side of the bed. "Amelia...," he repeated.

She hurriedly shook her head. "I... my name's Runt now. I haven't used Amelia for a long time. I'll see if I can warm up some food for us," she said.

Derik watched as she swiftly turned on her heel and exited the room. He grimaced, running his fingers through his hair before looking down at the gunshot wound in his side. He rubbed the fading scar. In another couple of hours, there would be no evidence of it at all.

"Terra and Cosmos are getting really good at coming up with new inventions," he mused.

He would have still been in the medical unit back on his world. Granted, he would have ended up in about the same shape he was in now, but it would have taken a lot more equipment and technology to get him there.

He looked up at the door when he heard banging. It sounded like Amelia was taking out her frustrations on the cabinets and cookware.

*Runt! For the last time, my name is Runt now!* she snapped.

*You'll always be my Amelia,* he responded.

*You make me sound like a song,* she growled.

His laughter was rewarded with more clanging pots. He pulled the blanket from his lap and slid off the bed. His tattered shirt hung loosely on his shoulders where it had been cut open.

Several minutes later, he had picked out fresh clothing from the room next door and was climbing the stairs. The smile on his lips grew when he thought about the kiss he and Amelia had shared. Soon they would be back on his world where he could keep her safe.

*And share much more than kisses,* he thought.

∾

Twenty minutes later, Derik tightly gripped the spoon in his hand. The afterglow of their kiss had been replaced with the desire to shake some sense into the woman sitting across from him. He studied Amelia's stubborn expression. In a matter of seconds, she had ruined all of his carefully laid plans.

He shook his head. Perhaps he had misunderstood her. Surely she had learned how dangerous it was to cross men like DiMaggio!

"What part of almost dying tonight did you miss?" he asked in a slightly incredulous tone.

"I wasn't the one who almost died, you were," she calmly pointed out, gesturing dismissively with a cracker in her hand.

"Yes... trying to save you, and you did almost die. If I remember correctly, you were being strangled," he reminded her.

"Whatever. I had a plan. *You* were the one who came blazing into a room full of guys with guns," she insisted.

"Plan... you had a plan? Getting kidnapped, dealing with a... a crazy man, and almost getting strangled was not a very good plan!" he growled.

She reached over and pulled several more crackers out of the open package on the table between them. She crumbled them into the bowl of chicken noodle soup in front of her, and silently stirred the crackers into the steaming liquid.

"I had it under control," she finally replied.

"Control.... Amelia, there was no control. Have you seen the bruises on your neck?" he snapped.

She shrugged and lifted her spoon to her lips. Derik was surprised that the spoon in his hand hadn't bent under the pressure of his grip. He reached over and pulled the package of crackers toward him. Removing half the contents, he crushed the crackers into his bowl.

"The bruises will heal. I've had way worse. Even after everything I went through, I was still in way better condition than you were," she added.

He opened and closed his mouth several times as he tried to think of a rebuttal. He dismissed each response as fast as they appeared. None of them would do justice to what he truly wanted to say.

"I won't let you do it," he finally said.

She released an inelegant snort and raised an eyebrow. "Oh, please! In case you missed it, I didn't ask for your permission," she replied.

He watched as she parted her delicate lips and popped a cracker into her mouth. His body tightened in response and he shook his head again. Now was not the time to think about how sexy she looked.

Instead, he drew in a deep breath, held it for a few seconds, and then released it. The small exercise helped him relax enough that he could speak without feeling like his jaw would break from the pressure. He tried to reason with her again.

"What part of nearly getting yourself killed do you think is smart? Isn't once today enough?" he growled.

She rolled her eyes. "I'm not going to get myself killed—at least not on purpose. Besides, I wasn't planning on going out again tonight. I've got things to work on," she muttered.

"Things that are dangerous. Things that will get you hurt! I had plans to return to my world," he said.

The spoon in her hand paused mid-level, and she looked at him with a startled expression before she lowered her eyes. His heart was in his throat as he waited for her response, and he almost winced when it came.

"No one's stopping you," she mumbled.

He ground his teeth together when she continued to eat. "With you," he added.

She shook her head. "Not happening. I told you, I've got things to do," she responded.

"Amelia…," he growled.

"Runt! I told you that my name is Runt now," she snapped, glaring at him.

He placed his spoon in his bowl, reached across the table, and gripped her hand. His expression softened when he saw a flicker of uncertainty in her eyes. She tried to pull her hand free at first, but stopped when she realized he wasn't going to use his grip to pull her from her seat, he just wanted to hold her hand. The tension in her body melted and she sighed deeply.

"Why is it so important that you stay here? Can't Avery and Cosmos take care of finding this man you are searching for?" Derik asked.

She shook her head and looked down at her soup. He tenderly stroked the back of her hand with his thumb. Her hand trembled and she looked up at him again.

"They can't. It's... personal," she whispered.

There was a moment of silence before he breathed a long, audible sigh and squeezed her fingers. He released her hand and shot her a crooked smile.

"In that case, what can I do to help you then?" he asked.

A flash of uncertainty crossed her face before she gave him a tentative smile. He sat back in his seat and picked up his spoon again. He loved the way her face lit up.

"Let me think about it and I'll let you know," she replied.

CHAPTER TWELVE

**Suburb of Washington, D.C.**

*A* brief knock on the door drew Afon's, aka Aaron Dolan's, attention from the report he'd been reading. He gave permission to enter and looked up when the door opened. His head of security stood in the doorway.

"What is it, Marcelo?" Afon asked.

"Mr. DiMaggio is here to see you," Marcelo replied.

Afon clenched his jaw in irritation. While he had never done business with the man, Afon knew of him. His whole life had once revolved around men of DiMaggio's stature. The question was—why was the man in his home?

"Show him in," Afon calmly ordered.

"Yes, sir," Marcelo said.

Afon rose from his seat and walked over to the window that had a view of America's capital. He'd carefully chosen each of his residences around the world. Here, he was near the powerful men he wanted to keep an eye on and he had the ability to use them if necessary to protect his new identity. In fact, the papers in his hands were one of his insurance policies.

Afon turned when Marcelo briefly knocked on the door again to warn him that he was about to have company. He critically observed the large, nervous man who entered the room.

"Mr. Dolan, sir," Ramon greeted.

Afon looked over DiMaggio's shoulder to Marcelo and gave his security chief a brief nod, then waited until Marcelo quietly exited the room, shutting the door behind him, before he walked over to replace the report in the folder lying open on his desk. He closed the cover, and motioned for DiMaggio to sit in the plush leather chair across from him.

The bulky man hurried over to the chair, wafting scents of cigar smoke and sweat as he came closer. He sat with a huff, clearly relieved to get off his feet. Distaste and irritation filled Afon when the smell caused a slight burning sensation in his sinuses.

"What brings you to my home, Mr. DiMaggio?" Afon asked, sinking into his own chair after his guest was seated.

DiMaggio swallowed several times before he reached inside his sport coat. Afon stiffened, then relaxed when the man pulled out a white handkerchief and mopped at his sweaty brow.

"Yes, well… I hate to bother you, Mr. Dolan, but I felt like I should be the one… I'm here as a professional courtesy. One good turn deserves another… or so they say," Ramon stammered with a strained smile.

Afon formed a steeple with his fingers. Impatience flared inside him when DiMaggio did not continue. The man appeared to be having difficulty speaking.

"Would you care for a glass of water?" he dryly asked.

"Yes…. Water… would be nice," Ramon hoarsely agreed.

Afon reached under his desk and pressed a button. In seconds, Marcelo appeared. He had one hand on the door and the other behind his back. Afon signaled Marcelo to put his gun away.

"Please have a carafe of water and a glass brought in for my guest," he ordered.

Marcelo raised an eyebrow, but he tucked his gun back into the low-back holster underneath his jacket and nodded. "Anything else, sir?" he inquired.

Afon looked at DiMaggio, who was mopping his brow again. "No, I believe that will be all," he replied.

"I'll have one of the kitchen staff deliver it," Marcelo said.

Afon studied DiMaggio as they waited for the water to arrive. Less than five minutes later, a middle-aged woman entered the room, pushing a cart with a clear carafe of water and two glasses. Small slices of lemon, lime, and oranges floated in the chilled liquid.

The blonde staff member poured water into the glass and handed it to DiMaggio. DiMaggio took the offered glass and drained it in one long gulp. He held the empty glass out for a refill. The woman glanced at Afon, and he motioned for her to refill DiMaggio's glass.

"That will be all, thank you," he dryly stated.

"Yes, sir," the woman replied.

She left the cart in the room, and Afon once again waited until the door was closed before he leaned forward and stared intently at the man who was draining his second glass of water. He pursed his lips when DiMaggio refilled the glass again. The man's hands shook as he replaced the carafe on the serving cart.

"I want to know why you are here," he demanded.

DiMaggio's gaze locked with his, and Afon let the man see that he was growing impatient. DiMaggio nodded and placed the glass on the tray.

"There's a hack named Runt. She's trouble. I should have taken care of her years ago, but she's smart—not like other hacks. She can do things others have only dreamed about," DiMaggio explained in a rushed voice.

"What does this have to do with me?" Afon demanded.

DiMaggio reached up and pulled on the collar of his dress shirt to get more air against his heated skin. "She broke into my computer tonight. She—and she took something from me. She wasn't alone either. There was this—well, I don't know what he was. He looked human, but he wasn't. Runt called him an alien vampire. He moved too fast to be human, and his mouth...," he muttered.

Afon tensed. He glanced at the folder on his desk before he returned his focus to DiMaggio's face. The man was draining another glass of water.

"I want to know everything that happened—and, Mr. DiMaggio..." Afon waited for DiMaggio to look at him before he continued. "Do not lie. Do not leave anything out."

DiMaggio slowly nodded and lowered his glass. "Yes, sir. I have a business... a very successful one. I... provide security and financial loans among other things," he said.

"I am well aware of the nature of your business. I want to know how our paths interconnect," Afon demanded.

"I recently acquired a file from a friend of a friend. Your name may have been mentioned during the exchange," DiMaggio reluctantly admitted.

Afon sat back in his chair. "Why?" he bluntly asked.

"You see, I was hoping we could do business in the future. I haven't exactly had much luck opening the file yet, but I was hoping that it might contain some useful information, if you know what I mean," DiMaggio explained.

"Oh, I know exactly what you mean. Tell me about this hacker," Afon instructed.

DiMaggio gave him a weak smile. "So, this hacker—they call her Runt because she's always been small for her age—she stole some money from me a couple of years ago. It caused me a lot of headaches 'cause the money wasn't exactly mine. She disappeared, and I've been looking for her ever since. Well, tonight, one of my men saw her and brought her to me so we could have a bit of a talk," he said.

"And did you... have a talk?" Afon asked.

DiMaggio's nervous countenance became frustrated. "The conniving little bitch gave my money to charity! Charity! She gave over five million dollars to feed some homeless animals!" he exclaimed.

Afon would have been amused if it hadn't been for the seriousness of the situation. He did feel a slight interest in this tiny young woman who had stolen from DiMaggio. He couldn't remember ever meeting a hacker with a conscience.

"A noble cause, I'm sure. What I want to know is what was on the file that contained my name," he responded.

"I don't know. Howard, my tech guy, wasn't able to open the file. The man that originally had it—well, let's just say he forgot to give anyone the password before his accident. Howard was working on the file before the girl came, and now it's gone—disappeared," DiMaggio finished.

Afon watched the man nervously rotate the glass in his hands for a moment. Irritation flared inside him at DiMaggio's ineptness. He pushed his chair back and rose to his feet, needing to put some distance between him and the stench of the man sitting across from him. He walked around his desk and made his way to his favorite window. There was just something about seeing the capital from this height that gave a man perspective. He turned to face DiMaggio at his leisure. DiMaggio was growing more nervous by the second.

"Who gave you this file?" he quietly asked.

"He's called Bobby the Blade—'cause he's good with a knife, you know. Bobby said a fella named Digs gave him some old stuff. He found the thumb drive in an envelope that was stuffed inside one of the cases the guy gave him. Bobby was going to ask Digs about it, but we think the guy who gave Digs the stuff died a few months back," Ramon replied.

"The man who died—what was his name?" Afon impatiently demanded.

DiMaggio's brow creased. "Digs doesn't give out info like that—all his sources are hush-hush, you know—but Bobby was able to do enough digging around. He thinks it may have belonged to a man named Wright—he isn't sure what the guy's first name was. Things got difficult and he told me he couldn't help me no more. That's when

I hired this smart-ass college kid, only he ain't as smart as Runt," he added.

"You no longer have this file, you said? The hacker, Runt, has it now?" Afon questioned, carefully scrutinizing DiMaggio's expression.

"No, sir, I don't have it, but Runt probably does. Like I said, that girl ain't right in the head, givin' away five million to a bunch of homeless dogs and cats. If anyone can open that file, she can, and then heaven only knows what she'll do with it," DiMaggio swore.

DiMaggio carefully placed his glass on the cart, the clink of glass against metal emphasizing the finality of his point, and he heaved himself out of the chair. Afon walked over to the man and stopped less than a foot from him. DiMaggio moved uneasily from one foot to the other.

"Let me be very clear about this, Mr. DiMaggio. I don't like people who try to stick their noses in my business. I suggest for the sake of your health that you remember that when you leave here," Afon quietly stated.

"Yes… yes, sir, Mr. Dolan," Ramon hoarsely replied.

"Do you have another name for the girl?" Afon asked.

"Yes… Her dad did business with me. He called her Amelia—Amelia Thomas. If you find her—well, I wouldn't be upset if you were to pass on the information to me. The two of us have some unfinished business that I'd like to take care of," Ramon said.

"It is time for you to leave, Mr. DiMaggio," Afon coldly stated.

He moved back to his desk and pressed the button for Marcelo. A second later, the door silently swung open. Marcelo looked from DiMaggio to him.

"Escort Mr. DiMaggio off my property," Afon ordered.

"Yes, sir," Marcelo replied, stepping aside and holding the door open wider.

DiMaggio's lips parted in protest, but he remained silent as he quietly turned and walked to the door. He paused and looked back at Afon with a determined glint in his eyes.

"There's one more thing you might want to know about the girl," Ramon said.

"What is that, Mr. DiMaggio?" Afon inquired in an icy tone.

"She ain't working alone. Besides that alien creature with her, she's working for a man named Cosmos Raines. He might even be the reason that alien vampire creature is here. Something just don't feel right about Raines and his company," Ramon said.

## CHAPTER THIRTEEN

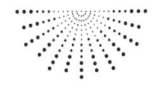

"How is it going?" Derik asked.

Runt looked up and blinked at him, her gaze unfocused. It took a moment for her brain to disconnect from the encryption code that she was unraveling and reconnect with the world around her. She glanced at the clock on her screen and realized that she had been working for nearly two and a half hours without a break.

She swiped the holographic image off the computer screen and turned her gaze to the steaming mug in his hand. She wiggled her nose and sniffed the air, her eyes lighting up with delight when the delicious aroma of chocolate teased her senses.

"Is that for me?" she asked in a hopeful voice.

"Yes. I forgot that your replicator does not truly replicate, it only warms your food and beverages, so it took me a few tries before I understood how it worked," he said with a wry grin.

Runt frowned. "Replicator... Oh, you mean the microwave! There *is* a replicator in the kitchen. It's behind the pantry door, I think. I forgot all about it. Cosmos and Terra installed replicators in the apartments at CRI last year, too. Avery was worried at first about bringing too much alien tech to Earth, but RITA convinced her that it would give Rose, Trudy, Maria, and me better meals since we tend to forget to eat when we are working. I still haven't used mine there yet," she confessed, taking the cup from him.

"Why not? They are very easy to use. All it takes is a simple voice command, and if the product is programmed into the memory, it will create the food or beverage for you," he explained.

"I know, it's just…," she replied with a sigh.

"Just what…?" he asked.

She scooted over on the couch when he sat down next to her, and took a sip of the chocolate before she answered him. The hot chocolate warmed her stomach, but Derik was causing a different kind of heat inside her. She could feel his thigh pressed against hers through the material of her jeans, and she liked it—a lot!

Her reaction to him made her feel edgy, off-centered, and just a little bit self-conscious that he might be able to sense what she was feeling. She tried to ignore her reaction and focus on what they were talking about.

*Replicators and food are good, neutral topics,* she reassured herself.

She released a soft sigh. "I don't know—it just feels like cheating," she finally confessed.

"Cheating?" he curiously repeated.

She shifted slightly, trying to put some space between them. It didn't help. He immediately moved his leg until it was touching hers again.

"Yeah, you know—there's no work involved in making what you want, so you don't appreciate it as much. You just say I want this and it appears," she mumbled.

"Why should there be work? The replicator is supposed to take away the difficulty and time needed to make a meal so that you can focus on more important things," he stated.

Runt looked down at the mug of hot chocolate cupped in her hands. Memories of her mom slowly stirring milk into a pot of melted chocolate filled her mind. She remembered standing on one of the worn kitchen chairs, waiting with anticipation. Her mom would hand her the wooden spoon, stand behind her with her arms wrapped protectively around her waist, her chin touching her shoulder, and quietly instruct her on how to stir the mixture until it was perfect.

Their meals were often simple—a grilled cheese sandwich, gooey peanut butter and banana on warm toast, a can of chicken noodle soup like they'd had for dinner tonight, or her favorite—making cookies from scratch. How could a replicator ever capture those kinds of memories?

"Sometimes making things is important," she quietly replied.

"What happened—to the woman you are thinking of?" he asked.

Startled, she locked gazes with him, then lowered the mug to her lap as she stared back at him without blinking. She didn't talk about that, not ever, but this time….

"They wanted *me*," she said, surprising herself.

"Who wanted you?" he asked.

"DiMaggio, this badass Russian mobster Boris Avilov, the government, my father—anyone, really, who thought I could be of use to them, even Cosmos and Avery if you think about it. I was—am—different…. I see computer code as if it's alive and talking to me. When I am in the code, I can travel anywhere, do anything, be… anything," she awkwardly tried to explain.

"I know what you mean," he said with a nod.

Surprise swept through her. "You do?"

"Yes. When RITA appears, her code is very pronounced. The code is….," he paused, trying to think of how to explain it.

"… beautiful. It is constantly changing," she excitedly answered.

"Yes, and very complex—the dynamics of her algorithms are the most advanced I've ever seen," he replied with a nod.

"Then, you see it, too? You see the lines of code streaming," she breathed with growing eagerness.

"And the underlying code threaded within it," he chuckled.

Her hand trembled as she placed her mug on the coffee table. She touched the wristband lying beside it and the screen she had been studying minutes before reappeared. Her gaze followed the binary language.

"You asked me what happened. The woman was my mom. She

knew I was different—and loved me all the more for it. She loved going to our local library, and I remember her looking up books about the things I could see. She was trying to understand me—and help me. No one understood who I was or what I could do—at least not at first, but once my dad realized how much money he could make from using my gift…. That's what my mom called my ability—a gift…," her voice faded.

She reached out to touch the holographic screen. Lines of code marked her skin like tattoos. She turned her hand until they showed up against her palm. Mixed among the ones and zeros was the mark that had appeared the night she and Derik had touched. Her fingers curled into a fist and she pulled her hand away, dropping it in her lap.

"My dad wasn't all that smart about *how* he used me to get rich, and if I refused to help him, he would lock me in the closet, start drinking, and beat on my mom. He'd tell me that it was my fault, though he hit her whenever he felt like it, not just when he was frustrated with me, but he said… he kept promising that if I did what I was told that he wouldn't hurt her anymore," she quietly shared.

"Your father…. He is no longer alive?" he asked.

Runt sneered and shook her head. She absently studied the code in front of her, one part of her brain registering the information it depicted while another part was arrested by the distant memories of her childhood.

"No, he crossed the wrong person. I'm pretty sure what happened is Left-hand Lou—that's what my dad was called—overheard DiMaggio talking about Boris Avilov, and Lou made the mistake of thinking a Russian billionaire wouldn't miss a few hundred grand—or be able to figure out where it went. Even if he did, he lived on the other side of the world, so Lou thought he'd be safe. Thinking wasn't Lou's strong suit," she bitterly chuckled.

"What happened next?" Derik asked.

"Well, if there was one thing Lou did well, it was bragging. He told anyone who would listen that I was his not-so-secret weapon. He flaunted the money he had stolen—and spouted off about who he'd embezzled the money from. If Avilov hadn't killed him, someone else would have. It was only a matter of time. In the end, I was glad he was gone. The world is a better place without him in it," she said in a voice devoid of emotion.

"Amelia...." Derik said compassionately, reaching for her hand.

She shook her head and stood up, stepping around the coffee table with a burst of nervous energy. She turned to face him. Her face felt stiff. She was surprised to see that he had risen to his feet as well. Standing across from him, she was once again conscious of how tall he was compared to her, a good foot taller than she was, but she didn't feel the least bit intimidated or overwhelmed by him.

"My name's Runt, Derik. I don't go by Amelia anymore. That... that was what my mom called me," she quietly insisted.

"You are more than a hacker to me, Amelia. You are a beautiful woman who has seen and dealt with more things than you should ever have had to endure, but that's not all you are, either. You don't have to cut yourself into pieces," he said, his voice earnest and loving.

She warily held his gaze as he stepped around the coffee table until he was standing close to her. She shivered when he reached out and tenderly ran his hands up along her arms. The warmth of his body drew her closer.

"My mom used to tell me that it isn't what happens to you in life, it's how you deal with it that matters," she murmured.

He touched the smooth skin of her neck, and she softly gasped when her body reacted to his tantalizing touch. He applied the slightest bit of pressure to the back of her neck and her body eagerly pressed against his. She lowered her gaze to his lips.

"Kiss me," she breathed.

She hadn't planned to say that out loud, but with the need surging through her, she was standing by her unexpected request. She looked unflinchingly into his eyes, and mentally challenged him—and herself—to find out if what she'd felt in their previous kisses was just... surprise at being kissed on the lips for the first time ever and then *French* kissed for the first time ever. He smiled, lowered his head, and captured her lips. She could sense the tight control he was trying to exert over his raging hunger.

She wanted more. As she parted her lips beneath his, she slid her hands up along his arms. Her eyes remained open as she focused on the sensations sweeping through her, processing them and trying to understand why he had this effect on her.

He was warm and hard, and he tasted so good. She could feel his biceps flexing as they kissed. He was also very solid, she noted with added pleasure.

His eyes changed colors as their kiss deepened. The swirling silver reminded her of storm clouds before a heavy snow in winter. Tiny flames danced in the middle of his pupils. Her fingers played with the soft strands of hair along his nape until she felt the chain he was wearing.

She stiffened when reality reared its ugly head through the haze of her desire. Derik reluctantly released her lips when he sensed the change in her. Slowly she pulled the necklace free from his black shirt, and her gaze lowered to the silver locket.

He reached up to undo the clasp, but she stopped him, interlacing her fingers with his. She pulled his hand back down between them, and stroked the locket in her other hand. She licked her tingling lips and stared at the locket for several seconds as she fought to organize her chaotic thoughts into an understandable reason for what she was about to say.

"Keep it. I want you... to keep it safe for me," she whispered in an uneven voice.

"Amelia...."

His voice faded when she shook her head and looked up at him. Her eyes burned, but no tears came. She took in a deep breath and shook her head more firmly this time.

"Don't get attached to me, Derik. People... people who get too close to me...." She released the locket and slid her hand down his chest and to the spot on his side where he had been wounded. "People who get too close to me get hurt. Go back to your world before it happens to you... again. You... you might not be so lucky the next time," she forced out in a voice that grew harder and more determined as she spoke.

"Amelia...," he protested.

"No. Earlier you asked me what you could do to help me. You can leave. I can't be watching over your ass, and you know what happens to your kind if you get caught. This world isn't ready for aliens, Derik, and neither am I," she said, stepping away from him.

"Liar," he growled, closing the distance between them. "I've seen inside your mind. I've felt your touch. You wanted me to kiss you as much as I wanted it."

She looked him in the eye and nodded. "Yes, I did. You're a nice guy—kinda cute, too, for an alien and all. I'm still young—too young to be in this kind of relationship with anyone. My mom...." She stopped and looked down at the locket glimmering against his black shirt. "My mom was my age when she met my dad. She never had a chance to discover the world. I... I've got things I want to do and being tied down isn't one of them," she said, looking back up at him.

"I can show you the world—my world. I can show you the universe! What we have is very special, Amelia. You have no idea what it means to a Prime warrior—to me—to find my bond mate. We are destined to be together," he implored.

She took another step back when he reached for her. As much as she wanted to believe him, the memories of her mother's bruised face and despondent voice reminded her that her father had promised the same thing. She didn't think Derik was anything like her father, but....

"If you really want what is best for me, then you'll go home, Derik," she quietly instructed.

Turning around, she scooped up her wristband and mug of hot chocolate from the coffee table. She could feel Derik's denial. The intensity of his emotions—concealed on the outside, but raw on the inside—shook her. Their connection was growing stronger. Afraid he would be able to sense the matching pain coursing through her; she shielded her thoughts as she hurriedly exited the room.

## CHAPTER FOURTEEN

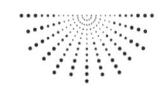

Across town, Afon sat at his desk, deep in thought. Ramon DiMaggio was right—there *was* something off about the public image of Cosmos Raines. Fortunately for Afon, he knew the real man behind the persona of the geeky billionaire. Cosmos Raines was as dangerous as he was brilliant.

There was a brief knock at his office door and Afon turned in his chair to look as the door opened. Marcelo's expression was carefully crafted to hide his emotions. The man did an excellent job, but they had known each other a long time and Afon could sense his curiosity. Marcelo must have overheard DiMaggio's alien vampire reference.

"What is it, Marcelo?" he asked.

"Mr. DiMaggio has left the premises. I've assigned a surveillance team to him—discretely, of course," Marcelo replied.

"Very good," Afon responded.

"Do you need anything else this evening?" Marcelo inquired.

Afon shook his head. "No," he answered, then a moment later he said, "On second thought, I want you to double check our security and add a few more men."

"I'll do it immediately. I wanted to check in with the guards to make sure everything is as it should be and will oversee the added security myself," Marcelo said.

Afon gave Marcelo a sharp nod in response, and Marcelo closed the door. He swiveled his chair around to face the windows. In his mind, he replayed everything DiMaggio had shared.

*The man will have to be dealt with,* he thought with distaste.

He returned his attention to the report he had been reading before DiMaggio's visit. He fingered the envelope in front of him before he withdrew the packet of papers. Stapled to the top document was a picture of a non-human male's flaming silver eyes, full of rage and a silent promise of retribution. Afon swallowed, and goosebumps shivered down his arms.

He slowly scanned the report, which included images—some sharply focused, others grainy—that reminded him of his former life, a life that had drawn him into contact with some of the darkest elements of humanity. A life that he had fought hard to leave behind once he found a reason to do so.

Avilov had been planning to have him eliminated. Afon knew the Russian oligarch had grown tired of his frequent questions regarding some of Avilov's decisions. Their professional relationship had become increasingly strained, especially after the alien, Merrick, was captured.

While a warped sense of loyalty made it almost impossible for Afon to kill the man who had taken him off the streets, he had not been above letting Avilov suffer the consequences of his own poor decisions—and leaving him to face them alone.

The alien called Merrick had been working with Tansy Bell. Bell was an undercover agent for CPAT, a secretive government program whose acronym stood for the Collaborative Partnership Against Terrorism. She was determined to take Avilov down, but after her confrontation with Avilov heated up, she was trapped in Russia. That was when her friend, Cosmos Raines, brought his seemingly unlimited resources into the fight.

Turning to the next page, Afon paused on an image of Adam Raines—Cosmos Raines' father. Adam Raines' death was one of the few he regretted. He'd been wrong when he thought Avilov would refrain from hurting the elder Mr. and Mrs. Raines—at least until he had their son in his possession. Avilov did hurt them, and Afon had known at that moment that his own time on Earth was very limited.

What Afon knew, and Avilov refused to accept, was that Avilov was in over his head. His former boss was poised to take everyone close to him down with him—and he had in the end. Everyone that is except for Afon.

The next few pages of the report were devoted to the half-brothers Weston Wright and Karl Markham. Their deaths had proven that other aliens were on the planet, though the autopsy of Wright's body showed that he hadn't been killed by the alien Markham was after. Instead, he had been murdered by his own half-brother at Addie Banks' family vacation home in Oregon.

At first, he had been perplexed by Markham's reasoning, but Afon later discovered that Karl Markham wanted to hunt an alien for the challenge of it.

*As if advanced alien races are exactly the same as big game in Africa,* Afon sardonically thought.

By all accounts, Wright was the more cautious of the two. The brothers had probably disagreed about Markham's foolhardy quest and Wright had ended up dead. In any case, Markham got his wish when he kidnapped Cosmos Raines' Head of Security, Avery Lennox, to use as bait.

Afon shook his head. Lennox was a deadly opponent and Markham should have known that—if he had done his research. Toying with her was like toying with a hungry lion.

Markham also should have known about the alien's capabilities from all the testing that had been done on Merrick. In the end, it was his own extreme hubris that had doomed him. Markham's desire to pit his skills against Lennox and a man with alien abilities had been the equivalent of suicide.

He turned to the next page. The detailed autopsy and gruesome photos showed that Markham had suffered a particularly grisly death.

Nearly a hundred men and one of the most advanced security systems on the planet hadn't been able to protect Markham from his prey.

Afon turned to the last page, and his lips turned upward in a crooked smile, though he felt more exasperated than amused. All of his carefully laid plans—plans that had begun nearly a decade ago—were in danger of unraveling because of the young woman staring defiantly up at him in the photo. Now, thanks to DiMaggio, CRI—or at least one member of it—had found the end of the thread and was following it to the source.

"You, little one, are a problem. A problem that will have to be dealt with sooner rather than later, I'm afraid," he murmured as he considered his options.

~

Derik paced back and forth in the downstairs study. A quick glance at the clock told him it was nearly one in the morning. Amelia had disappeared earlier into another room and he'd been left feeling frustrated and confused.

One part of him argued that he should ignore Amelia's protests, kidnap her, and return to Baade as soon as possible. The other part of him realized that doing so could cause enormous complications—especially if she protested to the Council. His orders were to bring her back, but his heart told him that if he tried to press the issue, Amelia would resent his barbaric behavior.

He needed advice. He needed someone who could really understand Amelia. RITA might be a good choice, but she was a computer. His mother might be a better choice, but she didn't really understand human nature. He needed someone who understood human females.

He stopped and grinned—his brothers! They each had a human mate. Surely they would know the right thing for him to say and do! They had each faced different challenges with their bond mates and they were older than he was. Their experiences would give him an advantage.

He reached for the portable Gateway device in his pocket, then paused and pursed his lips in indecision. He didn't want to leave Amelia here alone. What he needed was someone who could keep an eye on Amelia while he was gone, but without her realizing it. He grabbed the communicator at his waist, activated the device, and waited for RITA and FRED to respond.

"Is everything alright, Derik?" RITA asked, materializing in front of him.

"Yes, but I need your help," he said.

"Of course, love. What can we do?" RITA asked, perking up.

"I need to speak with my brothers back on Baade, but I don't want to leave Amelia alone and unprotected. I should only be gone for, at most, an hour. Can you open a Gateway to their residence on Baade and watch over my mate for me until I return?" he asked.

"Of course, sweetheart. We'll keep an eye on her and make sure she stays put until you return," RITA promised.

"Thank you. I shouldn't be gone long," he stressed.

"I'll open the Gateway. Your brothers are still in the palace," RITA responded.

"Perfect. Set the Gateway to reopen in one hour. That should give me enough time to do what I need to do," Derik ordered.

"Commencing Gateway," FRED said. "Return portal will open in exactly one hour."

A shimmering doorway appeared in front of Derik. He looked over his shoulder at the closed door across the hallway. A dim light shone from under the door. He briefly linked with Amelia. He smiled slightly when he saw that she was completely absorbed in the encryption code she was trying to crack.

"I won't mess up what we have, Amelia. I swear I won't," he vowed before he turned toward the open portal connecting their worlds and stepped through.

∽

Runt blinked and leaned back in her chair. She rubbed her eyes and looked around the room with a confused expression. Something was different—she could feel it. There was a void, as if she had lost something and didn't realize it yet.

She lifted her hand and rubbed her forehead as the sensation intensified. Turning off her computer, she rose to her feet and stretched. Her hand moved to her stomach when she heard it growl.

"Food. Maybe that's what the feeling is. I need food," she concluded.

She picked up the micro-computer and slipped the band over her wrist. She could work on the encrypted file while she ate. As it was, decoding the first document in the stolen file from DiMaggio had taken her longer than she'd expected, which irritated her. Now that she was pretty sure she understood what was used to encrypt the other documents in the file, it wouldn't take her long to open the rest of them. What was weird was the code was familiar and really similar to her style of code. She shook her head. It was obvious she needed to take a break.

She unlocked the door to the den, opened it, and peered out. A frown creased her brow when she saw that the room across from her was empty. She shrugged her shoulders; maybe Derik had gone upstairs to bed. She tentatively reached out, but didn't sense him. He may have needed more rest to finish recuperating from his wound.

She padded down the hallway in her socks to the kitchen. It wasn't until she stopped and looked into the empty refrigerator with a grimace that she remembered the safe house replicator that she had mentioned to Derik earlier. Scratching her grumbling belly, she walked over to the pantry door and opened it. She paused in front of the alien unit mounted in the pantry cupboard and released a tired sigh. As much as she'd tried to avoid using the things, she was hungry and didn't feel like cooking.

Plus, there was a limited selection of food available in the house since she hadn't been scheduled to stay here. She wrinkled her nose at her reflection in the dark glass. Now, to decide what she wanted!

"Uh, macaroni and cheese," she hesitantly requested.

She bent forward and watched with fascination as the replicator produced her dinner. The door slid open and inside was a bowl of steaming, cheesy noodles just the way she liked. Her stomach growled in approval when the delicious aroma swirled around her.

"Okay, maybe I have to admit this is good, but how will it taste? *That* is the question," she grudgingly muttered.

She carried her dinner to the table, then returned to the replicator and requested a glass of milk. She grinned when it magically appeared. Taking a sip of the white liquid, she was surprised that it tasted just like milk—and that it was cold!

"Okay, I give. This is pretty cool so far," she sighed.

Returning to the table, she slid onto the chair and removed her wristband, placing the micro-computer on the table in front of her. She continued working on the encrypted documents in the file while she enjoyed the thick, creamy pasta. In minutes, she had the rest of the documents decrypted.

She studied the information that was now appearing on the projected screen. Someone had been as curious about Afon Dolinski as she was, and the style of the summarized notes was very… professional and brisk, like a reporter had written this.

Fascinated, she began reading the documents. Afon and his sister had been placed into an orphanage when they were babies. His twin sister had been adopted four years later, but he had not. By the time he was nine, he was living on the streets.

"No wonder the guy had issues," she muttered.

She opened the next file. Apparently Afon had stayed under the radar until he was sixteen. There was a grainy image of him as a teenager standing next to Boris Avilov.

*Obviously a bad decision,* she thought.

Afon must have thought the same thing. It wasn't the expression on his face that gave her that feeling. It was in his posture and the way his gaze was fixed on Avilov. He was definitely wary.

"Should have kept your head down and kept going, man," she jokingly advised.

There were short annotations in Russian that she had to translate. It mostly described Avilov's growing power. She swiped the document aside and opened the next one.

Her eyes widened and her fingers trembled when she saw the photo of a beautiful girl looking into the camera. Her long black hair fell over one shoulder. Her eyes glittered with innocence and curiosity. While the photo had obviously been taken many years ago, Runt felt like she was staring into a mirror.

She slowly reached out to touch the image, pulling back when her fingers went through it. Her throat tightened, and she fought to breathe. Desperately, she scanned the scrawled notes on the page.

*Arianna Dolinski, aka Anne Davis: age 15.*
*Adopted at age four from a Russian orphanage by Albertson and Anne Mae Davis— both deceased.*
*Arianna (Anne Davis) married Lou Thomas—deceased.*

The last word was circled. Runt dropped her fork and wiped her cheek, absently looking down at her damp fingers. Returning her gaze to the screen, she swallowed. The note about her parents being deceased must have been put in within the past two years.

She leaned back in a rush of emotion. She was related to Afon Dolinski! As far as she knew, he was her only living relative. That is... if he *was* alive and hadn't died in Hong Kong. Her damp eyes moved to the smiling face of her mother, and she touched the short strands of her own dark hair. If she let her hair grow out, it would be hard to tell them apart.

And just like that, she was furious. She quickly closed the document. Tears blurred her vision, and she angrily wiped them away with the back of her hand. Glaring at the screen, she drew in a swift breath, and opened the next document. It contained another photo. The photo was blurry and had been taken from a fairly long distance. There was no writing, just the image, which was dated six months ago.

"RITA, I need your help," Runt requested in a shaky voice.

RITA's face appeared on the screen. "What do you need, love?" RITA asked.

"Can you enhance the face of the man on the screen and run a search? I need to know who he is," she requested.

"Of course, sweetheart. It shouldn't be difficult," RITA replied.

Runt watched as face after face flashed across the screen at a dizzying speed. In less than a minute, a match came up. Her stomach sank, and her heart raced. Rubbing her hands against her jeans, she stared at the face of the man that she had been looking for.

"You were right, dear. Afon Dolinski didn't die in Hong Kong. He is now known as Aaron Dolan. Mr. Dolan appeared in Washington, D.C. a little over a year and a half ago, and it seems he wisely invested most of the salary he received from Avilov. His net worth is now roughly two and a half billion dollars," RITA said.

Runt swallowed again, and studied the image RITA was displaying. Dolan and Dolinski were definitely the same man. Dolan had a touch of gray at his temples, but everything else was the same.

"Where is he?" Runt asked.

RITA rattled off the address. "It's quite a nice neighborhood that he lives in. I'm currently downloading records of his security system and personnel," RITA said.

Runt stood up, disposed of her remaining dinner, and washed her plate and cup. Then she walked back to the table, and stood there for a moment, rubbing her damp hands against her jeans. She knew what she needed to do.

Reaching out with her mind, she tried to connect with Derik. She frowned when she felt a void. She tried again and still felt nothing. Panic began to course through her—something had happened to him! Maybe the wound from earlier hadn't healed the way they thought it had.

"Which room is Derik in?" she asked.

"Derik isn't here at the moment. He had to return to Baade," RITA said.

"Baade…." She clamped her lips together when she heard the dismay in her voice. He'd taken her earlier words to heart and left. She closed her eyes and bowed her head.

Taking a deep breath, she pushed her pain deeper within her mind where she wouldn't have to look at it. She should be used to people leaving her. Besides, how could she blame him when she was the one who'd told him to go?

She opened her eyes and lifted her head, her gaze settling on the image of Dolinski. He was the last connection to her mom that she had, whether she liked it or not. Now that she knew he was still alive, she wanted to know more about him—and find out who else was looking for him besides CRI and a few aliens who wouldn't mind seeing him dead.

"Derik will be back, honey. He asked FRED and me to watch over you and make sure you didn't go anywhere," RITA added.

"Yeah… well…," she shrugged in response.

"You aren't planning to go after Dolinski by yourself, are you?" RITA asked, clearly worried.

"I'm not going after him. I'm just going to take a closer look," Runt remarked.

"I don't think that is a good idea. Wait until Derik returns. I'll notify my sis about this so she can tell Derik… and Avery and Cosmos as well," RITA said.

Runt bit her lip, slowly walked back to the micro-computer on the table, and pulled up a program she had developed shortly after she started working at CRI. Her finger hovered over the enter button indecisively.

"No, I need to do this alone," she quietly responded.

"Amelia, Dolinski is too dangerous," RITA protested, suddenly appearing next to her.

Runt straightened and turned enough to block the screen. Her eyes burned with emotion when she met the AI's determined gaze.

"Forgive me," Runt murmured, lifting her hand to touch RITA's cheek.

"For what, love?" RITA asked with a puzzled expression.

Runt shook her head. A tear slipped down her cheek as she turned and pressed the enter button. Out of the corner of her eye, she saw the instant RITA realized what she had done. RITA's lips opened in protest even as she began to fade.

"Amelia!" RITA called in a hurt voice before she disappeared.

Runt closed her eyes. The betrayal hit too close to home—and the program wouldn't stop RITA for long. Cosmos would receive an alert that something was wrong and activate a reset. If she was lucky, she would have an hour head start, but she would plan on it taking Cosmos half that time to fix everything.

She grabbed the wristband from the table, exited the kitchen, and hurried down the hall. She stepped into the den, mumbling incoherent curses under her breath as she did. The curses were directed at herself. She felt like she was going to suffocate under the weight of her guilt.

"It isn't like I really hurt her," she comforted herself. "It's more like a short nap. She's just taking a little break."

She snorted, because after all, she'd named the program 'Sleeping Beauty'. Lifting her arm, she wiped her nose with her sleeve. Instead of pricking RITA's finger, Runt had engineered a massive dump of information to download all at once, which caused RITA's systems to overload and forced her to shut down—but Cosmos would do a manual reboot, and she'd be fine. She'd be fine.

Runt finished tying the lace on her boots, stood up, and grabbed the black leather jacket draped across the back of the couch. She pulled it on and picked up her backpack. If Avery hadn't fired her for taking off, Runt was sure Cosmos' Chief of Security would fire her for this little stunt.

Taking a deep breath, she scanned the room one last time before exiting the townhouse through the back door. She made sure that she secured the door before she crossed the small porch. Stepping lightly down the steps, she hurried over to the brick garage. She lifted her hand and pressed her palm against the interface next to the garage door, impatiently tapping her fingers against her leg as she waited for the door to open. Inside, there were several vehicles.

Runt bypassed the sports car, the SUV, and the sleek motorcycle. Instead, she grabbed the helmet for the motorcycle and walked over to the small red Honda Forza 300ABS scooter. She pulled on the helmet and secured the strap under her chin before she slid her leg over the seat. She pressed the start button, and the small engine came to life.

After pushing off from the kickstand, she paused outside the garage to shut the door. Yes, the little scooter wasn't as fancy or as powerful as the other vehicles, but she knew how to operate it. The cars and motorcycle were beyond her.

"I can bring down the most powerful computer in the world, and yet, I don't have a driver's license," she said with a shake of her head. "RITA will probably make sure I never get one now," she added with a sigh as she turned left and disappeared down the deserted street.

## CHAPTER FIFTEEN

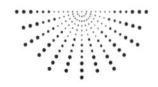

**Baade: Prime Home World**

Derik felt like he was getting whiplash from trying to keep up with the conversations going on around him. It had become obvious in the first few minutes after his arrival that he had made a mistake. He should have talked to their mates—or his mother or Tilly or even RITA!

As it was, all he could do was stare at his brothers with growing frustration. So far, he had learned about everything he shouldn't do and nothing about what he should!

"No, that is not how you woo her!" Borj argued. "Angus said you need to help with the household things. Hannah loves it when I help out."

J'kar scowled. "The last time I tried to do that, I turned all of our white clothes pink and Tink laughed her ass off at me—as did the warriors in the training room when I showed up in 'pretty pink'," he said with a shake of his head. "No, a box of candy works. The brown stuff called chocolate."

Mak folded his arms across his chest. "I've been banned from bringing any of that stuff into the house. The twins ate the last lot—well, I helped some. I don't care what the bag said, the twins were able to make them melt everywhere BUT in their mouths. We had rainbow-colored handprints in every room! Then, if that wasn't enough, they both got a tummy ache and pooped out a rainbow-colored river with these pellets in it that looked just like the candy. I'm not sure I'll ever be able to eat M&Ms without visualizing what was flowing into their diapers. Tansy was *not* happy with me," he stated.

Derik shuddered. After listening to his brothers' tales, he was even more sure he wanted *many years* alone with Amelia before they even discussed having children. Kids sounded more awful than fighting the Juangans! He would rather fight a dozen of the ruthless reptiles with one hand tied behind his back than clean a messy diaper!

Mak's description of the gooey stuff leaking out of the sides of their diapers and running down their legs was bad enough. When he added that the twins had painted the walls and their cribs with their liquid poop... it was obvious that Mak had a stronger stomach than he did.

From behind Derik, Teriff gave his own suggestion. "You should kidnap her, tie her up, and hope she doesn't get free like your mother did."

Derik turned to stare at his father. That comment had at least silenced the talk about children.

"I will not force myself on my mate," he growled with a disapproving glare.

Teriff scowled down at him. "I didn't force myself on your mother. I am an honorable warrior, not a...." He paused and shook his head. "Yes, I kidnapped your mother and tied her up—*but* she dared me to do it! Your mother said if I was willing to deal with the consequences, to go ahead and try to claim her! I wasn't about to ignore such a tantalizing challenge. Nothing else happened without her consent. Your mother can be surprisingly fierce and resourceful when she wants, and let me tell you, she packs a powerful punch when she gets angry.

Prime females are hardly the docile creatures that the elders would have you believe."

"So what do you propose I do, then? Wait until Amelia asks me to kidnap her?" Derik asked with a hint of exasperation.

Teriff rubbed his jaw and grinned. "I am suggesting that you spend some time with your bond mate away from distractions. I took your mother to Quadrule Five for a few days. There is a remote island on its moon there where you might learn more about each other," he said.

Derik ran his hand over his face. "I don't think that will work with Amelia," he quietly responded.

"How do you know until you try?" his father asked.

Derik started to respond when RITA2 and DAR appeared. RITA2 was clearly worried, and DAR looked grim. Derik was surprised to see they were not as defined as they normally were when they appeared. He could see the threads of code running through them. He stepped forward when both AIs started to glitch and sections of them faded.

"What is wrong?" J'kar demanded, rising to his feet.

"Amelia—shut down…," RITA2 stuttered. She disappeared and reformed.

"The human girl infected RITA, and she reached out to us…," DAR explained.

"The program… Runt uploaded… infected me…," RITA2 added.

"I was infected as… well—but RITA cut our link before it fully uploaded," DAR growled.

Derik watched in avid fascination when DAR wrapped his arm around RITA2. He could see lines of DAR's code merge with RITA2, repairing some of the broken and disrupted threads of code. RITA2's form gradually solidified. She sent a grateful smile to DAR, and smoothed her hair with her hand.

"I swear Amelia is part computer. Her programing is absolutely brilliant," she chuckled.

"She tried to shut you down," DAR retorted in a tone devoid of amusement.

"Nonsense; look at the code. She was merely creating a temporary overload. A simple reset and everything should be fine," RITA2 replied.

"A reset that only Cosmos can do," DAR pointed out.

"For my sis. I can't access the main computer system until RITA comes back online. That is the only way we can connect between our worlds. We must wait until RITA is repaired," RITA2 stated with a wave of her hand.

"Does this mean the Gateway is down?" Derik asked.

"No, the Gateway will work, but it will require manual programming. Cosmos and Terra developed a secondary system independent of RITA in the unlikely scenario that something like this happened," DAR answered.

"The portal device I have is already programmed for the safe house. It is supposed to activate automatically in… eight Earth minutes," Derik said, looking at the clock embedded in the device.

"The portal should open. The command would have been sent to the Gateway's queue," RITA2 replied.

"Is Amelia safe?" he quietly asked.

RITA2 hesitated, then sighed. Derik's stomach tightened as he waited for her to answer him.

"Well… yes, she was. We hope so. Before Amelia shut her down, RITA was able to convey that Amelia found Afon Dolinski," RITA2 said.

"Dolinski," Teriff murmured. "Wasn't he one of the humans responsible for Adam Raines' death?" Teriff asked.

"Yes. He worked with Boris Avilov," RITA2 answered.

The feeling that something was wrong blossomed into full-blown panic. He should never have left her! Why did he keep doing the wrong thing with Amelia? He should have worked it out himself—or with her. Now his stupid mistake could cost his mate her life!

"Can you open the Gateway now?" he asked.

"I'm afraid not. While I look like I'm functioning at full capacity, there is residual code interfering with my programming. DAR is working on repairing it," RITA2 explained with an apologetic expression.

"We are coming with you," Teriff said, motioning to J'kar, Borj, and Mak.

His brothers nodded in agreement. Derik wanted to protest that he could save her himself, but the words died on his lips. The thought of Amelia in danger again, this time from a human killer known for his cruelty, made his blood run cold.

Derik glanced down at the timer on the device in his hand, and gripped the warm metal tighter. The next four minutes were going to seem much longer than they really were.

"We find Derik's mate, and bring her and Afon Dolinski back. The man will pay for his part in Adam Raines' death and Merrick's torture," Teriff ordered.

"I agree," J'kar seconded.

"Amelia comes first," Derik tersely added. "If Dolinski threatens her, I want him taken out."

He looked up at his father when Teriff placed a hand on his shoulder. "We will not let anything happen to your bond mate. I promise," Teriff quietly stated.

Derik nodded. Pride filled him when he saw his brothers rise to their feet and look at him with the same grim expression of determination. He would take his father's advice and bring Amelia to Quadrule Five. It was far too dangerous to leave her on Earth.

"The Gateway will open in five, four, three, two...," DAR counted down.

Derik took a deep breath when the portal opened to the living room of the townhouse. He stepped through the opening, followed by his father and three brothers. He immediately reached out to Amelia —and felt down to his soul the silent void where she should be.

## CHAPTER SIXTEEN

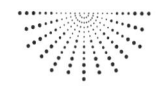

"RITA!" Derik called as the silence engulfed him.

Derik stumbled back several steps when FRED appeared in front of him, looking very unhappy. He shot the AI a fierce glare.

"Where is Amelia?" Derik demanded.

A tinge of red swept over FRED's glowing blue form, turning the AI's color to a dark purple. In the back of his mind, Derik wondered if Cosmos was aware of the extensive emotional adaptions that his AIs were developing. He made a mental note to take a look at the programming when all of this was over. Pushing his fascination aside, he listened as FRED answered him.

"Your female menace has gone to find Afon Dolinski," FRED informed him.

"I know that. What I don't know is where!" Derik impatiently snapped.

"FRED, be a dear and program the GPS in the… the SUV," RITA said, her voice slurring slightly. "The keys are in the locked cabinet in the garage." She added in a conspiratorial whisper, "FRED will unlock the cabinet for youuuuuu." Her last vowel seemed to get stuck for a moment, then she cheerfully said, "Oh! Never mind, Robert is here."

"I summoned him," FRED replied. "Avery reminded me that any attempt to retrieve Amelia should be done without drawing attention to the alien squadron behind it," the AI dryly commented.

"Avery... Oh, yes... I'm still re... re... recovering. Amelia's program makes me—sluggish. I feel like I'm on dialup!" RITA said.

"Dialup? That sounds like a very nasty word," FRED growled.

"It is, love. I feel like I'm running at about 40 kbps," RITA replied in a mournful tone.

"I'll bar Amelia from ever accessing you again," FRED threatened.

"Nonsense! I would much... much... much... rather have *Amelia* show us where our weakness is than some other little snip!" RITA dismissed.

The sound of footsteps outside of the room drew his attention. A moment later, Robert stood at the entrance to the room. Robert's eyes widened and he warily looked at their small group.

"Uh—Avery said you needed a ride," Robert said.

Teriff and Derik's brothers all moved in unison. Robert's face paled when Teriff pulled out his weapon. Derik held his hand out in front of his father.

"This is Robert, one of Cosmos' men," Derik quietly stated.

"Can he take us to your mate?" Teriff commanded.

"Yes," Derik replied, turning back to Robert with a fierce expression.

~

The scooter wobbled as Runt pulled it to the side of the deserted road. She placed her feet down on the ground and turned off the ignition. At the same time, she lifted her chin in surprise and relief. She could feel Derik again.

"Maybe I'll give him another chance," she mumbled.

She still had her mental walls up, but there was a reluctant smile on her face and an odd warmth in her heart because he'd been telling the truth—he *had* planned on coming back. Sliding off the bike, she pushed it into the shadows under a tree near the high, ivy-covered stone wall that surrounded Afon Dolinski's estate.

She lowered the kickstand and leaned the scooter against it, making sure it wouldn't fall over before she reached up and removed the helmet from her head. She looped the chin strap over the handlebar and stepped away from the scooter, scanning the wall. Confident that her mode of transportation was as safe as she could make it, she took off in the direction of the service entrance.

The damp grass, wet from the earlier rain, muffled her footsteps as she scanned the area. Light from the moon danced between storm clouds that still lingered, creating enough light to see and yet enough shadows to remain concealed. She grimaced when she felt her wristband vibrate. RITA was back online. She crouched and pressed the glass face of her micro-computer. In seconds, RITA's face appeared.

Always quick on the uptake, the AI had chosen to use a dark red, low-powered hologram to preserve Runt's night vision and emit as little noticeable light as possible.

"I have one of Cosmos' satellites aimed at the compound," RITA whispered. "There are two heat signatures within one hundred yards. They are walking away from you, going east along the inner fence. There are also two guards at the service entrance, and cameras mounted every forty feet."

Runt blinked in surprise. "You aren't mad at me?" she exclaimed in a soft, surprised voice.

"No, love. I know why you did it. You're good, but I'm better. I've read the file," RITA replied.

"Oh. I didn't know he was—that I was...," her voice faded.

"The fact that Afon Dolinski is your uncle does not negate the fact that he is a very dangerous man," RITA gently advised.

"I know," she murmured, bowing her head to hide her expression. "I don't want anyone to know about Dolinski yet. I need to...."

"You want to have a chat with him first," RITA prompted.

Runt nodded. "I have to know," she replied.

"So, what is the plan? I take out their security system and you sneak in?" RITA asked.

Runt thought about Dolinski and everything she had learned about him. A suddenly brazen idea formed in her head. It was totally crazy and probably just a little suicidal, but.... She rose to her feet and started to retrace her steps back to the scooter.

"Are you leaving?" RITA asked with surprise.

Runt shook her head. "Nope, I'm going to wake up Dolinski and introduce myself. I'll let you know if I need any help," she said with a half grin.

"Oh my," RITA replied in a faint voice.

Runt pressed the top of the micro-computer, pulled her helmet free of the handlebar, and put it on. Then she slid back onto the scooter, started it, and pushed it forward to release the kickstand.

Making a wide U-turn, she decided that if she was going to make an entrance, she would do it through the front gate. She had done a lot of crazy things in her life, but this had to be one of the craziest.

*Derik, are you there?* she tentatively reached out.

*Wait for me. I am on my way,* he instructed.

*No, I don't want to risk you getting hurt again. I'll be alright. I just… wanted to say I'm sorry,* she said.

*For what?* he demanded.

*For thinking that you had left me. I wouldn't have blamed you, you know, for leaving,* she murmured.

*I am coming for you, Amelia,* he said.

Runt smiled wryly. *I know. Just wait for me this time. I'll let you know if I need you to come in guns blazing,* she instructed.

*I hope you have a better plan than your last one!* he retorted.

Rolling her eyes at the exasperation in his tone, she didn't say anything. There was no doubt in her mind that Derik would have a cow—or a herd of them if aliens had such things on their world—if he knew what she was about to do. Still, while she did pull away and shield her thoughts from him, she was comforted by their muffled connection. If the worst happened, it might be nice to have some of that alien healing technology on hand.

Taking a deep breath, she turned the small scooter into the driveway and pulled to a stop when a guard stepped up to the gate.

She stared at the man for a second before she looked at the weapon in his hand. Doubts filled her mind, and she wondered if perhaps there was a better way to meet Dolinski. Perhaps she should schedule an appointment after all—one that wasn't in the middle of the night.

"This is private property," the guard stated.

She pulled off her helmet and looked at the guy with a wry expression. "Yeah, I kinda figured that from the wall, the gate, and the gun you're holding. Tell Mr. Dolan I want to talk to him," she stated.

"Take off, kid. Mr. Dolan doesn't talk to punks like you," the guard jeered.

"You'd be surprised. Tell him this is about Arianna Dolinski," she said.

The guard shook his head. "Get lost," he ordered, shifting his weapon until it was pointing at her.

"What is going on?" a deep voice demanded.

The guard lowered his weapon and turned to the man who stepped out of the shadows. Runt studied Mr. Tall, Dark, and Expensive Suit, and recognized him as Afon's Chief of Security.

*Now*, she thought, *I'll get somewhere.*

"This kid is demanding to see Mr. Dolan, sir," the guard replied.

Runt sat back on the scooter and returned Marcelo Moretti's scrutiny, silently waiting for him to finish his assessment of her.

"What do you want?" the man asked.

"Tell Dol…an that I'd like to speak with him about a woman named Arianna Dolinski," she replied, silently cursing herself for almost saying his real name.

"Why should I disturb Mr. Dolan at two in the morning to discuss this woman, Ms.…?" He waited for her to tell him her name, but she remained silent.

"Maybe because I'm here now, Mr. Moretti," she finally answered.

The guard's snort was cut short when Moretti stepped closer to the gate. She didn't flinch when she saw his expression harden, nor when his hand moved to the inside of his jacket. He was much more intimidating than DiMaggio, but when it came down to it, he was still made from the same fabric that she'd dealt with all her life—a thug.

"Open the gate," Moretti ordered.

"...Yes, sir," the guard grudgingly replied.

"Allow me," Runt said. "RITA, please open the gate."

Moretti froze when the security gate suddenly hummed and began to move. The guard's mouth hung open, his eyes wide with shock.

Runt pulled her helmet on and started the scooter before she slowly entered when the gates parted far enough. She couldn't help showing off, but it occurred to her that she had revealed two of her aces to get inside—knowing who Moretti was and having RITA open the gate. She would have to be careful moving forward.

"Follow me," Moretti instructed.

Moretti strode over to the UTV that had been idle in the driveway while the driver waited for the Chief of Security to return. Moretti sat on the back seat, facing her with his pistol in his lap. She drove her scooter several feet behind the UTV.

Less than five minutes later, the driver stopped the UTV beside a beautiful mansion. Moretti slid off the seat and waited for her to park the scooter. She turned off the engine and pulled the bike onto the kickstand before she slid off. Removing her helmet, she gazed at the impressive house.

"Nice digs," she commented.

"This way," Moretti said in a curt tone.

Runt rolled her shoulders in response. Moretti's grouchy tone didn't bother her. Long ago, she had learned the knack of irritating people, and by now she'd practically turned it into an art form. She slid the strap of her helmet onto the handlebar and gave the driver of the UTV a sharp nod.

"Make sure nobody touches the bike. It doesn't belong to me," she instructed.

The UTV driver shot her a startled look before he looked at Moretti for instructions. Marcelo nodded to the man, and Runt kept her expression blank when she saw the Chief of Security's barely concealed irritation.

"Is there anything else?" he dryly inquired.

"Nope, just take me to your leader," she quipped.

## CHAPTER SEVENTEEN

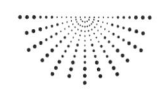

*A*cross town, the black SUV raced through the empty streets. Robert's skillful driving wasn't lost on Derik. The man handled the vehicle with impressive ease.

"How much further is it?" Teriff demanded.

"Six miles if you're a bird, ten if you're in an SUV navigating Washington's love of one-way streets," Robert cheerfully replied.

"I'll be glad when human technology improves," Borj muttered as he tightly gripped the armrest.

Derik tightened his own grip when Robert rounded a corner and the back of the SUV slid on the wet pavement. His breath caught on a curse when he saw their vehicle sliding toward another car parked along the curb. Robert straightened their vehicle mere inches from the parked car.

"Hello, everyone," RITA announced through the car's audio system.

"RITA, are you functioning at full capacity yet?" Derik asked, leaning forward and grabbing the back of Robert's seat.

"Yes, I'm fully functional. I wanted to give you an update on Amelia," she stated.

"Is she safe?" Derik ground out.

There was a brief pause before RITA responded. "Define 'safe,'" she said.

The SUV filled with a chorus of groans. Derik ran his hand over his face. One night! He had been here for one night and his mate was in danger again! He never should have left her alone. One thing was certain, when he got his hands on her again, he was sweeping her off her feet and taking her to Quadrule Five like his father suggested!

*What's Quadrule Five?*

Derik dropped his hand to his lap when he heard Amelia's question in his mind. He really needed to figure out how she was able to slip in without him knowing. Surely that wasn't the way their connection was supposed to work. He should be able to know at all times if she was there with him.

*You have a very noisy brain. It's easy to come and go,* she informed him.

*Noisy brain? I don't think I have ever heard that description before,* he dryly retorted.

*One of the counselors I used to go to said that. I thought it was funny,* she explained.

*Please tell me you are somewhere safe,* he pleaded.

*Well, no one is shooting at me, trying to strangle me, or threatening to do all of the above,* she joked.

*Why would you go after Afon Dolinski alone? You know what he can do —what he has done. Merrick alone would be happy to kill him, not to mention my brother Mak,* he said.

Silence greeted his statement. For a moment, he feared that she had withdrawn from him again—or worse, something had happened that prevented her from answering him. When she spoke, he exhaled the breath he hadn't realized he was holding.

*I told you, this is personal. I need to do this on my own. If I need help, RITA is with me. If I really need help... well, I hope you brought more backup than just Bert and Robert. These guys are a lot more serious about their fire power than DiMaggio's goons,* she said.

"You are killing me, Amelia," Derik groaned, unaware that he had spoken out loud.

"How is she killing you? Does she have some kind of special powers?" Teriff demanded, twisting in his seat to look at him.

"It is a human female thing," Mak said with a chuckle. "My mate did the same thing. If there was a way to make my heart stop and my stomach sink, she figured out how to do it," he wryly added.

"Mine as well," Borj quietly agreed.

"Mine is a danger to anyone who gets in her way," J'kar muttered.

"I saw that when she snuck into the Council Room and attacked Merrick and Core," Teriff remembered.

Derik ignored them—including Robert—as they chortled it up about how their mates drove them crazy. Instead, he focused on his mate. She appeared to be cool, calm, and collected. He didn't know if that should make him more or less worried.

*Less. I've got a pretty good feeling about this,* she reassured him.

He might have felt better if she had not said 'pretty' before she said 'good'. For once, he wished the Gateway could work like Cosmos had originally intended. If he could open the portal from here to there, he would have done it in a heartbeat.... *Blas ja de Juangans! Why didn't I think about this sooner?* He groaned in self-disgust and turned to his older brother with a grim expression. Two could play this game. If Amelia wanted to casually walk into the Juangan's lair, then so could he.

"What is it?" Borj asked.

"I have an idea," he quietly said as Robert slowed the SUV and pulled over to the shoulder of the road down the street from Dolinski's estate.

~

"Wait here," Marcelo ordered.

Runt didn't reply. It wasn't like she was going to go anywhere. Between the thick, dark wood doors in front of her and the two guards that had magically appeared to trail behind them when

Marcelo escorted her through the kitchen area, she was literally stuck where she stood.

She looked around her. The mansion was beautiful. It was tasteful, not gaudy like some she had seen in magazines or DiMaggio's office earlier. It was definitely on the masculine side, though. The walls were framed by dark mahogany baseboards. Brilliant Post-Impressionist artwork hung in heavy frames along the walls.

She wiggled her nose when she recognized a painting called Young Italian Girl Resting on Her Elbow by Paul Cézanne. She had seen copies of it in one of the art history books in the library. She'd loved looking at the details of the paintings. It reminded her of computer coding. Each programmer had their own unique stroke when it came to writing code.

Music, art, and computers had a lot in common. She loved how her mom used to make a game out of guessing the artist when they went to the museums. She did the same when she saw a hacker's code and analyzed their style. In this painting, the depth and number of layers of paint needed to achieve the color desired by the artist told her that this wasn't a reproduction.

One of the heavy wooden doors opened, and Marcelo looked grumpy. Obviously, his boss wasn't opposed to seeing her despite the late—or earliness—of the day. A part of her wished she'd been a fly on the wall when Marcelo had mentioned her mother's name to Afon.

"He will see you now," Marcelo coolly stated.

"I figured he would," she responded.

She took a step forward only to pause when Marcelo held out his arm. She tilted her head to one side and looked at him with a quizzical expression. He gestured impatiently.

"The backpack," he said.

She clenched her jaw and shot him an annoyed look. Talk about déjà vu! She shrugged off her backpack, and held it out.

"I want it back—with everything in it," she snapped.

"Now you have me intrigued," Marcelo replied.

"I paid a lot of money for my headphones, and don't go fingering my lace undies. I already need to wash them all because of one pervert putting his grubby paws on them a few hours ago," she growled.

"Duly noted," Marcelo dryly responded, taking her backpack and handing it to the guard behind her.

Runt stepped around him and into a very elegant—and overwhelmingly masculine—office. The guy's space really could use a woman's touch! A little splash of color would go a long way. Her mom had been good at that.

A shaft of unexpected grief hit her at the thought of her mom, and she locked eyes with the man standing near the window. His expression was intense... and in his face, she could clearly see her mother's features. Afon had the same eyes, nose, chin, and black hair. If there had been any doubt in her mind, it evaporated the moment they locked gazes. Tears suddenly burned her eyes.

"You...," she started to say, then trailed off, her wide eyes clearly showing her shock and turmoil.

He studied her for several seconds before he signaled Marcelo to shut the door behind her. She shoved her hands into the front pockets of her jeans. He raised an eyebrow and indicated with a casual wave of his hand that she should have a seat.

"To what do I owe this pleasure, Miss...?" he asked.

"Runt... My name—everyone calls me Runt," she murmured.

"Please, have a seat. Runt—that is an unusual name," he replied.

She warily followed him when he took a seat in one of the plush cushioned chairs situated before an unlit gas fireplace. She sank down onto the chair across from him. She rubbed her hands on the knees of her jeans in an effort to warm them.

"It works for me," she said with a shrug.

"How do you know Arianna Dolinski?" he suddenly demanded.

Runt looked at Afon. "What do you know about her?" she countered in a soft voice.

His eyes narrowed. "Surely you did not wake me at two in the morning to ask me about someone you know nothing about," he dryly commented.

She released an inelegant snort. "You weren't asleep," she confidently retorted.

This time he pursed his lips, and she mentally filed away this latest reaction. As short as their chat had been so far, it was giving her some interesting information about Dolinski. If he was as ruthless as Avilov had been, he would have already strung her up and begun the torture.

A visual of what had happened to Cosmos' dad suddenly formed in her mind. She rubbed her damp palms against her jeans again, stood up, and restlessly paced a few steps before she turned and leaned against the fireplace. Perhaps she should have thought this out for a little bit longer before she came here.

She touched the micro-computer on her wrist and reached out to Derik with her mind, needing the reassurance that she wasn't completely alone here. Her heart skipped a beat when all she felt was the void she'd felt when he left the safehouse earlier.

*Where the hell did he go this time?* she wondered.

"You're the same age as she would be," she said, thinking out loud.

"What do you know about her?" Afon demanded, standing as well.

Once again, she was struck by his uncanny resemblance to her mother. She didn't know why she hadn't seen it before. It was impossible to ignore now.

"Why did you work for Avilov?" she blurted out.

He looked at her thoughtfully before he turned and walked over to a nearby bar. She watched as he silently poured himself a drink. He held up the bottle and looked at her.

She shook her head. "I'm under age. You... you shouldn't, you know, drink and drive. It's not safe," she stammered before she pursed her lips together.

He chuckled softly and replaced the decanter of amber liquor before he picked up the glass of bourbon. She was mesmerized by the way he swirled the liquor, lifted the glass to his lips, and drank half of the contents.

"You baffle me, Runt. A hacker with a conscience... You steal from thieves and give to animals—literally. Did you really donate five million dollars of DiMaggio's money to animal shelters or did you keep some for yourself?" he inquired.

She looked up at him with a startled expression. "It wasn't my money. I gave it all away," she replied. "How did you know about DiMaggio?"

"You are not the only one who does their homework. Does Raines know that I am still alive?" he asked.

"I don't know. He probably does by now. I didn't tell him. Things are kinda complicated at the moment," she honestly answered.

He studied her with a frown. "Complicated.... Yes, I would agree with that. You asked me why I worked for Avilov. No one has ever asked me that before," he mused.

He returned to his seat, sat back, crossed his legs, and silently studied her again. She ruefully wondered if she had inherited this particular characteristic from him. Sighing loudly, she returned to her seat as well.

"So, what's your story?" she asked.

He shot her an amused look. "My story.... You make it sound as if you are here to listen to a bedtime tale." His smile faded and he became solemn. "My story would give a young woman like you nightmares."

She leaned forward, placing her elbows on her knees. "I'm not afraid of nightmares," she softly said.

Afon contemplatively studied her serious face, then he said, "Life as an orphan is difficult in a country such as this. Life as an orphan in a place like Russia is much, much more dangerous. You learn young how to survive or you don't live long. I learned—and I excelled. I have done a lot of things in my life that I should regret," he shared, staring down at his glass.

"But you don't. Regret what you've done, that is?" she asked in a tight voice.

He looked up at her. "Twice—I've felt regret only twice in my life," he stated.

"What happened those two times?"

He gave the barest hint of a smile. "Adam Raines died... and he died terribly. I knew that Avilov would use Raines' parents against him, but I was not expecting...." He shook his head. "My time with Avilov was already coming to an end, and though there was little I could have done to help, I did what I could to give Cosmos more time to save him. Unfortunately, it was not enough," Afon murmured.

"Cosmos wants justice," she warned.

"I'm sure Cosmos Raines is not the only one who wishes that I really had died in Hong Kong," Afon said with a wry smile.

He drained his glass and rose to his feet. She twisted in her chair when he walked by her. He stopped at the bar and poured himself another drink. He looked over his shoulder and lifted an eyebrow.

"Would you care for anything?" he politely inquired.

"Hot chocolate—with whipped cream if you have it? Or is it too late?" she said, biting her lip.

"Hot chocolate... No, I have a full staff on call," he reassured her.

He walked over to his office door and opened it. She could hear him talking to Marcelo, and she grinned when she heard the security chief's grumbled response. She quickly concealed her amusement when Afon closed the door and walked back to his seat.

"So... you said two things. What's the second one?" she asked.

He raised an eyebrow. "Are you never going to tell me what you know about Arianna?" he inquired.

"I will. First, I need to... well, I can hack what's in your accounts, but I can't hack what's in your brain," she admitted.

"Yes, conversation isn't often as illuminating as a person's paper trail. I've researched *you*," he admitted in turn, his gaze never leaving hers.

"You wouldn't have found anything except what I wanted you to find. You're a lot like that, too." She paused and narrowed her eyes. "What is the second thing? I hope it isn't killing me," she lamely joked.

He shook his head. "No, if I do that, killing you would be the third thing," he said.

She wiggled her nose at him. "Well, I hope things don't run in threes for you," she quipped.

He grimaced. "The second thing was losing my sister," he quietly said.

"Arianna.... What happened?"

"Arianna, my sister, my twin... She was born a few minutes after me. As children, we were very close. Unfortunately, the orphanage did not share that information with the American couple who adopted her," he calmly stated.

"Did you ever try to find her?" she asked.

He frowned at her. "The orphanage burned down three years after Arianna was adopted. Even if it hadn't, Russian orphanage record keeping was never very accurate—which leads to my next question. Why are you interested in Arianna?" he demanded.

Runt was deciding how to answer Afon's question when several things happened. Her wristband vibrated. Distracted, she looked down at it just as Afon released a muffled curse. She looked up, unsure if she had heard what he said correctly above the sudden knocking on his office door.

He had dropped his glass and stood up. She turned toward the door and noticed a familiar shimmering Gateway opening in the middle of the office. She gaped in shock when Derik stepped through, and gasped when she registered that his weapon was aimed at Afon. She instinctively moved in front of her uncle.

"No!" she cried out at the same time as another feminine voice cried out in shock and horror.

When Runt heard the woman's voice and the clatter of the dishes falling, she turned so swiftly that she lost her balance. As she tipped backwards, she took in every detail of Marcelo and the woman where they stood just inside the door.

The group of men behind Derik surged forward with their weapons drawn. One of the men fired, striking Marcelo in the chest. Afon's Security Chief fell back against the door, closing it, before he sank to the floor. The woman who had brought in the tray lurched sideways.

Runt felt a pair of strong arms wrap around her waist and steady her. At the same time, Derik released an animalistic growl that sent a shockwave through her. His face was a mask of rage. His teeth had lengthened and his eyes swirled with the silver flames she had seen earlier.

*I really have slipped into a time vortex,* she thought numbly.

"Release her," Derik said, his aim unwavering and his eyes cold.

"No," Afon stated.

"No," she repeated.

"No," the woman's trembling voice added.

"Did your mate just say no?" Mak asked with a startled expression.

"That is what it sounded like to me," Borj commented.

"Is that the human we are after or not?" Teriff demanded.

"Oh, that's Afon Dolinski," RITA replied, suddenly appearing beside Runt. The AI turned and smiled at her. "Hi, sweetheart," RITA said.

"It would appear we are at a standoff," Afon tersely remarked.

"That is where you are wrong, human," J'kar said, appearing from a shimmering doorway behind him.

Runt opened her mouth to protest but no sound came out when the blonde woman slowly walked toward her with frightened, tear filled eyes. A hiccupping cry escaped Runt when the woman removed her wig to reveal neatly pinned, black hair.

"Amelia... Afon," the woman said in a voice that shook.

Runt shook her head in denial. She was glad that Afon was holding her, otherwise she would be a puddle on the floor. All of the men in the room had frozen in confusion—except Marcelo, who hadn't moved since he was hit with one of the aliens' blast of energy and fell to the floor.

"You.... It can't be.... I saw your body. I went to your funeral...," Runt mumbled in disbelief, her own eyes glazed with tears.

"I know," Anne Thomas replied.

*Amelia....*

Derik's gentle inquiry drew her attention to him. He still stood poised to fire at Afon. She desperately reached out to him with her mind, needing his calming strength.

"She's... my mom," she brokenly stated.

"But I thought...," Derik said as he looked from Runt to the woman and back. His expression softened when he saw that she was barely holding it together. She felt the warmth of his touch in her mind.

*I need you to step away from Dolinski,* he tenderly instructed.

*You can't hurt him,* she replied.

*He will harm you. He is responsible for many atrocities—including the death of Cosmos' father and Merrick's capture,* Derik said.

*He's my uncle,* she quietly explained.

Derik stared at her for a second before he lowered his weapon. Runt turned her attention back to her mother, and decided they all needed to go to a place where they could talk.

She stiffly pulled out of Afon's arms and turned to look up at him. His gaze remained focused on his twin sister.

"Arianna...," he murmured.

A watery smile appeared on Arianna's pale face, she took a step closer, and replied, "Yes."

Afon tore his gaze from Arianna to look down at Runt. "You knew?" he asked.

"No. At least, not that my mom was alive. I knew that you were my uncle. I didn't know...." She took in a deep breath, released it, and looked at her mom again. "I didn't know my mom was here."

"We need to leave. Reinforcements are on their way," Borj commented, looking out of the window.

"Oh, dear. I should have disabled the alarm system. I am obviously not as alright as I thought I was," RITA fretted.

Mak walked over to Marcelo, located the small black box that looked like a primitive comlink on the floor near him, and kicked it across the floor. Runt was just relieved to note that Marcelo was still breathing.

*I guess nice aliens set their phasors to stun,* she thought.

She jumped when she felt an arm slide around her waist and pull her close. Looking up, she realized Derik had moved without her noticing. Her hands went to his shoulder to balance herself.

"What should we do?" Derik asked his father.

"RITA, let Cosmos and Avery know that we have the situation

under control. Borj, open the portal. We take everyone back with us to Baade. We'll deal with it there," Teriff ordered.

"Including this one?" Mak asked, nudging Marcelo with his boot.

Teriff nodded. "Yes. Unfortunately, he has seen too much," he said.

"Amelia…," Anne Thomas said with alarm when the shimmering portal appeared.

"I won't let them hurt you," Runt declared in a low voice. "I promise."

## CHAPTER EIGHTEEN

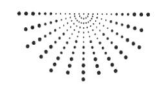

Six hours later, Derik quietly stepped into his living quarters. He rubbed his face and yawned, then blinked in surprise when he saw Amelia sitting on a lounge chair on the balcony. He felt a wrench in his heart when he saw her wipe her cheek.

*Are you alright?* he murmured.

She turned her head and gazed at him through the glass with eyes that were red and swollen. Her face was pale. The dark shadows under her eyes made her look very young and vulnerable. Regret that he couldn't protect her coursed through him.

She shook her head. *I'm good. You can't protect me from life, you know. I wouldn't want you to, even if you could,* she quietly informed him.

*That doesn't change the fact that I wish I could,* he ruefully told her as he walked through the living area and out onto the balcony. She twisted around until she was sitting on the edge of the lounge chair. He sank down beside her and opened his arms. She tilted her head to the side and studied him for a moment. She gave him a rueful, watery smile and leaned into him.

"I want more," he playfully teased, lifting her up and placing her on his lap.

"Yeah, well, keep dreaming," she retorted.

Derik wrapped his arms around her waist and buried his face against her neck. He tightened his hold when he felt her tremble. Closing his eyes, he drew in a deep, calming breath. The tension inside him slowly began to recede.

"What's going to happen to us?" she asked in a soft voice.

He lifted his head and rested his chin on the top of her head. "Us.... I like the sound of that," he said.

She leaned back and scowled at him. "I meant me, my mom, and Afon, not you and me. That's still not going to happen," she said.

"I'll ignore the last part and answer the first," he said with a sigh. "The Council will make a decision. Have you talked to your mother about what happened and what she wishes to do?"

She lowered her head and nodded. "We talked—a little," she mumbled.

She placed her trembling hands on his arms, her pain and confusion very clearly coming through their mental link. She was exhausted, but her mind refused to shut down.

"She will be protected and cared for," he assured her. "My mother has taken her under her wing and Tilly will be close by. As far as what will happen to Dolinski and the other man we brought, the Council is still undecided. If Cosmos does not request the Right of Justice, my brother Mak or Merrick may," he explained.

"What does Right of Justice mean?" she asked, meeting his gaze again.

"If the Council determines there is enough evidence, your uncle will face one of the three men in a fight to the death. If he survives, he will go free," he reluctantly explained.

"But… you said to the death. Does that mean…? Oh!" she hissed in dismay.

"Yes," he replied.

"Well, I won't tell you how messed up that is, because I hope you already know!" she muttered.

"It is our way, Amelia," he said.

He reluctantly released her when she pulled out of his arms and stood up. He followed her with his gaze when she walked over to the balcony railing and looked out over the city. In the distance, they could see spaceships lifting off from the ports.

"You know, for such an advanced, civilized world, you really aren't any better than we are," she bitterly remarked.

"Amelia," he started to say.

She turned to look at him. Fresh tears dampened her cheeks. She wrapped her arms defensively around her waist and gazed back at him. He rose to his feet and walked over to her.

"She faked her death because of me. My mom—she told me how she realized my dad and others would *always* use us, no matter where we went." She paused, gathering her remaining fortitude to tell him everything her mom had said, because she really needed to talk to someone about it. "It started with this one night, somehow my dad found out I was doing side jobs to earn extra cash. I wanted to save up enough so that we could run away together, Mom and me. He beat up my mom and told us there would be more if I ever tried to escape. I didn't really understand—I thought he meant more for her, more bruises, broken bones, stuff that would make me feel so guilty because she was injured and I was fine, but stuff that would heal, you know? We could still run away together and we'd be ok, eventually. We just had to be more careful, so he wouldn't hit her again. But... he told my mom that I didn't need my legs to hack computers. He threatened to cripple me for life if she tried to take me away." Her voice broke on the last word.

Derik tenderly wiped the stray tear running down her cheek. She sniffed loudly and looked down. He could sense her trying to withdraw from him, but she took a deep breath and continued.

"Usually he just locked me in the closet while he hurt my mom and never lifted a hand to me, but after we stole from Avilov, that was the first time he hit me. She was lying on the floor where he'd left her, and she had to watch. I could barely walk for a week," she murmured, flinching away from those memories.

Derik flinched with her, and forced himself to remain silent. It was hard enough for her to tell him this. He pulled her into his arms and held her tight. She hugged him back, rubbed her nose against his shirt, and continued the story her mom had told her to explain why she'd let her little girl think she was dead for years.

"She said she knew then, that she couldn't risk us leaving together, and she couldn't stand it anymore, the way things were. She needed a permanent solution... a solution that didn't involve her becoming someone else's weapon against me... but the thing is, she always would be. She believed that. The person abusing us could be different, but as long as I was me, as long as I was *useful*..." Runt's tears were flowing steadily down her cheeks now, but she was holding in her sobs with deep breaths.

"Why? Why did your mother not seek help? Surely someone would have assisted her," Derik murmured, keeping his voice soft with great effort.

"Who could protect us? The local homeless shelter? The police that weren't on DiMaggio's payroll? At the time we couldn't be sure who was and who wasn't. The local welfare office workers were overworked and underpaid. They didn't have the time or the energy to follow up, much less a way to protect us from the kind of powerful people we were dealing with. It was easy for my dad to move us around so that we slipped through the cracks. No, there was no one, and when DiMaggio found out about my dad stealing from Avilov, he sent Karl and a couple of his goons to our apartment. My dad had taken me on another job. When we got back, the police were all over the place. Dad pretended we lived in the apartment next door. Through the open door, I could see a body... covered with a bloodstained sheet. I couldn't see her face, but I saw... I saw the chain of my mom's locket—the matching one to mine—tangled in her fingers. My dad pulled me out of there," she said in a numb voice.

"And your mother? If that was not her body, whose was it?" he angrily asked.

She swallowed and looked away from him. "The woman was one of my dad's 'lady friends'. My mom had been at the library doing research on Avilov when Karl and his friends showed up at our apartment. Life really does work in mysterious ways. My dad's greed had connected him to DiMaggio and then to Avilov—and my mom's twin brother was working for Avilov. Mom found an image of Avilov with Afon standing next to him. She recognized Afon immediately—especially since his name hadn't changed yet.

"When she came home, she overheard Karl tell DiMaggio that he'd delivered the message. My dad and I would find our dearly departed wife and mother when we came back to our apartment, and we'd be putty in DiMaggio's hands if we didn't want Lou to be next. That's what she heard him say… and she realized this was it, her only chance to disappear and search for some way to help me escape while everyone thought she was dead. My dad had a type, you know, so his lady friend kinda looked like my mom from a distance, and when my mom left her necklace with the body…. It turns out my mom isn't such a bad hack herself, so she was able to stay 'dead' all this time. All those hours in the library trying to help me were a great learning experience for her." She took in a shuddering breath before continuing. "Left-hand Lou moved us to a cheap motel in a neighboring city. Avilov declared he would painfully eliminate anyone who stole from him and anyone who knew about it. By the end of the year, I had lost both of my parents and was living on the streets. I changed my name to Runt, kept moving, and connected with a very powerful friend named RITA," she said with a small smile as she remembered her first meeting with RITA.

Derik let that sink in for a moment, then said, "I wish now that I had killed Karl—and DiMaggio—when I had the chance. I can take care of that mistake. Avilov is dead. He is no longer a threat to you, and once Dolinski is dead, you would truly be free if you were ever to return to your world," he growled.

She snorted and shook her head. "You don't get it, do you? I don't want people dead, not even slime balls like Karl or DiMaggio. Avilov, well, I'll give you that one. He deserved whatever he got. Everyone makes choices in their lives. I know Avilov didn't regret a thing, and would have done worse if given a chance, but others do regret what they've done, try like hell to do better, and have to live with their lowest moments 'cause they did those things to survive and it worked. I think my uncle is one of those guys," she insisted.

Derik shook his head in disagreement. RITA had gone over the long list of crimes that Dolinski had committed. The fact that the man had faked his own death and lived a crime-free life for two years did not erase what he had done before—including facilitating Adam Raines' murder. Amelia and her mother were going to have to accept that the man had to pay a price for his choices.

"There is nothing I can do, Amelia. This is a decision for the Council," he said with regret.

She stared up at him, her eyes glittering with anger and grief. He pulled her into his arms and held her tightly against his chest. She remained stiff for several seconds before she relaxed against him. Amusement swept through him when he felt her pulling up a mental wall to hide her thoughts. She was already planning something.

## CHAPTER NINETEEN

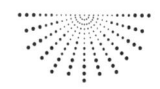

Runt woke to the feel of warm arms encircling her. She lay on her side, facing the window. The sun was just beginning to peek over the horizon, and vivid colors splashed across the sky like a child's watercolor.

"I love this time of the day," she whispered.

"Why?" he asked.

"It's that moment between light and dark—when the world seems at peace," she said, rolling over so that she was facing him. "You didn't need to do this, you know."

"Do what?" he murmured.

"Hold me," she said.

"I happen to like holding you. You fit just right against me," he teased.

She shook her head in response, and parted her lips to retort when his communicator chimed. He grimaced, rolled onto his back, and picked it up from the nightstand.

"This is Derik," he responded.

"I need you in the Council chambers now. We have a problem," J'kar tersely announced.

"I'm on my way," Derik replied.

He placed the communicator back on the nightstand and turned to face her. She studied his troubled expression with an unwavering gaze.

"Is this about Afon?" she asked.

"I don't know. I'll be back as soon as I can. Then, we are going to talk," he said.

She blinked when he leaned forward and pressed a hard kiss to her lips before he pulled away. She watched him slide from the large bed. Then she sat up and ran her hand through her tousled hair.

"I'll have some clothing and breakfast brought to you," he said, removing his shirt as he spoke.

"Swee… Sweet," she mumbled.

Suddenly feeling too warm, she pushed the bedspread down. Derik's muscles rippled across his back and shoulders as he shrugged off the shirt he'd worn last night. He tossed it into a basket near the door.

She gaped at him when his hands moved to his pants, and softly gasped when the waistband slid down, revealing a very nice set of buttocks. She moistened her lips. The guy had a seriously cute ass! If he turned around….

"If you need anything else…," he was saying.

"Uh-huh," she responded, having no idea what he was saying.

"Are you alright?" he asked, looking at her over his shoulder.

She forced her gaze to move from his ass to his face, and flushed when she saw his amused expression. He was doing this on purpose! Swallowing, she nodded.

"Of… course, I'm alright. It isn't like… like I've never seen a naked guy before," she muttered.

He rumbled in displeasure. "Remind me to ask you more about that when I get back," he said before disappearing into the bathroom.

She sank back against the pillows and shook her head as she gazed up at the ceiling. "Damn, but I may never wash my eyes again," she muttered.

It was true that he wasn't the first guy she had seen naked. The difference was she had never wanted to look at the others—much less do other things to them. Just the thought of touching Derik's smooth skin, cupping his firm butt cheeks, and seeing what he looked like from the front was enough to make her ache in places that had never ached before.

*I can hear you*, he mentally told her from the other side of the door.

*Shit! Get out of my head! I'm having a private fantasy*, she replied with a disgruntled hiss.

His chuckle swept through her already heated body and sent her scrambling from the bed. She ran her hands through her disheveled hair again.

*I really need to know when this link is turned on and when it's off!* she thought.

*We will always be linked from now on*, he mentally stated.

*Great! Just great!* she growled.

Her body was reacting to him with a vengeance. She could feel every motion of his hand when he slid it over his body. She looked down at her tingling palm. The mark on it was clearly visible.

*Well, two can play this game*, she thought.

*What game?* he asked.

*This one*, she retorted mischievously.

Lifting her palm to her mouth, she ruthlessly ran her tongue over the mark. She gleefully scrunched her nose and smiled in satisfaction when she heard Derik's sudden yelp followed by a loud crash and a string of curses. She added a little teeth to the action.

The sound of his footsteps heading for the door sent her scurrying for the exit. She looked over her shoulder as he appeared in the doorway to the bathroom. His hair was standing up in all different directions, still foamy with shampoo. Small globs of soap ran down his temple. Water dripped from his elbow as he fought to keep his grip on the towel that was loosely bunched around his waist. She froze, her parted lips millimeters from the mark.

"Don't... you... dare!" he growled.

She licked from the edge of her palm all the way to the tip of her fingers in defiance. He jolted as if she'd sent a shock through him. The towel he was holding fell to the floor as he surged toward her—just as his communicator chimed again.

"Derik, where are you?" J'kar demanded from the communicator's location on the bathroom counter.

"I'll be there in two minutes," he said in a loud voice, never taking his glittering gaze off of her. "This is not over."

He stooped, grabbed his towel off the floor, and returned to the bathroom. Runt stood rooted to the spot by the door. Her hand remained frozen in front of her mouth while her eyes were fixated on the area below his belly button. She didn't need to wonder what he looked like from the front anymore.

"Holy Moly, but he's well-endowed!" she mumbled to herself.

Shaking her head, she looked down at the mark on her hand. In that moment, she knew that her life would always be tied to this unusual alien male—and it scared the hell out of her. Lifting her head, she stared at the empty doorway. She needed to talk to someone. She needed to talk to her mom.

Turning on her heel, she silently fled down the hallway and out of Derik's living quarters. She ran along a long corridor, passing startled alien warriors and strangely dressed women, her heart pounding as she zipped through corridor after corridor. Only when she realized that she didn't know where she was going did she slow to a stop. Stepping into an alcove, she pressed her back to the cool wall. Her fingers trembled as she reached for the micro-computer on her wrist.

"RITA, I need help," she breathlessly murmured.

She blinked, startled when a female AI appeared with a strange man beside her. This RITA looked significantly different from the one she was used to seeing—much more than just a change in the outfit. Runt's gaze moved to the man. He was definitely different.

"Oh, dear, is everything alright, Amelia?" the AI asked.

"You're not RITA," she blurted out.

"No, love. RITA is my Earthly sis. I'm RITA2, the Prime version of AI perfection," RITA2 cheerfully greeted.

"Absolute perfection," the male AI agreed with a warm smile.

RITA2 winked at her. "DAR and I have been working on a flirtation program. I think it is working marvelously," she chuckled.

Ruth studied the beautiful AI standing in front of her, and frowned when she saw an unusual strand of code running between the woman and the man. She opened her mouth to ask about it, then decided it was none of her business.

"Can you help me find my mom?" she asked instead.

"Of course, love. Would you like us to escort you? I swear the palace has more corridors than the Pentagon back on Earth!" RITA2 said.

"Have you been to the Pentagon?" Runt asked.

RITA2 looked at her with a startled expression. "No, but my sis is always complaining about it. Ever since the Vice President of America and Tansy's former director at CPAT turned out to be baddies, RITA and FRED have been spending a lot of time there—and other government buildings too, but none as large as the Pentagon," RITA2 explained.

"Oh, yeah, I can see that. Cosmos asked me to design and run a program to review all personnel, contractors, and subcontractors who may be receiving funds from unregistered entities," Runt murmured.

DAR smiled. "RITA is always gushing about how brilliant you are, which is why my mate and I were wondering…," DAR began.

"Not now, sweetheart. Can't you see that Amelia has enough on her mind?" RITA2 interrupted.

"Of course, love. I'm just concerned about your delicate programming issue," DAR murmured, his eyes heating up.

"Wait until you see what Tilly is working on," RITA2 murmured with a flirty glance.

"Is this like some kind of sex planet or something? I mean, is everyone here like horny all the time or what?" Runt asked in a bemused voice as she watched them and listened to the innuendo of their banter.

RITA2 burst out laughing, and Runt looked up when the lights began to glow really bright. She looked at RITA2 again and could see the swirling code multiplying. There was something seriously wrong.

If she didn't know better, she'd think that RITA2 was infected with malware. Shaking her head at her ludicrous thoughts, she reached out to touch the AI.

"Oh my. I think I might need to power down for a bit," RITA2 said, lifting a hand to her head.

"I think that would be wise," DAR agreed.

"My mom?" she quietly reminded RITA2.

"Of course, honey. Go down to the end of this corridor, make a left, and she is in the last room on the right," RITA2 instructed before she abruptly faded.

Runt looked at DAR. "Is she okay?" she asked.

"No. I would like to speak with you later," DAR replied.

Runt nodded, and the male AI disappeared. For a brief moment, she wondered if she'd fallen into an alternate universe. That feeling intensified when two warriors who were walking by paused to stare at her as if *she* was the alien…because that's exactly what she was now.

"I've ended up in a frigging Sci-Fi movie," she muttered as she scooted by them and took off down the corridor.

## CHAPTER TWENTY

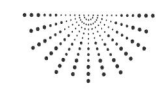

"Derik, you need to see if Amelia can do something—anything—to help RITA2 and DAR," Teriff ordered.

"Preferably before we end up with a dozen miniature RITA2s and DARs running around the palace," J'kar said.

"What happened?" Derik asked, sliding into an empty chair.

J'kar scowled. "Didn't you notice the power surge?"

Derik shrugged. "I must have missed it," he replied in a distracted voice.

"I've seen that look before," Mak muttered under his breath.

"Mate trouble," Borj agreed.

"Mate trouble," Mak grinned.

"She is not happy about Dolinski's future. Has the Council made a decision?" he asked.

"Yes, they've made a decision. Cosmos has declined the Right of Justice," Teriff stated.

"But I accepted," Mak added.

Derik frowned. Afon Dolinski might be a skilled killer, but against his older brother, there was no way he'd survive—even with a weapon. Derik was glad that Cosmos had declined. Terra was about to give birth any day now, and that would have been a big factor in his decision.

"There is only one problem," J'kar dryly added.

Derik frowned. "What? The fact that my mate and her mother will be devastated that you killed their newly discovered family member?"

His father shook his head. "No, the fact that Dolinski and the other human male escaped during the night, because your mate's mother helped them," Teriff replied.

Derik sat back in his seat in disbelief. "How did she do that?" he demanded.

"My mate assisted her," DAR replied as he appeared in the room.

∽

"You did what?!" Runt asked in disbelief.

She now understood why her mom's expression had been so resigned before she'd looked up and realized it was Runt, not the guards coming into the room. A part of her was grateful and extremely impressed by what her mother had done. The other part wanted to know what *else* was different about her mom since they'd last been together.

All thoughts of Runt's own problems had taken a back seat when she'd found her mother's heavily guarded room. Her quiet requests to be let in had been denied, but she wasn't going to give in and she'd been threatening heinous acts of violence when some guy named Brock had finally appeared from around the corner of the hallway. He had taken one look at her and groaned as he raised his eyes to the ceiling in a 'heaven help me/why me?' kind of way. Apparently some things were universal. Then he issued a terse warning to not try anything, and nodded to the guard to open the door.

"Well, RITA2 helped, but yes, I was the one who hacked into their system and I am responsible for their escape. I couldn't release one without the other, but I think they might stand a better chance together," Anne explained, reaching out to grip Runt's hands.

Runt looked down at their clasped hands. Her mom had changed so much in the two years since she'd disappeared. The changes both confused her and made her happy, but it was also overwhelming on top of everything else that had happened.

Meeting her mother's eyes, she could see fear in Anne's expression, but also the knowledge that she had done the right thing. Runt gave her a lopsided smile. She would have done the same thing—in fact, she had already been planning to do it!

"Did RITA2 open a portal back to Earth?" she asked.

Anne shook her head. "No, she couldn't without risking disconnection while they were still travelling through," she said.

Runt pulled her hands free and walked anxiously over to the window. "Do you have any idea where they might have gone?" she asked, turning back to look at her mom with worried eyes.

"No. RITA2 showed the men a map of the area, and gave them minimal security clearance—just enough to get out of the palace, I believe. I asked RITA2 to deactivate all the cameras in the city when we disabled the security around their cell. I had to distract the guards in person, of course," Anne confessed.

"What have you done to my mom?" Runt joked.

Anne gave her a wavering smile. "I finally pulled on a pair of cast iron panties," she chuckled.

Runt walked back over to her mother and hugged her. "I'm glad," she whispered.

"Me, too, Amelia. I only regret that I didn't do it sooner. Bert kept me up-to-date with how you were doing, and once I discovered you were working with CRI, I knew you would finally be safe," Anne admitted.

"Bert! That wily old man," she muttered with a shake of her head.

Anne laughed. "He was the only person who knew that I wasn't dead. I don't know what I would have done without him, if you know what I mean." She chuckled as she used one of Bert's favorite phrases.

"Yeah, I know what you mean," Runt agreed, thinking of all the times that Bert had helped her as well. "So, what now?"

Anne quickly snapped back to her previous worries. "I don't know.

I haven't exactly been making friends with the head of security around here," she said.

"I won't let anything happen to you," Runt declared.

Anne gave her a strained smiled. "I don't regret what I've done. I can only hope that Afon and Marcelo are able to find a way back to Earth. I'm not sure there is a way without RITA2's gateway, though," she said.

"I don't think so either," Runt agreed.

They both turned toward the door when a knock sounded on it. Runt's stomach knotted when the door opened and one of the guards stepped inside. She slipped out of her mom's embrace and stepped protectively in front of her. The guard stepped aside to reveal Derik.

"The Council wishes to see your mother," he grimly informed her.

"Yeah, well, they'll have to see us both," Runt retorted.

He released a long breath. "I figured that. That is the reason I am here," he said.

"Amelia, I don't want you to get involved," Anne insisted.

Runt turned and met her mother's determined glare with one of her own. "There is no way I'm letting anything happen to you," she growled before returning her gaze to Derik.

*I will do everything I can to protect her as well. I cannot promise the same for Dolinski or the other human, though,* he silently informed her.

"I know," Anne said, stepping forward to grasp Runt's hand. She looked at Derik. "I'm ready."

Derik briefly bowed his head in acknowledgment and stood to the side. Runt followed her mother. When she passed Derik, she reached out and touched his hand. He gave her a reassuring smile.

*Will they keep her locked up?* she asked.

*If that's her sentence, how would you feel about a life on the run?* he teased.

She barely suppressed her snort of laughter. *I think I can do that.*

He smiled, and sent her a thought crackling with intensity. *Seriously though, I swear on my life you will never have to run again.*

Runt swallowed, and looked at her mother's stiff back, wishing that she could have had more time to talk to her about this. Her feelings for Derik confused her, and she wasn't sure what to do. Were they real or caused by some kind of alien pheromone? Was it normal to want to constantly touch him whenever they were near each other? And what was it about him that made her want to… do things to him? Things that she'd purposely shied away from doing before.

She liked what she'd seen earlier this morning and wouldn't mind seeing more—and doing a little hands-on exploring. Last night, all they had done was sleep, but… he'd made a difference. Normally when her nightmares started, she woke herself up immediately.

Last night had been different. She had been beyond exhausted, her body so heavy she'd felt like she was wearing a lead suit. The dream started with a small stream of blood that had turned to a river. No matter how she'd tried to escape the red current, she had been tossed and turned until the thick, copper waves pulled her under.

At first, she had seen an image of her mother lying on the floor covered in a thin blood-soaked white sheet. Her hand lay outstretched with the silver locket tangled among her lifeless fingers.

The image changed as she tried to swim away, and she was violently wrenched to a halt when she bumped into something. Her hands instinctively grabbed the limp body. Horror swept through her, and her lips parted for an ear-piercing scream when she saw Derik's lifeless face and blank eyes.

She'd awoken gasping and sobbing. Her chest hurt and she'd felt like she was splintering into a million pieces. Pain unlike anything she had ever known held her locked in the dream. Only his calm, soothing voice and warm, gentle caress had finally broken through the paralyzing terror of her blood-drenched nightmare. He had held her the rest of the night.

Deep down, she knew he meant what he'd said. He wouldn't let anything happen to her mom—or to her. A sense of rightness filled her when she reached out again and cupped his hand in hers. He looked down at her with a tender expression of pleasure.

"I'm glad you're on our side," she murmured.

He lifted her hand to his lips. "Always, Amelia," he promised.

"You're never going to call me Runt, are you?" she mused.

"Nope," he replied, slowing as they neared a set of large double doors. "Do not be afraid. No one will harm you or your mother."

"I'm not afraid," she murmured.

Derik released her hand and stepped ahead of her mother. He waited for the guard to open the door before he entered the room. Runt moved close to her mother and grasped her hand. In the back of her mind, she could still sense Derik's presence. This time, she quietly embraced it.

"The Council is called to order. Have the human woman come forward," Teriff loudly ordered.

Runt took a deep breath when she felt her mom's hand tremble in hers. "Everything will be okay. Derik says he'll run away with us if we need to take off," she whispered.

Her mother nervously giggled. "Well, it isn't like we haven't had a little practice at it," she murmured in return.

Runt squeezed her mom's hand to comfort her. Together, they approached the row of men sitting behind a long, curved desk. There was only one empty seat, and she suspected it wasn't for a woman unless her name was Rav.

Her lips twisted in sardonic amusement. *Even alien worlds can't get it right when it comes to choosing leaders,* she thought as she scanned the group of men.

## CHAPTER TWENTY-ONE

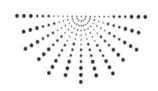

"Hello, everyone. I'm sorry I was late. The kids are growing at a phenomenal rate," RITA2 stated, suddenly appearing beside Runt and her mother.

"Well, at least they haven't multiplied. Why are you dressed like that?" Teriff asked.

"I'm Amelia and Arianna's—Anne's—legal counsel, of course," RITA2 replied.

"Legal counsel?" a large warrior to the right asked. "Teriff, didn't RITA2 help the human males escape?"

"That is what we are trying to clarify, Brawn," Teriff snapped.

"And that is why I am the counsel of the counsel," DAR stated, appearing beside RITA2.

"You are such a sweetheart.... but who's watching the children?" RITA2 asked under her breath.

"Tink and Tilly," DAR replied.

"Whose kids?" Runt asked, turning her shocked gaze to RITA2. "What is going on with your code? It's like… going crazy."

"You see it? What is it doing? For some reason, neither DAR nor I can figure out what is going on," RITA2 excitedly exclaimed.

"It looks like a duplication loop," Runt reflected, pointing to the lines of code she meant.

"Can we get back to business here? You can work on your—whatever—later," Teriff ordered.

"What did I miss?" another man asked, stepping up to the long table, pulling out the single empty chair, and sitting down.

*Score one for the human geek. No women on the Council,* Runt thought with disgust.

"Nothing," Teriff growled.

"*Hockta balmas!* I'd hoped you'd be finished already. Now I know why Merrick asked me to sit in for him, and Core wanted nothing to do with the Council. These meetings are as boring as a—" Rav suddenly interrupted himself when he noticed Anne, and he abruptly stood up, leaned forward, and growled, his dark silver eyes flaring with intense emotion.

"Rav! What has gotten into you? Sit down!" Teriff ordered.

Rav straightened and took a deep breath. He swallowed, and said, "Are you trying to say *she* is the one who released the human males?" He suddenly sat down in his chair on the dais with a thump.

"Yes, I am," Anne declared.

Runt noticed with surprise that her mom was glaring at the big guy with a ferocity of spirit that she'd never seen in her before. It took a fraction of a second for understanding to dawn. The guy was looking at her mom the same way that Derik looked at....

"*Shit!*" she hissed.

Derik's soft laugh and amused expression confirmed her suspicion. Was this some kind of sex-deprived hell, or what? The guy was eyeing her *mother* like she was some kind of scrumptious dessert, for crying out loud!

"She didn't do whatever you think she did. I claim her. Meeting adjourned," Rav said, slapping his hand on the dark wood table and rising to his feet again.

"Here we go again! Every time he sees a human woman, he thinks she is his bond mate," Hendrik muttered.

"Yes, but I seem to recall you think the same thing," Brawn chuckled.

"That's different," Hendrik growled.

"Rav, sit down. Hendrik, Brawn, I won't have any fighting today. I swear if any of you get blood on the floor or break a piece of furniture, I'll make you deal with my mate's displeasure," Teriff threatened.

Rav sank back down onto his chair. Runt blinked as the other men grumbled but calmed down. She looked over at her mother. Anne had crossed her arms in front of herself and was still glaring defiantly up at the large warrior.

*Wow!* That was all she could think as she watched the woman who had been beaten and almost broken blossom before her eyes. She listened as her mom explained what she had done and why, and the more she listened, the prouder she was of the woman her mother had become. She looked up at Derik when he silently held her hand.

*Everything will be alright now,* Derik reassured her.

*How do you know? They still plan to go after Afon,* she said.

*Yes, but I can tell from the way they are talking that they will reassess the situation. He will be given an opportunity to prove he deserves a second chance,* he said.

Runt looked up at the hard row of faces. She wasn't as confident about how things were going to turn out as Derik was, but she trusted him.

Shock coursed through her at that thought—she trusted him! She stiffened and drew in a deep breath.

*What is wrong?* he asked.

She shook her head. How did you explain to someone that you had just had a life-changing epiphany? Sure, there were people she had trusted before—all two and a half of them! Well, one and a half if you counted the fact that RITA wasn't really a person. She had always trusted her mom, but she had also held a part of herself back because as long as her mom protected her, others would use their love for each other against them. She had tried to shield her mother as much as she could.

The only other human she had given a small amount of trust to was Bert. Even then, she never let him know where she was staying or what she was doing. She didn't even rank Trudy, Maria, or Rose at CRI on her list of people she trusted. Sure, they were nice, but they were just people she worked with. She knew that if Avery or Cosmos gave the order to go after her, they would. Bert would at least think twice before he did.

RITA was different. Theirs was a special kind of trust. They were kindred spirits. If Runt could choose to be anything other than human, she'd want to be an advanced AI system like RITA. She could be herself around RITA without dealing with things as messy as emotions.

The loud sound of a hand pounding on wood drew her attention back to the council room. She blinked in confusion when she saw that all of the men were now standing. Gripping Derik's hand, she turned to look at her mother.

"The meeting is adjourned. Brock will search for the two human males. The Council will reconvene when they have been found. You will show us how you hacked RITA2 and will remain on Baade until the situation is resolved," Teriff stated.

"Under my supervision," Rav added.

Teriff rounded on the Rav. "We never discussed that," he snapped.

"I just did. Someone has to keep an eye on the woman—for her own protection," Rav stated.

"And you are eager to volunteer?" Brawn chimed in. "How about you two touch hands? If the mating mark appears, then I will second his request."

"I'll third it if that happens," Hendrik declared. "At least it will prove that Trudy is mine,"

Teriff frowned at Rav before he sighed deeply and turned to look down at her mother. Runt was about to object when Derik sent her a thought.

*Let her make the decision,* he suggested.

"But she doesn't know what it would mean," she hissed.

"If the mark appears, it means your mother will be loved and protected," Derik murmured.

"Will you accept his touch?" Teriff asked Anne.

Anne nervously looked at Rav before turning her gaze back to Teriff. "Touch how? If—and it is a big IF—I agree, what will happen?" she demanded.

"Can I speak to my mom for a moment—privately?" Runt snapped.

"She's going to scare her out of touching me, isn't she?" Rav muttered.

"If she is smart she will," Hendrik retorted.

Runt pulled her hand out of Derik's despite his obvious reluctance, gripped her mom's arm, and pulled her several feet away. Her worried gaze met her mom's wary one. The room suddenly became deathly quiet. Leaning forward, she began to speak in a quiet, but earnest tone.

"Look at my hand. Do you see this mark?" she said, lifting her hand so that the mark on her palm was showing.

Anne's eyes widened. "When did you get a tattoo? Oh, Amelia. You know we talked about this," her mom said.

Runt shook her head. "It isn't a tattoo—or at least not like the ones back home. This is called a mating mark. It's like this weird alien sign that two people are supposed to be right for each other. It *only* shows up if they are compatible. Don't ask me how it works. I just know that if you have skin to skin contact with him and it appears, some really strange shit starts to happen that you can't stop, even if you want it to," she whispered.

Anne gripped her daughter's hand, examining the mark closely, then she turned her head to glare daggers at Derik.

"He did this to you?" Anne hissed. She met her daughter's gaze. "You are not trapped, Amelia. I won't let you be tortured like that again; I swear it. I swore that when I left. I can take you with me this time. You'll be safe. I promise I'll keep you safe this time," Anne urgently said.

Runt closed her eyes when she felt her mom's hand against her cheek. Memories of the thousands of times she'd felt her mom's comforting touch washed through her. She covered her mom's hand with her own and opened her eyes.

"Derik would never hurt me. He would do everything in his power to keep me safe and—and he understands who I am—who I really am. It isn't me that I'm worried about. It's you. I know he isn't Lou, but we don't know…." she whispered. A single tear slid down her cheek.

"What did this man *Lou* do to you? Who tortured you?" Rav demanded.

Runt turned in surprise to see the large Prime warrior standing behind her. The retort died on her lips when she saw how concerned he was. She turned back to her mom, and issued one last warning, feeling the inevitability of their alien mojo. She had denied it for two years, hadn't she? And look where she was now.

"You have to be sure…'cause if the mark appears, it'd be a forever kind of bond," she said, glancing at Derik for a moment before she stepped back.

Anne held Runt's gaze, then reluctantly looked at Rav, the man standing in front of her with such an intense expression of hope and concern. Runt shivered when Derik wrapped his arms around her waist, pulling her close against his tall, muscular frame. She covered his hands with her own.

"Only the Goddess knows if they are destined to be together," he murmured.

Runt held her breath when Rav held his hand out. Her mother didn't move for several seconds as she searched Rav's expression. Then she slowly extended her hand towards his. Her trembling hand was a breath away from his when she paused and suddenly clenched her fingers into a fist. She pulled away.

"I can't," Anne whispered. The careful space between them was thick with tension, and Rav's dismayed frustration was difficult to watch. "I can't," she said again in a stronger voice. She turned on her heel and quickly walked toward the guarded exit.

Runt sagged against Derik. The nearby guard opened the door for Anne when Teriff waved his hand. Silent tears coursed down Runt's cheeks. She closed her eyes, bowed her head, and told herself this was for the best. Her mom was safe.

## CHAPTER TWENTY-TWO

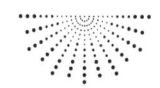

Derik held Amelia's hand as they left the Council room. He remained silent, knowing that she needed time to get her emotions under control. Her current thoughts were unprotected by the wall that she usually tried to keep between them.

Even without their connection, it would have been impossible to miss that the last few days had deeply affected her. It would be traumatic for anyone to discover that her mother was actually alive and she was related to someone like Dolinski!

"Being related to Dolinski isn't so bad," she murmured, answering his thoughts.

"Not bad?! Have you read about his crimes?" he asked in a shocked voice.

She gave him a crooked smile. "Yeah, but it could have been worse. I could have been related to Avilov or Markham. Trust me, having Lou for a dad was bad enough," she pointed out.

"I would have protected you," he swore.

She stopped in the middle of the corridor and looked up at him. Then she smiled and cupped his cheek, slowly trailing her fingers over his coarse stubble. She tilted her head to the side as she caressed his face.

"I can remove the hair if you do not like it," he said.

She shook her head. "It's *your* body. It doesn't matter whether I like it or not. If you like it, that's all that matters," she said.

"It matters to me if it causes you irritation," he murmured, turning his head so that his lips brushed her palm.

She studied him for a second, a curious smile curving her lips, then she stood on her tiptoes. She slid her other hand up his chest to balance herself.

"I guess I'll have to find out if it does," she replied.

He inhaled deeply when her glance moved from his eyes to his mouth. For a moment, she paused just a breath away from his lips, then she gently kissed him. He wrapped his arms around her and pulled her tightly against the hard frame of his body.

He'd let her explore as long as she wanted as long as she kept moving her lips sensuously against his. He enjoyed the sensation of their lips touching, the way their breaths mingled together, and when he slid his hand down her back, he loved the way she arched and pressed her breasts against him. He moaned and felt his cock swell. She softly moaned too, and parted her lips so he could deepen their kiss. Their tongues danced, touching, pulling back, and touching again in an erotic rhythm that increased in speed as their desire flared.

He trailed his fingers up her arm, then cradled the back of her head as he continued to explore her. She moved just enough to slip her leg between his, and took his breath away. His low groan suddenly seemed unusually loud in the hallway, and finally remembering that they were out in public, he opened his eyes. They weren't alone.

Derik slowly ended the kiss, his glare locked on the group of warriors he could see over her shoulder. They were observing him and Amelia with intense fascination and a lot of enjoyment. He instinctively drew Amelia's head to his shoulder to shield her.

"Uh, Derik," she whispered.

"Ignore them," he murmured.

She giggled. "That's kind of hard to do when we are surrounded." She pulled back and turned to look at the men with a raised eyebrow.

"Are you guys really that hard up? Why don't you take a photo? It will last longer," she suggested.

"Can we?" one of the warriors asked with a grin.

"Are all human females this affectionate?" another one inquired.

"Of course they are! Haven't you been attending Tilly's Chick Flick Friday Nights?" a third warrior asked.

"I like her Thirsty Hallmark Thursday nights. She serves different flavored beers with her popcorn," a fourth warrior proclaimed with a grin.

Derik was about to order them all to leave before they upset Amelia, but her burst of laughter stopped him. Her face was flushed a pretty pink and her eyes twinkled. His breath caught at how beautiful she was.

"You guys really need to get a life," she said with another giggle.

"We are trying! It is very difficult to find a mate without going to your world. We have to wait for the Council to resume missions that involve the Gateway," the first warrior replied with a wistful sigh.

Amelia shook her head. "What you need is an online dating site. That might help," she suggested.

"Online dating? Does RITA2 know what this is?" Derik asked with a frown.

"Probably. It isn't exactly that difficult to create. People back on Earth use them all the time to connect and find people they are interested in," she replied with a shrug.

"Would this online dating help us find our bond mates?" the second warrior asked.

"Theoretically. I've never used one, just saw them when I was surfing the web. The ads for them say they'll find your soul mate, but you know how that goes. Ads almost always make things seem better than they really are," she responded.

"How does...," the warrior began.

"That's enough for now," Derik interrupted. "I will mention this to the Council, but right now, I would like some time with my mate."

"Maybe Lady Tilly will know. She knows everything there is to know about human women and sex," a warrior commented as the group moved away.

Derik wanted to groan in embarrassment. He was sure that Amelia would put two and two together and deduce that he was about as clueless as the warriors walking away from them. She looked up at him with a contemplative expression, and he fought to hide his dismay.

"I take it you guys don't get much dating action here," she calmly reflected.

"No," he reluctantly replied.

She tilted her head and gazed at him for a few seconds. He could tell she was trying not to smile, but he also knew she was genuinely curious.

"So, are you, like, a virgin?" she casually inquired.

Derik knew what she was really asking. She wanted to know if he'd know how to pleasure her. All of his insecurities returned with a vengeance. He wanted to lie and say he had more than enough experience to do this right. The problem was—he couldn't lie to her without her knowing it.

"I've watched the instructional vidcoms RITA2 uploaded, and I have seen many of the movies Tilly presented," he stiffly replied.

She looked at him with wide eyes. "Wow!" she murmured with a shake of her head before she turned and began walking again.

"Wow?" he repeated with a frown. He turned and stared at her back. "What do you mean by 'wow'? Is that a good 'wow' or a bad 'wow'?" he demanded, quickly striding forward to catch up with her.

She looked at him with a mysterious smile. "Well, if you got to be that good a kisser by watching a bunch of dorky movies and *instructional material*, I wonder what else you are good at," she thoughtfully reflected.

He stopped as the meaning of what she'd said finally sank in. A goofy grin curved his lips. She liked the way he kissed her.

*No, I loved it,* she cheekily retorted.

Several days later, Amelia sat in her mom's new living quarters. They had spent the time since the Council meeting talking about things they had never talked about before. It was strange—and yet surprisingly comforting.

Their relationship had changed in these past few days. Before, they had both been cautious—more focused on surviving than living, but now they were slowly moving from just mother and daughter to friends. She looked up when she heard her mom's soft sigh.

"What's wrong?" she asked.

"You are so young and yet—so grown up," Anne commented, sinking down into the chair across from her with a cup of hot tea.

She gave her mom a quizzical look. "Yeah, well, that tends to happen when you grow up the way I did," she commented.

Runt regretted her rather flippant reply when she saw remorse flash through her mother's eyes before she looked down at her steaming cup of tea. Runt turned her gaze to the window when the shadow of a shuttle flying overhead caught her attention.

"I was a coward for staying," her mother whispered. "In the end, I abandoned you to save myself."

Runt turned and glared at her mother. "Don't!" she said in a sharp tone. "You protected me. Remember, it wasn't just Lou. Running wouldn't have done anything but gotten you—and probably me—killed. We can't change the things that happened. Things are different now. We don't have to worry about people like Lou or DiMaggio, or even the government. They can't touch us now," she said, waving at the window.

Her mom's eyes followed the motion of her hand. "This world is so beautiful," Anne murmured.

"You know you could stay here," Runt said. "You don't have to go back. There are other human women here. They seem happy."

Anne looked back at her with a startled expression. Runt grimaced as she anticipated her mom pouncing on that statement. She could see the question in Anne's eyes. What was worse was that she could feel her face heat.

"Is that what you are planning on doing? Staying here—with Derik?" Anne asked.

"Maybe…. Probably…. I don't know yet. I'm still working things out in my head," she mumbled.

"He seems like a nice young man," her mom continued.

"He's alright," she replied, wishing she hadn't brought this up.

"Have you and he…?" her mom started to ask.

"Not yet," she said.

"Oh. Well, if you have any questions," her mom awkwardly replied.

Runt shook her head. "I'm eighteen, almost nineteen. I think I have a pretty good concept of what goes on between a man and a woman—probably more than Derik does," she commented with an amused grin.

Her mom's eyes widened with surprise. "Are you telling me that he…?" her mom choked.

Runt nodded. "Yeah. They don't have a lot of women here, I guess, so the guys spend most of their time training to beat the crap out of each other and their enemies. Apparently there's this weird alien species called the Juangans that everyone hates 'cause they like to attack and eat people." She scrunched her nose.

"Oh, dear. I wonder if…," her mom started to say before she blushed.

"I wouldn't be surprised," Runt chuckled, knowing her mom was thinking of Rav.

Her mom's lips trembled for a moment before she giggled. The soft, bubbly sound was contagious, and soon they were both laughing. Life was definitely different on this planet! Even the sound of their laughter sounded strange and unusual. Her mom wiped away a tear near the corner of her eye and shook her head.

"Derik wants to take me away on a trip—just the two of us," she finally confessed.

"Where? For how long?" Anne asked.

Runt shrugged. "I don't know. A couple of weeks maybe. He was talking about this place called Quadrule Five. I think it would be pretty awesome to fly through space," she said, biting her lip and looking out the window again.

Silence followed her comment. She curled her fingers as she waited to see how her mom responded. It wasn't like she was asking permission. It was more like asking for acceptance.

"I think that would be a wonderful adventure, Amelia," her mom said.

She turned to look at her mom. "Yeah, that's what I was thinking too. But, what about you? Will you be alright?" she asked.

"Sweetheart, I'm a lot tougher than I used to be. I'll be fine. Besides, what could possibly happen to me here? Like you said, Lou and DiMaggio can't touch us anymore." Anne smiled.

"It's not them that I was thinking about," Runt said with a wry grin.

Her mom's eyes widened and she blushed again. "Trust me, I wouldn't get near one of these warriors with a ten-foot pole. Besides, I think the guy from the other day has finally given up. I haven't seen him lurking around anymore. I must have finally scared him off," Anne laughed.

"Yeah, I thought the same thing, and look where that got me!" Runt muttered under her breath.

## CHAPTER TWENTY-THREE

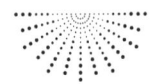

**Baade Spaceport:**
**Two days later:**

Runt waited in the shade of the covered walkway while Derik quietly spoke with a merchant who had delivered some last minute items that Brock had sent for their trip. She glanced over her shoulder at Derik and noticed that he was listening intently to what the man was saying. Given the way the guy was waving his hands around and excitedly pointing at the tablet he was holding, it looked like it was going to take a while.

She turned when she heard a strange buzzing noise. She grinned when she saw a boy go by on a really cool looking hoverboard. The city was filled with amazing things everywhere she looked and she had fallen in love with all the futuristic vehicles. Deciding to see if she could catch another glimpse of the boy, she walked over to the edge of the sidewalk in the hopes of seeing the boy again.

The boy had disappeared into the crowds, but a dozen other vehicles soon caught her attention. Her eyes lit up when she caught sight of a floating motorcycle that was coming down the street. For a moment, it didn't look like anyone was operating it. It wasn't until the motorcycle stopped in front of her that she could see the driver straddling the bike. The bizarre creature with multiple eyes and tan leathery skin stepped off the cycle onto the sidewalk in front of her, turned, and leered at her.

Runt shuddered when he opened his mouth and ran a long tongue over his lips. From the way he was acting and the expression on his face, it wasn't hard to translate what he wanted—her! She shook her head and quickly stepped away from him. The creature might have been shorter than she was, but that didn't make him any less terrifying when his expression changed to one of anger. He reminded her of some of the lowlifes back on Earth.

"Hi'mov," *Get moving*, Derik shouted with a growl.

Runt jumped and turned around when she heard the shout behind her. Derik was striding toward her, his glare locked on the alien who had been eyeing her. She saw the alien make a rude gesture before he climbed back onto the motorcycle and pulled away.

"What was that?" she curiously asked, watching the alien disappear around the corner.

"A Merflick. They are a pain in the ass to be around, but they are hard workers. You just can't trust them. They'll try to barter with a rock if they think they could turn a credit for it," he said.

"He sure looked weird. I think he was trying to pick me up," she mused.

He held her hand and grinned at her. "He might have looked at you with an appreciative eye, but he wouldn't have bothered you. The Merflick aren't known for their bravery, and he knows I would have slit his throat if he came near you," he added.

"I'm cool. I can handle myself," she quipped.

"I know. I've seen what you can do," he teasingly reminded her.

She gave him a mischievous grin. "You haven't seen anything yet," she retorted, patting him on his chest.

"You set my blood on fire," he suddenly muttered.

Runt's lips parted in a gasp when he wrapped his fingers around her wrist, lowered his head, and captured her lips. He swept his tongue possessively between her lips. She curled her fingers into his vest, pulling him closer as she returned his passionate kiss with one of her own.

"My lord—apologies, sir. I… didn't realize you were…," the male voice faded into a grunt.

Derik slowly released her lips with a heavy sigh. "One of these days I'm going to be able to kiss you without interruption," he quietly vowed, resting his forehead against hers for a brief moment.

"That would be nice," she muttered.

Derik pulled back, but kept a hold on her wrist. She tilted her head and looked at the warrior who stood next to them trying to pretend that he wasn't there. The poor guy wasn't doing a very good job of it because his curious gaze kept straying to her.

"Is my ship ready?" Derik asked.

The warrior nodded. "Yes, my lord. Everything you requested has been loaded into the cargo bay," the man stated.

"That will be all," Derik replied.

"And thank you," Runt stated, elbowing Derik and giving him a look.

"Thank you," Derik grudgingly added.

"It was a pleasure, my lord," the warrior replied with a smile.

Runt watched with amusement as the man walked away. He had a little more pep in his step. She blinked in surprise when Derik gently grabbed her chin and turned her head. She looked up at him.

"You really enjoy driving us Prime males crazy, don't you?" he teased.

She raised an eyebrow. "It's too easy," she retorted.

It took her a second to realize that they were flirting. She had never done that before. It was a strange feeling—kind of powerful in a weird way.

She had seen others flirt, and a few guys had even tried to chat her up once or twice. None of them had interested her mentally or physically. Derik was different. She normally didn't like to talk that much, but with him, she found herself opening up. Of course, she could listen to him talk all day. They had spent time talking about everything from computer code, to how the Gateway worked, and about daily life on each of their respective planets.

Since she'd come through the Gateway, he had taken her to dinner at some of the small cafes around the city and even taken her to a few of Tilly's film events. Her favorite was the day he set up a surprise picnic lunch in the palace gardens. He had invited her mom to go with them. She couldn't remember ever having heard her mother laugh so much when Derik shared tales of his brothers and himself growing up.

"What is it?" he asked.

She blinked, realizing that she was staring up at him. She frowned and tilted her head to the side as she studied his face. It suddenly dawned on her what he had been doing the past week.

"You're courting me," she suddenly blurted out.

He bent down and brushed a kiss across her lips. "It took you long enough to figure that out. I thought I was doing it wrong. DAR kept telling me that I wasn't," he chuckled.

She shook her head. "What does a computer know about courting?" she scoffed.

"Obviously, a lot more than anyone realizes. Have you seen the way he interacts with RITA2? I wonder if Tilly has been playing with their programming again, or if it is part of their adaptive code. That reminds me, when we get back, Father has asked that we take a look at RITA2's code. He is afraid she might have more replications with DAR," Derik said.

Runt's eyes widened as a new thought occurred to her. "The duplication code I saw, yeah. I'll have to see if I can replicate it so that I can narrow it down...," she said in a distracted voice.

He brushed another kiss across her lips. "When we return. For now, I want only us," he said.

She nodded and held onto his hand when he turned and walked through the crowded space dock. She looked from side to side as she took in the colorful, wondrous alien world. This was her first view of the space dock on Baade. There were so many aliens from other worlds that she couldn't help but wonder how they had all discovered one another.

The buildings were futuristic and took her breath away. Tall spires of glass and metal towered above them. Walkways meandered through the numerous atriums connecting the tall buildings at various levels. The atriums created the illusion of lush floating gardens. It was obvious that the architects and engineers on Prime used solar energy extensively. Vehicles of different shapes and sizes moved in coordinated patterns. A sleek monorail sinuously glided along, carrying its passengers like a serpent from one building to the next.

Her mind swirled with the possibilities of learning more code—and challenging herself to see if she could penetrate their systems as easily as she had the ones on Earth. It was like telling Charlie that he won the chocolate factory and could do whatever he wanted in the magical, mystical world inside.

This was her fantastical playground. This was her chocolate factory. She could gorge on the technology and never be sated. This was a world made for someone like her.

Emotion choked her at the thought. This was a place where she actually fit in, felt at home. It was an indescribable feeling.

"Are you alright?" Derik tenderly asked.

She nodded, unable to speak and a bit overwhelmed. Instead, she squeezed his hand. He returned her gentle grasp before he continued on. He guided her to a set of large sand-colored doors. She was admiring the intricate artistry depicting scenes from space carved into the doors when they suddenly opened. They stepped through the entrance into a wide area that looked like a hanger with no roof. Inside, two guards straightened and stood at attention.

Runt's lips parted in awe when she saw the sleek shuttle waiting for them in the hangar. She pulled her hand free of his and slowly walked around the ship. The silver glittered in the bright sunlight that was streaming down through the open ceiling. The teardrop-shaped spacecraft looked like it was built for speed.

"How fast will this thing go? Can it go into light speed? Do you have light speed travel? Will we float when we go up into space, or does it have some way of creating an artificial gravity?" she asked in rapid-fire succession.

He laughed. "It goes fast. Yes, light speed fast, because yes, we do have light speed travel. No, we won't float, because yes, it has artificial gravity. Do you have any other questions?" Derik asked with a chuckle as he followed her around the shuttle.

She turned and looked at him with wide eyes and a hopeful expression. "Can I drive it?" she replied.

He threw his head back and laughed. "Yes, I will show you how to pilot the shuttle—after we get to Quadrule Five," he promised.

"Yes!" she crowed, giving a fist pump and dancing around in excitement before she turned and threw her arms around his neck.

Her lips connected with his in a kiss that surprised them both. She pulled back and stared at him in wonder. He was holding her up off the ground. Her body was pressed tightly against his.

"I...," she whispered, mesmerized by his eyes.

"You what?" he asked in a rough voice.

"Can you make love in space?" she wondered out loud.

He tightened his arms around her until she could barely breathe. His eyes flared with the silver flames that she recognized whenever he was intensely angry or aroused. She looked at his mouth. His teeth were lengthening.

"I'm willing to find out," he choked in a thick tone.

"Good," she said before leaning forward and capturing his lips again.

She hadn't planned on asking him that. Deep down, she knew going away with him meant they would have sex. Her mind may not have been completely ready to register that fact, but her body was. Now, there was no doubt in her mind that she wanted it as well. She wanted him—mentally and physically.

She sighed when she realized that, once again, they were not alone. The two guards were getting a pretty good show at the moment. She had lifted her legs and wound them around Derik's waist. If that wasn't bad enough, she was rubbing against him like a cat in heat.

Breaking their kiss, she buried her face against his shoulder. Her body was on fire, and she didn't know if her legs would hold her. She kept her face hidden when Derik slid his arm under her buttocks and turned around. He growled out a command, but she didn't hear it because her heart was beating like crazy.

"You are dangerous," he murmured.

She finally lifted her head when he slowly released her. A glance over her shoulder showed that the guards had left, and they were now alone. He held her until he was sure her legs could support her.

"Me?! You've got this like—super nova thing going on between my legs," she muttered.

His low groan told her that he caught what she meant. He shook his head and gripped her hand. Together they walked up the platform and into the shuttle.

*I hope this thing has a bedroom with a nice big bed,* she thought as the door behind them closed.

*This doesn't, but my ship does,* he promised with a sexy grin.

## CHAPTER TWENTY-FOUR

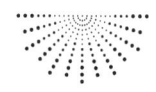

The journey into space was different from what she had seen on television back on Earth. They didn't need rockets that boosted them straight up with tremendous force. There was no shaking and rattling.

The sleek shuttle lifted off the ground like a Harrier jet before it took off like a speeding bullet. Derik guided the shuttle through the atmosphere with the same ease of someone driving a car along a highway.

Her breath got stuck in her throat when she looked down and saw the planet beneath them. Seeing the world below from space was like placing the final piece into a puzzle and seeing the complete picture. Baade was magnificent with its swirls of white, blue, purple, and green.

The approach to the Spaceport was just as electrifying. Derik pointed out the spaceship they would be transferring to in order to travel deeper into space. His spaceship was several times larger than the shuttle.

He maneuvered the shuttle to the side of the large ship. A bay opened as they approached and he guided the shuttle into the ship's landing bay. He skillfully rotated the shuttle until it was facing the open door and landed. She attentively followed the sequence as he powered down the shuttle and the door in front of them closed. A moment later, the flashing red lights around them turned to green.

Runt wordlessly followed Derik to the bridge of the huge spaceship, her wide eyes trying to take in everything at once, and she sat next to Derik as he settled into the pilot's station. She could see even larger ships through the window. Spaceships of all shapes and sizes glided past them.

"This is *Prime 521,* disengaging locks," Derik said into the comlink.

"*Prime 521,* you have clearance. Safe journey, my lord," the Spaceport controller replied.

And just like that, they were leaving the Spaceport. Her heart pounded when she saw the vast openness of space. Living in the city had never prepared her for what the world without artificial lights would look like.

"The stars look like twinkle lights." She smiled at the thought. "When I was a kid, there was a little café not far from our apartment. I loved walking by it at night and seeing the twinkle lights they had put in the trees. When I was little, I thought they were fairies," she murmured.

He reached over and cupped her hand. "You will love where I am taking you, then. I promise. Now, watch this," he said with a grin and released her hand.

She watched as he pressed a series of buttons, then pushed a lever forward. In seconds, she was pressed back against her seat watching the stars around them become a series of star trails. It felt like the universe was theirs and she wanted to hug the feeling close. For the first time in her life, she felt like a bird soaring free. There was nothing that could touch her here.

*Except me.*

*Except you,* she agreed with a cheeky grin.

∽

Three hours later, Runt stood in the galley of the ship. She had taken a shower and decided afterwards that she would like something warm to drink. She sighed in delight as she ran a finger through the whipped cream floating on top of her hot chocolate and lifted it to her lips. Sucking the creamy mixture off her finger, she turned when she heard a low groan.

"You have no idea what that does to me," Derik muttered.

She laughed and ran her finger through the whipped cream again—this time licking off the white cream with slow, measured swipes of her tongue. His muttered curse and the glint of playful revenge in his eyes made her laugh even harder.

She noticed that his hair was damp. "It looks like you had a shower, too. Who is flying this tank if you aren't?" she asked.

"What? Tank?" he asked in a distracted tone. He was mesmerized by her tongue as she licked a stray spot of whipped cream from her finger.

She snapped her fingers in front of him. His hand shot up and he gently snagged her wrist. He slowly pulled her closer. She took in a hissing breath when he lifted her hand to his mouth and touched his tongue to her finger.

"The spaceship. Who... who is flying it?" she asked, her voice trembling slightly with emotion.

"The computer. It will alert me if I'm needed," he softly replied.

"Self-driving spaceships... cool. We... back on Earth, the car... the car companies are experimenting with them—self-driving cars, that is. I want you, Derik," she added in a distracted voice, her eyes locked on his lips.

"Thank the Goddess," he breathed out with relief.

Their lips connected as they met halfway—all teasing forgotten. His hands ran up and down her sides before moving down to cup her ass. She wound her arms around his neck and pressed hard, frantic kisses to his lips, cheeks, and down his neck.

"Goddess, Amelia!" he groaned.

A rumbling deep within his chest shook him when she nipped his neck. He sounded almost like he was purring. One second she was standing in front of him and the next she was in his arms. He held her tight as he strode down the corridor to a cabin she hadn't seen yet. She had used the shower in a smaller cabin that she had found further down the corridor.

The door opened when he paused in front of it. The bedroom was larger than she'd thought it would be on a spaceship. A large bed was set up in front of them with built-in drawers on each side. Whatever else might be in the room, it wasn't nearly as important to her as the bed was right now.

He walked across the room, stopping next to the bed. She held on to his shoulders when he gently lowered her feet to the floor. Looking up at him, she could see the silver flames that she had come to love. They were burning for her.

He paused long enough to unsnap the straps on his boots. She watched him pull off each of them, along with his socks, before he tossed them to the side. She only had her socks on, so she was one step ahead of him. She tossed her purple socks on top of his boots with a wry grin.

She bit her lip when she noticed that his teeth had lengthened in the few short seconds that it had taken for him to remove his boots. Lifting her hand to his face, she slid her fingers lightly along his jaw until she touched the tip of his canine with the pad of her thumb. She hissed when she felt a sharp prick. She was shocked to see a small bead of blood was beginning to pool on the soft tissue.

She started to pull her hand away, but he grasped her wrist and guided her injured digit to his lips. He opened his mouth and ran his tongue over her thumb. She felt a strange, tingling warmth sweep through her thumb, spread through her hand, and up her arm.

"What...?" she started to ask.

"A Prime male's body changes when we are fighting—or in this case, when aroused. During arousal, my teeth will lengthen and I produce a chemical that causes a heightened sense of arousal. When I bite you, the chemical will mix with your blood and better prepare you for our joining. Afterward, I will seal the area using my saliva. It contains a healing coagulant," he explained.

She tilted her head. "You seriously have, like, Viagra for Women running through your veins, and you're gonna inject it into me by biting me?" she asked.

"I do not know what this Viagra for Women is, but yes, the chemical will mix with your blood and make you very sexually aroused. My bite should not be painful," he confessed.

"I guess if they ever came out with one on earth, it would be the Little Pink Pill—or is that birth control? Whatever…. So—it's just… ummmm, you're telling me that with one bite, I'll turn into some kind of horny hussy ready to jump you?" She laughed nervously, touching his tooth again.

"Yes, that sounds… very interesting," he croaked.

"It does, doesn't it?" She giggled. "I've never thought of being a horny hussy before, but then, I never thought I'd end up in an alien world with a sexy alien either," she observed.

"Is this foreplay?" he asked.

She tilted her head and grinned. "I don't know. I guess," she shrugged, her fingers sliding down to his shirt.

"I think it is time to move on to the after foreplay part," he suggested, soothingly running his hand up to her neck.

"About time," she muttered, pulling his shirt free from his trousers, up over his head, and throwing it behind her.

"Good," he groaned.

Runt moaned when she felt Derik brush his lips along the curve of her neck. There were some serious chemical reactions going on between them. When his teeth scraped against her skin, she arched closer.

"I like that," she moaned.

"I… can wait… if you…," he struggled to speak.

She turned her head and captured his mouth. His teeth had grown and she could feel them pressing against her lips. Her body felt hot and restless. They had waited for years. Now was not the time for him suddenly to be having second thoughts.

"You wait if you want. I'll help you get out of your clothes while you make up your mind," she mumbled against his skin.

His loud hiss filled the room when her hands slid down to work the fastenings of his trousers. The feel of her fingers between the material and his flesh drove him crazy. He kicked his trousers to the side.

When she touched his throbbing cock, his body took over with the primitive need to mate. He bent and pressed his mouth to the slender column of her throat again. He brushed his tongue against her silky flesh twice before he sank his teeth into the pulsing artery.

She released a startled cry that turned into a long moan. Her grip tightened around his cock and her hand moved up and down as he released the mating chemical into her blood stream.

"Derik!" she cried out.

They were locked to each other, one of her hands compulsively stroking his cock while her other hand cradled his head, her fingers threading through his hair. His arms tightened around her. At the moment, he couldn't have stopped what he was doing if he had wanted to.

His body shuddered when she tried to rub against him. He gently withdrew his teeth and ran his tongue over the mark, then he leaned back to study her face. Her cheeks were flushed and her eyes were closed. He swallowed and broke out in a cold sweat, so afraid that he'd done this wrong and she was in pain.

"My Amelia," he worriedly murmured.

Her lips quirked and she opened desire laden eyes to gaze back at him. "Now that—is some good shit. If the Prime bottled it, you'd have every woman on the planet wet and ready," she observed with a dreamy sigh.

His chuckle turned into a rumble of pleasure when she brushed her lips across the bare flesh of his chest. His hips began to rock to the rhythm of her strokes. The difference between reading about this and actually doing it were universes apart! He decided that the training vidcoms left a lot to be desired.

"You're thinking too hard," she muttered.

"How do you know?" he choked out.

"Because I can hear your thoughts," she giggled.

"Oh."

She leaned back. Her eyes glowed with the fire of the chemical coursing in her veins. His body was in meltdown. He didn't know how she was staying in control. The chemical—if he had shared it correctly—should have left her mindless with need.

"You really need to forget the videos," she recommended.

"How?" he asked, suddenly feeling overwhelmed.

She shook her head. "And people think I'm naïve," she muttered under her breath. "Hang on, I'm about to totally blow your mind!"

His mind was not 'blowing', whatever that meant, it was buzzing with questions, until she sat on the bed and pulled him closer—by his cock! He watched with growing fascination when she licked her lips before she leaned forward.

His brain short-circuited the moment she slid his cock between her lips. His mouth opened and closed before he swallowed the fierce cry that almost slipped out.

He clenched his hands by his side until he couldn't stand it any longer. He was going to come too soon if she did not stop. The problem was it felt so good—her tongue stroking him, the heat of her mouth firing his blood and causing his cock to swell even more, and the way her fingers were sliding lower.

"Goddess, Amelia!" he hissed when she cupped him.

He threaded his fingers through her hair. His head fell back and he rocked his hips back and forth. The need to claim, to penetrate more deeply, and to bury himself to the hilt pounded like a drum inside him.

She must have read his mind because she suddenly stopped and looked up at him with wild eyes. She kissed her way up his stomach until she was standing.

"Okay, your super horny hussy mix has kicked in," she informed him.

The feeling of sudden frustration dissolved into triumph. He pulled off her shirt and tossed it aside. His gaze followed the movement of her hands as she unfastened her jeans, pushed them down, and kicked them to the side. Needing to touch her, he knelt in front of her and pulled down her panties while she unsnapped the front clasp of her bra.

His breath caught in his throat when he looked up as she tossed her bra to the side. Her breasts were dainty with twin peaks that stood taut. His mouth began to water at the idea of how good it would feel to suck on them.

He wondered if she would enjoy it if he did the same thing to her that she had done to him. The need to know overruled his inexperience. He pressed her backwards, and gently pushed her down onto the bed. His hands slid around her thighs and he spread her legs wide enough for him to slip between them.

Her increased breathing told him that she was not immune to what he was doing. He leaned forward. Her body trembled when she felt the heat of his breath against her sensitive womanhood.

"I've never done this," she admitted, looking up at the ceiling.

"Neither have I. Tell me if it feels as good for you as it did for me," he instructed.

Her response was reduced to breathless cries as he slowly maddened her with the same thoroughness she'd used to torture him. He parted her soft lips to reveal the tiny nub that he had learned about. It was supposed to bring her intense pleasure if he caressed it.

Rolling his tongue over the nub proved that it indeed caused a passionate counter-reaction. Her cries grew louder and her thighs opened wider. Her fervent invitation was clear—feast as much as he wished.

He feasted—and feasted—and feasted until she was thrashing wildly on the bed and begging him to quit at the same time as her heels dug into his shoulders pulling him forward for more. Now was the time to prepare her so their joining would not be painful. He slid his fingers into her moist depths as he sucked and stroked her swollen nub. She was slick with desire and his fingers easily slid deep into her soft channel.

He paused when he felt the barrier that RITA2 had warned him about. Mentally reaching out to Amelia, he connected their thoughts.

Her mind was splintering as her first orgasm built. He sucked hard on her nub until he felt her body stiffen.

Pulling free, he stood up and leaned over her. He gripped his engorged cock and aligned the hard bulbous head with her channel. He pressed forward until he felt the barrier again. He rocked his hips forward, breaking through the thin barrier at the same time as he pulled her against his body and sank his teeth into her neck once again.

This time, the chemical flowed both ways. He could taste the tangy mixture within the coppery taste of her blood. The reaction of his body was instantaneous. A cry tore from his throat when he felt the sudden heady rush.

He reached down and pulled her left leg up so he could drive deeper. She was still locked in the throes of her orgasm, her body shuddering from the intense waves of feelings. Her eyes were closed and she was panting hard.

"You are mine!" he roared, losing himself in the driving rhythm.

The primal connection between them, forced to hibernate for the past two years, woke with a vengeance. Her nails raked across his skin as she tried to pull him even closer. Her mouth moved across his flesh, nipping, biting, and sucking on him as she fought to leave her own lasting mark of their joining. All doubts and insecurities melted as they gave themselves up to the pleasure engulfing them.

He could feel the slide of her hard nipples against his chest, and Amelia's orgasm was fisting his cock with the same force as her hand. The combination proved too intense and he thrust forward, emptying his seed deep inside her. His gasping breaths echoed hers.

"Yes!" he hissed.

His body stiffened as he drained himself into her. His head fell forward and he barely had the strength to hold himself up. He rolled over, keeping their bodies locked together. He didn't know if it was proper for her to be atop him, but at the moment he didn't care. The vidcoms hadn't included such a move, but how did a warrior keep from crushing the diminutive love of his life after such an intense release?

"You think too much. There is nothing wrong with the woman being on top. In fact, I've read it can be even better," she murmured with a sigh.

"Better?" he asked, his cock twitching back to life.

She lifted her head from where she'd rested it against his chest and looked at him with a bemused expression. He hoped that meant she was curious to see if what she had read was true. With the chemical pouring through their bodies, they would be ready again within a few minutes.

"What? Ready for what?" she asked before her eyes widened when he twitched again. "Are you serious?"

He grinned at her. "I'm an alien," he reminded her. "A very sexy alien, if I remember correctly."

She shook her head and lifted a delicate eyebrow, then groaned as his cock became rock hard inside her, its size engorged again. "Well you, my very sexy alien, had better be ready to have your mind blown again in round two," she said, spreading her legs and sitting up with him still inside her.

"I love the sound of that," he murmured.

"What? Having your mind blown a second time?" she asked in a low, sultry voice brought on by emotion.

He shook his head. "No, that I am *your* very sexy alien," he said before his hands cupped her breasts and he leaned forward to capture her swollen nipples.

## CHAPTER TWENTY-FIVE

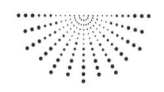

The spaceship's familiar hum surrounded Derik as he walked to the bridge. His body was humming as well. Any fears that he would not be a good lover for his mate had disappeared. He would have to thank RITA2 for her instructional videos. They certainly had come in handy, more than he'd expected—though at the moment he couldn't specifically think of any one lesson.

He wondered if Amelia had received instruction, as well. The different ways she had touched him with her hands and mouth had sent him spiraling out of control. Nothing in the vidcoms had prepared him for the intensity of her touch or his release.

*I'm glad you enjoyed last night so much,* she teased.

A flash of heat coursed through him. *The word 'enjoy' is too tame a word,* he retorted.

"Yeah, well, what can I say? Tame is for wimps," she cheekily replied, coming up behind him.

Derik laughed and wrapped his arms around her. He lifted her up against his body and pressed a lingering kiss to her lips.

"If we weren't almost to Quadrule Five, I would like for you to show me how untamed you can be," he teased, pressing against her.

"Maybe when we get down to the surface," she murmured against his lips.

"On second thought, Quadrule Five can wait," he responded, closing the distance between them.

~

Two hours later, Derik checked their approach to Quadrule Five. The medium-sized, blue-green moon that would be their final destination was simply known as the Moon of Quadrule Five. The small moon stood out against the large, bright orange planet that it orbited. Quadrule Five helped shield its smaller satellite in space from the powerful rays of the double suns.

While the planet never felt the total darkness of night, the small moon did thanks to the shadow of the planet. The moon was covered by water except for a few lush areas above sea level. The largest land area contained a resort for those looking to escape for a while. There was also a chain of islands off the coast for those looking for peace and quiet. His parents owned one of those island retreats.

He looked over his shoulder when he heard the sound of Amelia's footsteps as she approached the bridge. She leaned against the doorframe and smiled at him. He turned in his seat and beckoned her to sit next to him.

"We'll be landing soon," he said.

"Will we take the shuttle like we did between Baade and the Spaceport?" she asked, walking forward and sliding onto the seat next to him.

"Yes. We'll land on the planet, but take the shuttle to the moon. Where we are going, there is not enough space to land a ship of this size," he explained.

She watched as he checked a series of screens. "It still amazes me that you can fly this ship by yourself. Granted, the technology is out of this world and it isn't like there is a lot of traffic to worry about, but still, it's a pretty complex piece of machinery to know how to fix if something goes wrong with it," she reflected.

He shook his head. "Most of the ship's systems have duplicate backups in case of failure. I enjoyed working on ships from an early age. I used to slip out of the palace to go to the space docks. Mother and Father finally gave up trying to keep track of me and gave me a shuttle of my own when I was barely ten cycles old," he explained.

"Sweet! Did you know how to fly it?" she asked.

He laughed. "No. It wouldn't have mattered if I had known anyway. The shuttle was a discarded piece of wreckage. Father insisted that if I wanted to fly, I had to understand how the spacecraft worked. I spent the next two years going to the salvage yards, searching for parts, and rebuilding it. J'kar, Borj, and Mak told me when I finished it, that Mother and Father had done the same with them. I promise not to do that to you," he teased.

She sighed. "I don't even have my driver's license 'cause it never made much sense to get one. I didn't own a car. Even if I did, it wouldn't have mattered anyway. I wouldn't want to drive in Houston or D.C. traffic. There's never any place to park, people drive crazy, and you can usually get to where you want to go faster by walking. Now, if there had been shuttles like you guys have, that would have been different. The scooter was fun to drive." She groaned. "The scooter! Dang it, I forgot all about it. It's still at Dolinski's place," she grumbled with a shake of her head. "I hope Cosmos gets it back. I guess if he doesn't, he can always deduct it from my salary. It's not like I'll be back for my paycheck anytime soon."

"I'm sure Cosmos will understand. RITA would have notified him that you were on Baade. As for flying, I was nervous the first time I flew the shuttle. After all, I was the one who'd rebuilt it," he admitted with a chuckle.

"What was it like?" she asked.

He smiled as he remembered his first flight. He had been surprised when Mak showed up instead of his father. He learned later that J'kar, Borj, and Mak had conspired to keep him from having to go through the same thing they had—side-seat driving.

"My brothers decided that I should be spared the trial by fire. Father is an exceptionally skilled pilot. To the west of the city, there is a region in the desert with a vast maze of deep canyons. It is not unusual for warriors to train there. Mak volunteered to take me. I thought I was smart. I memorized the canyon layout. By the time we arrived, I was confident that I could handle any challenge," he boasted.

She raised an eyebrow and looked at him with a skeptical expression. "And how did that go?" she asked.

He shot her a wry grin. "I crashed on the first turn," he chuckled.

She giggled and shook her head. "At least you made it to the canyon," she said.

"That's what Mak said," Derik replied.

"It must have been a nice way to grow up," she murmured.

"It was," he agreed.

His heart ached for her. He could sense her joy for him; yet, there was a feeling of sadness as well. In his mind, he could see images of her alone, staring at the reflection of herself in the computer screen. A new face blended with hers—the reflection of a tall, lanky man with an expression of avarice on his face.

"He can no longer hurt you, Amelia," he quietly said.

She looked at him with a surprised expression before she shrugged. "I know. How long before we reach the planet?" she asked.

"At least an hour," he replied.

She nodded. "I'm going to get something to drink. Do you want anything?" she asked as she stood up.

"Only you, Amelia," he quipped.

She rolled her eyes. "Like I didn't already know that," she playfully retorted. Bending toward him, she kissed him. "And my name is Runt."

His lips tingled after she pulled away and disappeared through the door. He could feel the flames of desire burning through him. If they weren't so close to their destination, he would have followed her.

"You'll always be Amelia to me," he murmured before he forced himself to focus on piloting the spaceship.

Runt silently berated herself for thinking about the past, and then berated herself for berating herself. How many times did she have to tell herself to just let the memories come? Trying to shut out the memories just didn't work, she knew that. Listening to Derik, she couldn't help but wonder what her life would have been like if her dad had been different.

She shook her head in self-reproach. "You can't change the past. Cosmos hasn't invented a time machine—yet," she ruefully chuckled.

Stepping into the galley, she walked over to the replicator. She started to request a drink when she noticed there was something already inside it. Frowning, she opened the replicator and pulled out the tray of food. It was still warm.

"Weird," she muttered.

She shrugged. Derik must have requested the meal and forgotten about it. She lifted the tray to her nose and sniffed. The food smelled pretty good.

"His loss," she chuckled.

She requested a hot chocolate—with whipped cream. While the replicator hummed, she picked at the food on the tray. After a few bites, she realized that she was famished. Retrieving a utensil, she collected the cup of hot chocolate and picked up the tray of food.

Placing her items on the table, she picked up her spork and began to eat. Her thoughts immediately strayed to the night before. She remembered the feel of his arms around her, his hands gliding over her skin, her lips sliding over his....

*Stop or we will never reach the planet!*

*Don't read my thoughts if you don't like what I'm thinking,* she teasingly retorted.

*Oh, I like them,* he replied.

She grinned when a warm feeling spread through her after he added a few of his memories to hers. Shaking her head, she decided that she better focus on something else; otherwise, he was right, they wouldn't be landing any time soon. Sliding the micro-computer off her wrist, she pressed the top to turn it on.

"Let's see what is going on with RITA2's programming," she murmured.

Humming under her breath, she soon lost herself in RITA2 and DAR's code. Fascinated by what she was seeing, she pushed the rest of her meal to the side, oblivious to everything else. Her eyes widened as she realized what was happening. There was some seriously messed up code going on between them!

"And I thought I had issues!" she muttered.

## CHAPTER TWENTY-SIX

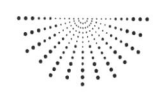

"Amelia, you may want to see this," Derik announced over the intercom system.

She quickly finished pulling on the T-shirt that she had grabbed from her backpack. Old habits were hard to break. Despite everything that had happened, she still wasn't used to putting her clothes in a drawer.

After reviewing the issues RITA2 was having, she had cleaned up her mess in the galley before heading back to their cabin to take a quick shower. Her mind was still racing with what she had discovered about RITA2 and DAR as she hurried back to the bridge nearly an hour later.

Stepping through the doorway, all thoughts of RITA2 vanished as she stared in awe at the huge orange planet. The view through the front glass made her feel like she was in a virtual game. Swirling bands of color, ranging from bright yellow to dark red and all the hues in between, covered the entire planet. She tightened her grip on the edge of the door frame when the ship rocked.

"Is it safe to go down through that?" she asked.

Derik looked over his shoulder. "Yes, but you might want to strap in. It can be bumpy. The planet has a sustainable atmosphere. The cloud covering looks thick, but it isn't. Most of the color is a reflection from the surface. The dark red lines are a vast mountain range that circles most of the planet. The orange is a shallow ocean. The yellow is primarily forests or sand dunes," he explained.

She walked over to the seat next to Derik and sat down. Reaching for the harness, she snapped the buckles into place. A dark, billowing line rising up through the clouds caught her attention.

"What is that?" she asked.

"It looks like smoke," he commented.

"Look to the right. It looked like something just exploded," she said.

"Something is wrong," he muttered.

"What do you think it is?" she asked, watching in morbid fascination as another explosion lit up the swirling clouds.

"I don't know, but we are going to find out," he grimly replied.

She shot him a wary look. "Uh, you know, usually when there are explosions, people tend to go in the opposite direction," she pointed out.

He flashed a grin at her. "Maybe a human does. Prime warriors tend to charge in," he replied.

"We'd call that competing for the Darwin Award," she muttered.

"Awards are good," he responded.

Runt shook her head. "Not this one. You only win it for dying in the most stupid way," she commented.

"I guess that we won't try to compete for this award, then," he decided with a sheepish expression.

She curled her fingers into the arms of the chair when the spaceship tilted and accelerated. She ground her teeth together. Her first thought was that instead of going faster, they should be decelerating as they approached the ground.

A harsh gasp slipped from her lips when she saw a dark shape emerge out of the clouds heading toward them. Derik veered to the left with a low curse. The two ships passed each other with less than twenty feet to spare.

She turned her head with a jerk, trying to get a good look at the smaller spaceship. There were markings on the side that she didn't recognize. She turned to ask Derik if he knew what they meant. The question died on her lips when she saw his expression.

"This is *Prime 521* to Baade Command," he said.

Static greeted them. His lips tightened. Runt gripped the arms again when he suddenly pulled up.

"They must have taken out the communications systems," he said.

"Who?" she asked.

"The Juangans," he replied just as the alarms came on.

"Shields full, defensive measures have been engaged," RITA2 said.

"RITA2?" Runt called out.

"Yes, dear, though I'm afraid I am only a fraction of my full program. Derik, there are ten fighters locking in on your location," RITA2 stated.

"Have you alerted Baade Command?" he demanded.

"The electromagnetic field of the planet is blocking all outgoing communications. Once you break out of the atmosphere, I'll be able to use the ship's internal radars to link up with the nearest relay satellites and send a distress signal," RITA2 answered.

"Um, the Juangans are the species everyone hates 'cause they eat people, right?" Runt demanded.

"Yes, they are a nasty, murderous reptilian species—and they aren't above eating their victims even if it is one of their own. We've been at war with them for centuries," he explained in a tense voice.

"Great! Looks like humans aren't the only bloodsuckers out there —no offense. What are they—Look out! There's another one," she warned.

"I see him," Derik muttered.

Several red energy balls struck the Juangan fighters. Derik's ship soared through the exploding fireball. She winced when she heard debris from the wreckage bounce off the shields as they passed through the fragments. She didn't want to think what else was mixed with the bits of metal that were bouncing around them.

She was thankful for the harness holding her safely to her seat after she was thrown forward when several bursts hit them from behind. Derik turned the ship at a sharp angle and headed for a dark red band. They broke through the clouds. The scream on Runt's lips froze when she saw a cliff in front of them.

"Let's see how good they are," Derik muttered.

Runt sat with her mouth hanging open and her eyes glued to the scene in front of them. Her stomach dropped when the ship suddenly lunged down and twisted to the right. They barely managed to pass through a narrow gap between two canyon walls before straightening out on the other side.

"I've changed my mind. I don't want to learn how to fly. This is worse than driving in rush hour traffic during a major event," she muttered.

"That took care of another two of them, Derik. I have DAR on the weapons system," RITA2 said.

"I'm bringing up the targets on screen now," DAR said.

"Do—do—do—you want me to take over… navigation?" RITA2 asked in a stuttering voice as she began to glitch.

"What's wrong with her?" Derik demanded.

"It looks like her duplication code is speeding up," Runt replied.

"Shut her down," Derik ordered.

Runt nodded. "Sorry, RITA2," she said, pulling up her microcomputer.

She worked as fast as she could. As much as she hated the idea of shutting DAR down as well, he was infected with the same code as RITA2. She initiated the shutdown program that she had used on RITA. Hopefully, the slight modification she'd made to it would be enough to keep RITA2 from stopping her.

"Hold on," Derik growled.

Her stomach rolled when he tilted the ship to the side. She watched as he fired at a rock ledge a short distance ahead of them. They passed under the cliff as the ledge began to collapse. She winced when she heard rocks raining down just behind them, and then heard them hit the Juangan fighters.

She looked at the screen. Three brilliant flashes of light appeared before the shapes of the Juangans' fighters vanished. She wanted to whoop with excitement, but there were still five more fighters.

"Faster—no, slower—no up, I mean down. Oh hell, I'm closing my eyes," she muttered.

She lifted her hands to cover her eyes, but never quite made it. Her heart was in her throat as Derik maneuvered through the narrow canyons, trying to shake the last fighters.

"Weapon systems damaged. Manual override necessary," the ship's computer said.

"What does that mean?" she demanded.

"That means we have no auto weapons. I can't fly the ship and operate the rear cannons," he answered through clenched teeth.

"I can do it. I mean, I can shoot things. I'm a gamer," she said.

Derik shook his head. "It is too dangerous," he tersely replied.

She waved her hand at the front screen. "And this isn't?" she retorted. "Where are the weapons?"

He started to protest when another alarm sounded. "Shields at forty percent," the computer stated.

"There are three. Use the top one. There is a lift up to it in the center of the ship," he said.

"Oh, that's what that thing is," she said.

She fumbled with the release on her harness. As she stood up, she fell against Derik's seat when he had to swerve around a large rock formation. He briefly looked up at her with a troubled expression on his face.

"Be careful," he instructed.

She wiggled her nose at him. "I've got this. You focus on not smashing us into a million pieces," she urged as she pushed off toward the door.

"I've got this," he replied, mimicking her response.

"You better or I'm really going to be pissed. I finally met a guy I like so I'm not about to let some alien lizards screw it up," she retorted as she stomped down the corridor.

Her mutterings turned to curses when she was knocked off balance.

She grabbed the conduit running along the left bulkhead to keep from falling. She looked at the small lift down the corridor. It looked like one of those hand truck carts the delivery guys use. Seeing it from a different perspective, she now recognized how it worked—stand on the flat section, hold onto the hand grips, and the two bars lifted you up to a hatch that, she assumed, opened before you ran into it.

"It better, or I'm going to have one hell of a headache," she muttered.

She took a deep breath and lunged for the vertical bar. Of course, that was when Derik did one of his rolling turns. A cry of alarm slipped from her lips as she felt her body leave the floor. For a brief second, she was weightless before the ship righted itself and gravity made its ugly appearance.

Her body instinctively stiffened in preparation for what was bound to be a bone-jarring impact with the metal floor. Runt released a short, sharp scream when a pair of arms suddenly encircled her waist, catching her in mid-descent. Her arms and legs swung around like a rag doll in a puppy's mouth.

"You shouldn't be moving around without the right equipment," a voice murmured in her ear.

Runt turned her head and looked over her shoulder in disbelief at Afon. The sound of footsteps on metal pulled her attention to Marcelo coming down the corridor. Looking back and forth, she felt her body sag for a moment.

"What in the hell are you guys doing here?" she demanded.

Marcelo grinned at Afon. "I told you that computer thing didn't tell her about us," he said.

"Not now, Marcelo. What the hell is going on?" Afon demanded as the ship tilted again and the lights flickered.

"Some evil lizards are trying to kill us. I have to get to the weapons because the auto-shooter thing died," she said, grasping hold of his arm when the ship rocked back and forth.

"Where is it?" Marcelo grimly asked.

Runt pointed to the lift almost directly across from them. "There are two more at the end of the corridor. I'll take this one if you two can take the others. Do you know how to shoot—of course you two know how to shoot! It has been a crazy day," she groaned.

"We'll find them," Afon said with a nod to Marcelo.

Marcelo nodded in response and retraced his footsteps. Afon carried her over to the lift and placed her feet on the floor. Once she had a good grip on the handles, he released her.

She turned and looked at him. "Don't get killed. I want to know how you two got here," she ordered.

Afon chuckled. "I'm still trying to figure that out myself," he replied before stepping back.

Runt pressed the button on the handgrip and felt the lift glide up. She tilted her head as she neared the ceiling and held her breath. Sure enough, the hatch slid open. She easily passed through the opening. Once the bottom of the lift cleared the hatch, it shut again.

She turned and gripped the arms of a chair that reminded her of a gamer's seat. Sliding into it, she quickly pulled the harness over her shoulders and clicked it into place. Her fingers wrapped around the two toggles on the arm of the chair.

A screen surrounded the chair, and Runt swiveled around, briefly in awe at being able to see 360 degrees around the ship. That wonder quickly changed when she saw one of the alien fighters closing in on them.

Pursing her lips in determination, she aimed, and squeezing the firing control, she released a stream of powerful bursts on his ass. Either the bastard didn't have his shields up or they were no match for the power of a Prime laser cannon. The shots she fired tore through one section of the wing and the fighter spiraled out of control before exploding in a fiery crash.

"Wahoo! Take that, you ugly alien lizard!" She grinned.

She swiveled when she saw additional laser fire. It looked like her uncle and his security man had found the other two weapon areas. Twin explosions proved they also knew what they were doing.

Given what she remembered about how many fighters had been initially following them and how many were now down, she calculated that there should only be a couple of fighters left. She slowly rotated, looking for them. Her eyes scanned the shadows in the rocks even as her mind played out where she would attack if she were on the other side.

"Derik, can you hear me?" she asked.

"Yes, what the hell is going on? There were three coming up behind us and they just disappeared. I saw the one hit from your cannon. How did you get the other two systems online? The auto-weapon controls are still down," he said.

"I'll explain later. There are still two fighters out there," she replied.

"The sensors aren't showing anything," he answered.

"How likely are they to turn and run?" she asked.

"Zero chance," he said.

"That's what I was afraid of," she muttered.

She slowly rotated her seat. She had almost made a full circle when she caught a faint glimmer of light out of the corner of her eye. Turning her chair, she depressed the button on the control and opened fire.

The fighter hiding in a crevice below them angled upward. Runt's stomach twisted when she recognized the pilot's intent. The son-of-a-bitch was pulling a kamikaze. She'd seen it on some of the World War II games she'd played.

"Like hell," she cursed.

Afon and Marcelo must have seen the fighter at the same time as she did. Between the three laser cannons, he didn't stand a chance. It wasn't until the fighter exploded that she realized the guy was a sacrificial decoy.

*Up!* she snapped to Derik.

The ship suddenly climbed at a steep angle. The last fighter was weaving back and forth. This guy was more skilled than the last ones.

The smaller fighter was gaining on their ship. Derik cleared the top of the cliff. For a moment, Runt lost sight of the Juangan following them. It didn't take long to find him again. Her eyes widened in terror when she saw a ball of energy heading straight for her.

She sagged and closed her eyes when it exploded before reaching her. Unfortunately, the explosion was still close enough to cause damage if the smoke suddenly pouring out of one engine was anything to go by.

*Shields are down,* Derik informed her.

*I figured that. This bastard is pissing me off! How bad is the damage?* she asked.

*Bad enough that I need to find a place to land,* he replied.

Runt could feel him pulling away from her. Her finger hovered over the button on her toggle. The crafty bastard behind them was weaving again. He was also staying just low enough that Marcelo and Afon's weapons couldn't get to him.

"One, two, three—side. One, two—side. One, two three—side. You've got a rhythm going there, dude," she murmured, recognizing what the pilot was doing. "You—should—never—mess—with—a—gamer," she slowly stated as she counted out the rhythm until he came back into view.

She depressed the button, sending a stream of laser fire at the spaceship while swiveling in her seat to keep up the heat. The fighter's left wing exploded. The ship spun out of control and hit the top of the plateau, rolling dozens of times before it disappeared in a cloud of dust.

"Yes!" she hissed in triumph.

"Got him!" she crowed into the comlink.

"You are one amazing mate," Derik responded with a chuckle.

"Yeah, and don't you forget it. I am *the* number one shooter on this ship," she bragged.

"I'll second that. Once we land, you'll have to share how you were able to operate all three weapon systems at once. Until then, I'm going to find a place to land in the valley south of the city so I can see how much damage there is. We are going to need to contact Baade Command and let them know what is happening," Derik said.

"I'll stay here in case there are any more," she said.

He was silent for a second before he spoke again. "I'm glad you are safe," he said.

She felt a wave of warmth, and a pleased smile curved her lips. "We make a good team," she teased.

"Yes, we do," he responded, not teasing.

She sat back in her chair. Her gaze moved to the smoke coming from a section on the back of the ship. Behind them, she could see the faint outline of the crashed Juangan fighter.

"Well, I've never been on a vacation before. If this is what they are like, I think it might be safer to just do a staycation on Earth." She paused. "Except I can get shot there, too," she sighed as the ship began to descend once again.

## CHAPTER TWENTY-SEVEN

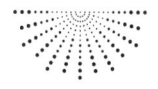

Derik looked up when Amelia came out of the ship. She had a bemused expression on her face. He wondered if she realized just how much of what she felt was reflected in her expressions. She raised an eyebrow at him when she caught him staring at her.

"How is it going?" she asked, walking over and sitting down on one of the cargo bins he had pulled out of the storage bay. She could see he had removed the damaged cover from one of the rear panels of the ship. The inside was a melted mess of wires.

"Good—and not so good. I have a replacement panel and most of the items I need, but," He held up a melted piece of metal. "I need to go into the city tomorrow and see if there is anything left."

"That doesn't look good," she murmured.

"Yes… not good. I need to replace the coupling and don't have the right one," he replied.

She turned to study the sky with a frown. His gaze followed hers. While it wasn't dark, it was definitely not as bright as it had been earlier. Dark clouds swirled above them with increasing speed.

"Is it going to rain?" she asked.

Derik shook his head. "No, it looks like a sandstorm. We should be safe. The cliffs above will shield us from the worst of it," he said.

"I've never been in a sandstorm before," she commented.

"Another first," he teased with a grin.

She snorted. "Not the kind I want to experience. By the way, I think I fixed the issue with RITA2 and DAR. The versions we have onboard are the offline ones downloaded to the ship's computer system. I figured they would be good to experiment with. If the changes I made work, the new code should upload once they reconnect with their primary versions back on Baade. We should know before then if everything is back to normal," she explained.

He frowned. "Did you reboot them?" he asked.

She nodded. "Yeah, I can't exactly test them if they aren't working. I have them helping Afon and Marcelo," she said with a sigh.

"I can't believe DAR helped them get on my ship," he muttered, returning his attention to the compartment he was working on.

She giggled. "It's the reasoning behind it that gets me—'in case you needed some male instruction on how to deal with a human woman'! I think DAR's been spending a little too much time with your brothers. Did Hannah really hit Borj in the head with a frying pan?" she asked.

Derik laughed. "Borj would never admit it. You should have seen what Tink did to J'kar's entire ship! When she was telling us about…," he stopped and flushed.

She leaned back and looked at him with an amused expression. "You mean the scene from When Harry Meets Sally? DAR showed me the video. You guys really needed to get a life. I've seen juicer stuff online," she remarked.

He looked over his shoulder at her. "Is that where you learned the things you did last night?" he inquired with a fiery glint in his eyes.

She lifted her chin. "I learned a lot more than that," she replied in a low suggestive purr.

Derik heard the invitation in her voice, and set down the melted part on a torn piece of metal, threw his gloves on top of it, and closed the distance between them. Her legs parted so he could stand between them. Her arms slid up his arms as he wrapped them around her waist and pulled her close.

Their lips met in a passionate kiss. The intensity was magnified by the danger of the day. Deep down, they both knew that last night could have been their only chance to be together. The light banter between them had been covering their need to reassure each other that they had survived.

"I want you," she frantically mumbled against his lips.

He pressed a series of hard kisses to her lips, then followed the line of her cheek down to her throat. She tilted her head back and to the side to expose the slender column. His teeth lengthened at the invitation. His hand slid down to her ass and he cupped her buttocks.

"Do either of you know where I can find a...," Afon's voice shattered the moment.

Derik's savage snarl drew a giggle from Amelia. Her hands clung to his shoulders as if she was afraid he might rip her uncle's head off his shoulders. The idea was very tempting. He closed his eyes and counted to ten. His body was throbbing with the need that he had been trying to keep under control.

"What... do you need?" he ground out between clenched teeth.

"DAR said a splicer," Afon responded before he looked up at the sky. "It is going to rain?"

"Sandstorm," Runt replied, looking over Derik's shoulder.

Afon's expression turned grim. "Will it cause more damage?" he inquired.

Derik released a loud sigh. "No, but I need to seal the panel before it hits. Sand in the electronics doesn't do well in space," he acknowledged.

Afon returned his gaze to Derik's face with a pointed look. "Then I guess you should quit groping my niece and finish working on it," he suggested.

Derik growled. Afon's eyes narrowed, but he didn't back down. Derik really was tempted to just rip the human's head off. He sighed when he felt Amelia's hands tighten on his arms.

"I'm not going to kill him," he muttered.

She laughed and patted his chest. "I can read your thoughts," she reminded him.

He stepped back when she slid off the bin, and looked over his shoulder again. Afon was watching them with a narrowed-eyed gaze and folded arms across his chest. He sighed and picked up the splicer he been using. He tossed it to Afon. The other man caught it in midair.

"I can't do any more until I get a part. Hopefully, the city wasn't completely destroyed," he said before looking at Amelia. "You better go inside. The storm will be here soon. We all need to be inside the ship when it hits."

She held onto his arm and rose on her toes to brush a kiss across his lips. "I'll check on RITA2 and DAR," she murmured against his lips.

He nodded. His gaze lingered on his mate's back when she turned and walked past Afon. When she disappeared into the ship, he turned his attention to the man still watching him.

"I don't care what RITA2 or DAR said, I know what you are. I don't trust you and if you try to get between me and my mate again, I will kill you and leave your body to rot in the sands," he snarled.

Afon's expression hardened. "I've seen what your kind can do. I won't let you harm the girl," he stated in a cold voice.

Derik's eyes narrowed. "Why do you care? You've never cared before," he demanded.

Afon was quiet for a second before he answered. "I lost the only family I ever had once. I couldn't stop it then, but I can now. I won't let that happen again," he quietly vowed.

"The decision is not yours, it belongs to the Council. You know that I have to take you back," Derik said.

Afon shrugged. "You can try. I prefer to make my own destiny," he countered.

A blast of chilled air swept down from the cliffs. The storm would be upon them soon. Afon must have sensed it as well because he bowed his head and turned. Derik watched him disappear inside the ship.

He shook his head. "I need my head examined," he said under his breath.

He picked up the panel cover and fitted it over the area he had been working on, quickly securing it before he picked up his tools. The winds were picking up, swirling the sands until they delivered a sting when they struck his exposed skin. He retreated up the platform and turned to watch the storm as he pressed the button to close the hatch, though his mind was on Amelia, not on the storm beginning to rage outside. He had brought her to spend some quality time, just the two of them, learning more about each other. Instead, he had placed her in mortal danger. Space was a dangerous place.

"So is Earth," she quietly reminded him.

He turned to see her standing a few feet behind him. Her dark eyes held an emotion that took his breath away. She silently walked toward him before stopping just a few inches away.

"You could have died today," he said.

She shrugged. "I could have died weeks ago in DiMaggio's club. If I had to choose between the two, this was a lot more scenic," she half-heartedly joked before her expression became serious. "We never really know when our time is up, Derik. We can only embrace each day and keep putting one foot in front of the other," She took in a deep breath. "When I thought my mom...," her voice choked up and she bowed her head, taking a deep breath before she looked at him again.

"How did you get to be so smart at such a young age?" he tenderly asked.

She touched his chin, her gaze focused on the motion, but he could tell her mind was far away. He saw flashes of memory—her father, her mother, the other homeless people—Bert.... They had all played a role in shaping who she was and who she would become.

"I don't ever remember being young—until last night. Last night I forgot about everything but you," she whispered.

He reached over and placed his bag of tools on the control box for the door, then his arms swept around her and he tenderly pulled her close. Her arms wound around his waist. They embraced each other for several minutes.

"I want to give you more of those nights," he said.

"I know."

Her quiet response shook him. She believed in him. He pressed a kiss to the top of her head. She tilted her head back and slipped her hand between them to the opening in his shirt. It took a moment for him to realize that she was touching the locket that he still wore.

"I keep forgetting to give this back to you," he said.

She shook her head. "I want you to keep it. I like being near your heart," she confessed.

"You are always near it, Amelia," he said.

"You have grease on your chin. I think you need a shower, and I know the perfect person to help you take one," she suggested, pushing his hair back from his temple.

He released a low hiss of pleasure. "So help me, if Dolinski tries to interrupt us, I'll throw his ass out into the storm," he vowed.

She giggled. "I'll open the door for you," she teased.

He grinned and swept her up into his arms. Striding across the bay, he climbed the short set of steps and passed through the opening to the main corridor. He could hear Afon and Marcelo quietly talking. They were in the galley.

"Shush!" she whispered near his ear.

He grinned and nodded. They both fought to keep from laughing as he carried her past the galley door. Once they were past it, he sped up as Amelia buried her face against his neck and giggled.

He turned into their cabin and gently placed her feet on the ground. Waving his hand over the door panel, he closed the door. His gaze locked on her shimmering eyes.

"I love you, Amelia," he murmured.

She touched his cheek. Her lips parted, but no sound emerged. He pulled her into his arms and kissed her with all the pent-up emotions raging inside him.

Her fingers fumbled with the fastenings of his shirt. Their heavy breathing filled the room. His hands moved to the hem of her shirt and he broke their kiss long enough to pull it over her head.

"Thank you," she said in a breathless voice.

"For what?" he asked in a rough tone.

"Thank you for not ripping my shirt. It's one of my three favorites," she said as she pushed his shirt off his broad shoulders.

"How many shirts do you have?" he curiously asked.

"Three," she replied with a grin.

"I'll have to find you more," he chuckled.

"Last one in the shower gets to be washed first," she laughed, twisting away from his hands.

He turned, watching her as she kicked off her shoes and began to wiggle out of her jeans. A low growl of approval slipped from him when she kicked them aside and bent to pull off her socks. Seeing her clad only in her lacy silk panties and bra, his body filled with need. He imagined standing behind her, taking her from behind while his hands were filled with her firm breasts, squeezing her hard nipples between his fingers….

"Hey, are you coming?" she called from the bathroom.

He blinked and shook his head. "I will in a minute, and so will you—multiple times," he chuckled.

He quickly stripped out of his clothing, his body throbbing with need, then he paused and looked at the hidden compartment near the head of the bed. His gaze moved to the bathroom, and he wondered….

A moment later, he stepped into the bathroom and stood by the door. Amelia was standing in the shower. A heavy mist surrounded her. Her head was tilted back and her eyes were closed. Water trailed down her shoulders and a single droplet clung to one taut nipple.

He'd never seen anything more beautiful in his life. Drawn to her like a moth to flame, he opened the door and stepped inside the shower cubicle.

"What were you doing? Daydreaming," she answered herself without opening her eyes.

"You were made for loving, Amelia," he murmured.

"Does this mean I get to be washed first instead?" she requested with a hopeful look.

"Place your hands on the wall," he instructed.

Her eyes widened at his rough tone and sudden demand. She turned toward the wall. He could sense her growing excitement. She liked it when he was a little 'bossy' with her, as she would say.

"Have you been watching bad-boy vidcoms or what?" she inquired.

"If you mean what I think you mean, yes, those particular instructional vidcoms were quite exciting," he said.

She snorted. "I've heard them called a lot of things, but instructional videos were not one of them," she chuckled before she released a startled yelp when he suddenly pinched one of her hard nipples.

"Hey," she hissed in surprise, looking down when the pressure didn't stop after he removed his hand.

He moved behind her and held one hand under her jaw while his other hand moved to her right breast. She squeaked again when he pinched it.

Derik slowly slid his right hand down over her wet skin while he kept his left hand under her chin. He caressed her right buttock.

"How much do you trust me, Amelia?" he murmured in her ear.

"How—How much should I trust you?" she asked in a voice that wavered.

"Completely," he said.

He pressed a kiss to her neck as he continued to caress her ass. His hand slid across to trace the delicate line separating her right cheek from her left. Tonight was about savoring each other. They had come together in passion. Now he wanted them to come together in love.

"That's a lot to ask," she weakly protested.

He turned her toward him. "Is it?" he quietly probed.

She stared up at him, her eyes conveying how conflicted she was. Disappointment filled him when she didn't immediately respond.

He raised his hand to remove the nipple charms he had placed on her. Her hands covered his—stopping him, her hesitancy replaced by a tender expression.

"I trust you—completely," she whispered.

She held his gaze, never wavering. He took in a deep breath. For a moment, they were not in the shower on his ship, but the only two people in the universe. He could see the threads of their bond glow with a luster that only their true feelings could power.

"I want to explore you," he warned.

"As long as you agree that it's an equal opportunity exploration," she cheekily retorted.

He looked down at the nipple charms and grimaced. "Maybe not completely equal," he muttered.

She laughed softly and he captured the sound with his lips. His hands slid over her body, cupping her breasts, and tracing a path down her stomach to the soft curls glistening with water from the shower. She lifted her arms above her head and opened to his touch.

She never flinched as he learned every inch of her body. He washed her hair, traced the path of her ears, and marveled at her tiny toes. He learned that she was very ticklish on the bottoms of her feet and had a small birthmark on her left hip in the shape of a crescent moon.

"My mom said I was sent to her from the stars," she whispered when he traced it.

"You were destined for the stars," he murmured.

When it was her turn to explore him, he remained still. He absorbed the feel of her hands on his body. When his passion threatened to overwhelm him, he focused on the droplets coursing down her body.

"Where did you get this scar?" she asked, stroking the long line on his left thigh.

"Juangans attacked my brother's ship when I was seventeen. That is when Tink, J'kar's mate, suddenly appeared through the Gateway. I thought she was the Goddess come to save me," he confessed.

"And the one on your arm?" she murmured, standing so she could trace it as well.

"The same attack. I would have died that day if not for Tink and her hammer," he explained, sharing the memory with her.

Her eyes darkened. "I would never have met you," she reflected.

"Nor I you. I thought I would never have a chance to find my bond mate. I am glad I was wrong," he admitted.

She lifted her hand and touched his cheek. "Make love to me, Derik," she whispered.

He reached over and turned off the mist. Warm air surrounded them, drying the water from their bodies. Once the dryer turned off, he opened the door to the cubicle and stepped out. He reached out a hand to help her.

They silently walked to the bedroom. The restraints he had laid out before stepping into the bathroom hung from the corners of their bed. He had thought to have some fun, but now he wanted to hold her —and have her hold him.

"The fun will come later. For now...," she said.

He bent and picked her up. Stepping close to the bed, he gently lowered her to the mattress, and followed her down. They clung to each other, kissing, and touching until she pushed him onto his back.

Climbing on top of him, she straddled his waist. His cock throbbed between them. She reached down and pulled his hands to her breasts. Her gaze never left his when she rose far enough to align his cock and slowly impaled herself on his thick shaft.

"I love you, Amelia," he declared.

"I know," she said.

He pulled her down until their lips connected. He could feel her love for him. She wasn't ready to say it and that was alright. She didn't have to say it out loud. When the time was right, she would—and he vowed that he would be there when she ready.

## CHAPTER TWENTY-EIGHT

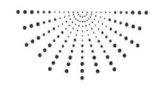

They had left an hour ago to travel to the city, and by now, Derik could see the smoldering outline of the city. He scanned the horizon for threats, pointedly ignoring the most recent of Afon's disapproving glares. Neither he nor Amelia needed to answer to the man. It wasn't like Dolinski didn't 'have a few skeletons, literally, in his closet' as Amelia liked to say. The irony of Afon's displeasure made him smile.

"What's so amusing?" Amelia asked him.

She must have felt his silent chuckle. Her arms were wrapped around his waist and she was resting her chin on his shoulder. He placed a hand over hers and squeezed it before refocusing on navigating the skimmer.

"I was just thinking of the phrase you mentioned last night—about skeletons and closets. Your uncle is not pleased that I have claimed you," he blithely reflected.

She looked over her shoulder to check on Afon and Marcelo. They were riding on the trailer that Derik had attached to the skimmer, each holding a laser rifle at the ready. So far, no one had seen any evidence of other Juangans.

Turning back to him, she rested her chin back on his shoulder. "Sounds like a personal problem to me," she quipped with a shrug.

He laughed. "I love your human phrases," he replied.

She pressed a kiss behind his ear. "I've got loads to share," she teased before releasing a sigh. "Do you think the Juangans are still here?"

"Yes," he replied.

"What are we going to do if we run into them?" she asked.

"Kill them. If they are in the city, they will show no mercy for any of the residents—young, old, male, or female. As a Prime warrior, it is my duty to protect those who cannot protect themselves," he explained.

"Uh, you do realize there are only four of us, right?" she pointed out.

"Three—I don't want you in harm's way," he said.

She snorted. "Is that why you insisted I come with you?" she retorted.

"I didn't want you there alone and I may need your uncle and Marcelo," he admitted.

"Yeah, well, remember who the best shooter on the ship is. I totally blasted the lizards out of the sky," she reminded him.

"You may have to remind me a few more times," he joked.

A rumbling laugh slipped from him when she playfully pinched his arm. They fell silent as he slowed the skimmer near a rock outcropping, and stopped, powering it down.

Her arms loosened from around his waist. He stepped off the skimmer and turned to help her down. Afon and Marcelo slid off the back and walked over to them.

"What now?" Afon asked.

"Now, we go on foot," he said.

"Wish this damn planet had night," Marcelo cursed under his breath.

"Keep your coverings on. They will conceal you and protect you from the suns and sand," Derik cautioned.

He adjusted his own sand-colored coverings before he reached out and tucked a strand of Amelia's dark hair under her protective headgear. Then he reached for the laser pistol stored inside a compartment of the skimmer. He checked the charge on the pistol before he handed it to Amelia.

"Don't think twice if you see a Juangan. Shoot and run. Headshots only," he instructed.

She gave him a weak smile. "I've got this," she said with more confidence than she was feeling.

"I know you do," he murmured.

He leaned forward and pressed a hard kiss to her lips before he straightened and looked at the other two men. They returned his gaze with piercing determination. These were men accustomed to fighting —and not afraid to kill if necessary.

"Protect Amelia at all cost," he ordered.

They nodded. Without another word, he picked up the laser rifle attached to the side of the skimmer and turned. He scanned the area before motioning for the others to follow him.

∼

Amelia could see the heavy devastation to the city as they entered it. She followed Derik while Afon and Marcelo took up the rear. Debris from buildings that had been blown up littered the road, making it difficult to traverse. The ruins reminded her of the pictures of war zones that she had seen on the television.

Afon steadied her when she stumbled over some loose rock where a hole had been blown in the road. She bowed her head in thanks even as her gaze moved back to the buildings. All around them, there was nothing but destruction and wreckage.

Afon and Marcelo checked several buildings that were still standing. They both emerged and grimly shook their heads—they'd found no survivors. Runt had witnessed a lot of misery in her life, but she had never seen anything like this. It was as if the Juangans had purposely targeted each and every building.

The buildings and the residents inside hadn't stood a chance against the Juangan's deadly laser cannons. Her hand slid across the rough exterior of a wall. The coarse sands had been mixed with water and combined with thick, bright red reeds to form bricks for building. Each building was connected to the next. Now, gaping holes in the structures revealed the colorful debris of the residents' lives. The contrast was heartbreaking.

Her stomach roiled when she saw the arm of an alien sticking out from under a pile of crumbled stone and the stain of green blood. She averted her eyes when she saw a small toy covered in dust lying in the road. Amelia waited in the shadows of a crumbling stone wall while Derik moved across the narrow road to another burnt shell of a building. He scanned the area before waving for them to move out. She darted across the open space and turned until she was next to him. They were slowly working their way deeper into the city. The farther they went, the more extensive the damage.

Sporadic fires burned—fueled by the reeds, the materials inside the structures, or something worse—the remains of those who couldn't escape. She didn't want to know. She covered her nose with her head covering to keep from gagging as the acrid stench of smoke burned her throat and made her eyes water. She saw the look of concern on Marcelo's face when he fell in beside her.

"Where is everyone?" Marcelo hissed under his breath.

They all turned as a ship flew low over the smoking remains. It rotated a hundred yards from them and landed. She shivered as an ominous feeling swept through her.

*This must be what it means when they say someone is walking over my grave,* she thought.

*I don't like that saying,* Derik absently commented.

*Me either,* she decided.

She hadn't meant to broadcast that thought to him. Afraid she might distract him, she pulled the wall up around her thoughts. She knew from experience that a single unintentional distraction could be the difference between life and death.

"That is a transport ship. They must have rounded up the

remaining residents and are planning to transport them off world," he quietly explained.

"What will they do with them?" Afon asked.

Derik turned and looked at her uncle. The expression on his face sent another shiver through her. He glanced at her before turning his attention back to the transport that was landing.

"They will use them as food," he said in a dispassionate voice.

"Food?!" she hissed with horror.

Her stomach knotted at the idea of the residents' horrible fate. She bit her lip to keep from crying. Bowing her head, she realized that no matter where you went in the universe, there would always be those that preyed on the weaker. She looked up when she felt Derik's tender touch.

"Are you going to be alright?" he asked.

She nodded. "Yeah, I'm good," she murmured.

He motioned for them to continue moving through the debris. Ten minutes later, they were peering through a narrow slit in a wall at the center of the town. On the north side, a large enclosure had been erected. Inside, terrified residents pressed to the back as far away from the opening as possible.

Her heart broke when she saw mothers and fathers holding their weeping children to them. Older residents had taken a fruitless protective stand in the front of the younger residents. Two guards paced in front of the entrance. A single heavy bar held the gates shut. There was no need for a lock when you were that big, ugly, and had a reputation for eating your prisoners.

This was her first up close look at the creatures. Her stomach turned. They were over eight feet tall and thickly built. Their skin was dark green with tan, black, and light green blotches that made them look like they had been splattered with camouflage paint. They had long tails, long legs, and short, stubby arms. They wore armor made of leather and metal, and they each held a glowing sword that had to be four or five feet long!

She silently counted as a dozen more of the creatures jumped out of the transport and spread out to stand guard at different points around the town center. It was obvious that something else was going on. There was a distinct tension in the air as the Juangans gazed warily up at the sky, focusing on another shuttle that was landing. With so many Juangan soldiers, she didn't know how they were going to free all the prisoners without anybody getting hurt—or worse, them getting killed.

"What is the plan?" Afon asked.

She swallowed and looked at Derik. "We are going to free the prisoners, aren't we?" she asked in a voice that wasn't quite steady.

His lips curved upward and he nodded. "We're going to free the prisoners," he repeated.

She heard Marcelo release a long breath. "I knew I should have taken the security job at the mall," he muttered with a rueful expression.

His response made her smile. "Naw, teenagers are a thousand times worse," she joked.

"You're probably right. I wouldn't have been allowed to kill them," Marcelo retorted with a wink.

"It would be best if we split up. I'll move out to the right and around to the back side," Afon said.

"I'll take the left," Marcelo added.

"Amelia and I will cover this side. The communicators are on a secure frequency. Stay in touch," Derik agreed.

"I should take a side. The more firepower, the more confusion," she said with a shake of her head.

Derik's lips parted in protest. She touched his lips with her fingers, and shook her head again.

"I'm fast and I can hide if things go crazy. I've got this. It isn't my first rodeo with bad guys. Besides, if you guys can create a distraction, I might be able to free the prisoners," she reasoned.

"She's right. If we can get them to focus on us, Runt might be able to slip in and open the gate," Marcelo agreed.

She winced when both Derik and Afon turned to the other man with an outraged glare. She touched Derik's arm. He reluctantly turned to her.

"We have a unique ability to communicate with each other. I won't go until you tell me it is clear," she murmured.

"If things get out of control, I want you to head back to the skimmer and the ship. RITA2 and DAR can operate it. It is hidden and you should be safe. If we don't check in within a few days, a recon ship will be sent," he ordered.

"Deal," she agreed.

She could tell he wasn't happy, but they didn't have a lot of choices considering there were only the four of them. It didn't make sense for her to be Derik's shadow when she could help. Her fingers tightened on the grip of her pistol.

"Move out," Derik reluctantly said.

She took a deep breath and followed Afon. They wove their way through the damaged remains of the buildings until they were behind a pile of debris next to the fenced compound. Peering over the wall, her eyes widened when she saw a formidable creature standing across from where they were hiding. He must have been on the last shuttle that landed since they had not seen him during their first sweep of the area. Given the expressions on the guards' faces, they were very leery of the newcomer.

The Juangan's authoritative manner had the other soldiers standing at wary attention. This new Juangan wore a uniform of gold-plated armor and was shouting orders in a language she didn't understand, but in a tone that left no doubt that he was furious.

"That has to be the man in charge," Afon murmured.

She nodded. "He doesn't look pleased," she observed.

"He's about to get even more upset. Wait for Derik to signal you. We'll take out the guards and draw attention away from you. Stay close to the cage and come up the right side. There aren't any lizards on that side and there is enough debris you can use as cover if you need it. Once you get the signal, open the gate and get the hell out of there. We'll provide as much cover fire as we can for everyone else," he said.

She looked back at him with a worried expression. "But… there are bound to be casualties that way! The women with kids…. There is no way they will be able to run fast enough, especially if either one of those transports lift off," she hissed.

He reached out and gripped her hand. She blinked back the sting of tears when she saw the look of resignation in his eyes. He'd already come to the same conclusion as she had—there would be collateral damage.

She turned back and looked at the frightened faces. Bowing her head, she forced herself to think. There had to be a way to stop the Juangans. Even if they escaped, the aliens would hunt them down. If there was a way to stop them—all of them, then that wouldn't be an issue.

"Runt, if you don't think you can do this, tell me now. It is better to retreat than to freeze. That will only get you—and the rest of us—killed," he said.

She looked at him with a stony expression. "I won't run and I won't freeze. You get to the other side and don't miss," she said in a tight voice.

Afon studied her face before he gripped his weapons tighter and disappeared into the shadows. She turned her gaze back to the prisoners, then the transports. She might not be as good as they were in a physical fight, but she was damn good at fighting with her brain. Slipping behind a pile of debris that gave her cover yet still allowed her to see what was going on, she touched the micro-computer on her wrist.

"RITA2, I need your help. DAR's too," she whispered.

## CHAPTER TWENTY-NINE

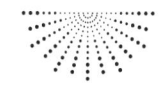

"I'm in position," Afon stated.

"I'm in position as well," Marcelo said.

Derik's gut tightened. "Amelia, are you ready?" he quietly asked.

"Yes."

Her immediate response sent a shot of adrenaline through him. He rolled his shoulders and then lifted his laser rifle to a firing position. He flicked the switch to silent mode.

"I'll take out the first guard when he turns the corner. Marcelo, if you have a clear shot, you take out the second guard. Afon, get ready," he ordered.

"I'm aiming for the guy in gold. Something tells me he is the leader," Afon wryly responded in his ear.

"Affirmative," Derik responded.

He waited until the guard on the right side of the enclosure turned and walked back to the corner. He fired as the warrior rounded the corner and was briefly obscured from the other soldiers.

His blast struck the back of the Juangan's head and the force of the impact propelled the creature forward. He collapsed next to the cage. Several old men inside the enclosure looked at the Juangan in surprise before they looked around the area. Three of them quickly concealed the dead soldier by standing along the fence in front of where he was lying. From his position, Derik could see one of the men reach through the bars and pull the soldier's weapon from his limp fingers.

Marcelo fired the second shot almost at the same time. He had waited until the Juangan on the left began to turn and retrace his steps. A young man inside the enclosure jumped to his feet and grabbed the soldier's clothing before the Juangan could collapse to the ground. He held the creature upright, using the dead Juangan's body to conceal himself.

Turning his attention back to the main area, Derik could see the man that Afon had identified yelling orders. He recognized the uniform and armor the Juangan was wearing. He was the Starship Commander. It was unusual for the Commander to leave the ship. There was always the chance of a mutiny, and he could return to find himself the new item on the menu.

"Where are the fighters that were deployed?" the General demanded.

"They intercepted a Prime spaceship that entered the atmosphere, General Tusk," a soldier replied.

General Tusk turned on the Juangan who had answered him. He sneered. Derik could see the Juangan's sharp, yellow teeth glisten against his dark blue gums.

"What happened? Where is the Prime's ship?" General Tusk snapped.

The Juangan warily watched the General as he stepped closer. "Five fighters moved to intercept. Colonel Tusk reported that it was a transport and not a warship before we lost contact. With the planet's communication system destroyed, there is no way the Prime ship could have sent out a distress signal. The last signal we received from Colonel Tusk came from the Red Canyons. A sandstorm developed shortly after and we've received no communications since, General Tusk. We only have three transports and a single fighter remaining on the planet, sir. We did not want to conduct a search without proper equipment in case the Prime ship survived. We were waiting for additional forces to arrive," the soldier reported.

General Tusk scanned the area. He roared in anger and extended his sword arm, separating the soldier's head from his shoulders in one fluid movement. He kept his arm up in the air as he looked at the prisoners.

"That is for waiting. Load the prisoners in the transports and prepare the fighter," the General ordered.

It took Derik a moment to register the connection between the General's name and the Colonel's. He had never expected any Juangans to give a damn about their heirs, but it was obvious that this one did. He vaguely wondered which one of the pilots they had killed yesterday was related to the General. It didn't really matter. The General was about to join his relative.

"Amelia, get ready. Afon, if you have a shot, kill the bastard," Derik said.

Derik saw the flash from Afon's weapon. The General's head jerked in Afon's direction at the same time. The shot cut a deep slice through the scaly skin near the General's neck instead of striking him through the temple.

General Tusk's loud roar of rage filled the air. Derik took that as a signal to begin firing. Marcelo and Afon did the same. He moved along the wall that he was using for cover, picking off the Juangan soldiers.

"Make sure you aim for their heads. Their skin is too thick and it will only slow them down!" he snapped into the comlink.

"I only shoot to kill," Afon growled back.

Three of the Juangans' heads snapped back as Afon, Marcelo, and Derik simultaneously fired. Out of the corner of his eye, Derik saw Amelia come around the corner of the enclosure, grab the bar across the front gates, and pull it free. The men in the front rushed to push open the doors.

Derik fired on a Juangan who had noticed what was happening at the gates. Pieces of rock flew up as a barrage of laser fire riddled the wall he was standing behind. He ducked and sprinted for a hollowed-out building, only to be thrown back when it suddenly exploded.

He rolled and shook it off. Pushing up from the ground, he stayed low as he darted for another building. He had barely cleared the area when the wall behind him exploded as well. Twisting around to an opening in the mortar, he aimed the rifle and fired.

The Juangan's head snapped back, and he fell backwards. The laser cannon in his hands fired as his fingers tightened in death. One of the fireballs streaked through the open door of one of the transports.

Terrified screams combined with the deafening sounds of the spacecraft exploding into a fiery ball. Derik darted to another section to see if he could locate Amelia. He frantically glanced around, trying to find her slender form among the chaotic mass of bodies fleeing into the ruins of the city.

"Shit! I'm hit," Marcelo's pain-filled curse sounded in his ear.

"How bad?" Derik demanded.

Marcelo huffed out a harsh laugh. "I won't be running any marathons for a while," he grunted.

"Afon, do you see Amelia?" he asked.

"Negative. I'm taking heavy fire. This piece-of-shit hole I'm hiding in is about to collapse," he tersely replied.

"The Juangans caught about a dozen women and children. They're herding them onto the transport that is powering up. I was trying to stop them," Marcelo said.

"Keep firing," Derik ordered.

"I'm out," Afon said.

Derik heard a spate of shots. "I'm on empty as well," Marcelo groaned.

Derik looked down at his weapon. The charge was low. He had one more power pack. He peered through the smoke. Without reinforcements, it wouldn't take long before the transport was able to notify the Command ship in orbit to send more fighters. They would hunt them down and round up the residents again.

"Did someone call for reinforcements?" Amelia asked.

"What the hell…?" Afon's stunned voice hissed in his ear.

Derik watched in wonder as hundreds of small attack bots flew over the ruins like a swarm of angry wasps and began firing, limiting its targets to the remaining Juangans. He chuckled. Lifting his rifle, he aimed at the Juangan General's head. He slowly squeezed the trigger.

The General turned in his direction just as he fired. A dark hole appeared in the center of the creature's forehead. The glowing sword in his hand slowly lowered before he fell forward—dead.

Brock's attack bots quickly eliminated the rest of the Juangans in the center of town. The only ones that remained were the Juangans on the transport that was now soaring over the town. Derik turned his rifle to fire at the engine but slowly lowered it when he realized that if the transport crashed, no one would survive. That brief hesitation cost him the only chance he had of stopping the vessel.

"Check in," he ordered.

He released the spent power pack and replaced it with the last one he had. He held the rifle to his shoulder as he stepped out from behind the wall. Out of the ruins, he saw small clusters of residents emerging. Among one group, he saw Afon helping a bloody Marcelo.

He lowered his rifle and walked over to them. "Where's Amelia?" he asked.

Afon frowned and looked around. "I haven't seen her," he said as he helped Marcelo lie down on a section of rock.

"Who sent the swarm of attack bots?" Marcelo asked before he groaned when he straightened his leg.

RITA2 suddenly appeared next to him on the rock. She was dressed in a flowing white dress with a large white floppy hat. Dark sunglasses shielded her eyes.

"I did, of course. Amelia asked me if we had anything on the ship that could help, and I remembered the boxes of training bots. It wasn't hard to reprogram them as deadly attack bots. Brock sent a new, improved batch in case Derik struck out with Amelia, and needed to work off some frustration. It really is amazing how much better I function when I'm not suffering from glitches!" RITA2 said.

"RITA2, where is Amelia?" Derik demanded with growing alarm when he couldn't find her.

"Oh, she and DAR are on the transport with the women and children," RITA2 said with a grin.

"She's on the….," Derik let loose a heated string of curses.

He turned and looked in the direction he'd last seen the transport. His heart was in his throat as he thought of Amelia in the hands of the Juangans. If he had fired the shot….

*I'm fine. DAR is showing me how to fly. We dropped the women and children off in a small camp that DAR discovered. Looks like the beginning of a rebel camp. We are heading to your ship with the part you needed,* she cheerfully reassured him.

Derik swayed with relief. He glanced from the transport to the fighter. He looked at RITA2, then turned to Afon.

"Here," he said, slapping an injector into Afon's hand. "Give Marcelo this. He'll be healed in a few hours. Once he can travel, get to the skimmer and head back to the ship," he ordered, turning away.

"Where are you going?" Afon called out behind him.

"To have a private conversation with my bond mate," Derik yelled back.

"Oh, dear," RITA2 murmured with a delicate laugh.

∼

Afon watched with a frown as Derik jogged over to the Juangan fighter, shaking his head in disbelief when Derik lifted off, leaving him with RITA2 and an injured Marcelo. He turned his attention back to Marcelo when the other man softly moaned.

"How the hell are we supposed to find our way back to the spaceship?" Marcelo groaned.

RITA2 waved her hand. "Oh, no worries, I'll guide you. Afon, love, be a dear and give your friend the injection. The nanobots will heal him in no time, just like Derik said," she instructed in a distracted voice.

He pulled the injector out of the pouch and studied it for a second before he pressed the tip of the injector against Marcelo's leg through the torn section of his trousers. He pressed the button.

Marcelo hoarsely uttered a string of curses before his eyes rolled back in his head, and he started to fall to the ground face first. Afon reached out and grabbed Marcelo. With the help of a couple of men who had hurried over carrying a modified stretcher, they lowered his friend to the ground.

He looked up to ask RITA2 if that was normal, but stopped when he saw her eyes glowing red. She had removed her sunglasses and was staring intently at the Juangans' transport. A shiver ran through him when he saw the satisfied smirk on her red lips.

"What are you doing?" he quietly inquired.

She looked at him. It took a few seconds before the red glow disappeared and was replaced with vivid green eyes, but once her irises were a more normal color, it was hard to tell that this was not a real woman.

"I'm sending the Juangan Command ship a present," she cheekily replied.

Afon looked over his shoulder as the transport slowly lifted off the ground and turned. In seconds, it was heading out of the atmosphere. He looked back at her.

"What did you do?" he pressed.

She snapped her sunglasses open and placed them on her pert nose. He gritted his teeth when she patted her hair and adjusted her hat. Only after she had checked her lipstick in a mirror, which had magically appeared in her hand, did she look at him with amusement.

"I sent a message to Baade Command. Then I instructed the transport to dock with the Juangan Command ship—where an unfortunate programming issue will cause the engines to overheat, which will cause a spectacular explosion," she calmly informed him.

Afon looked up when he heard several gasps from the residents. Above them, the exploding ship looked like a brilliant display of fireworks. The debris changed colors as it entered the planet's atmosphere, then disintegrated.

For the first time since his capture, Afon felt the enormity of his situation. This wasn't Earth. This wasn't human technology. He gazed at the growing crowd around him. Without the protective covers over their faces, he could see that there were people of all different shapes, sizes, and species. None looked remotely human—except for RITA2.

He looked down at Marcelo. The man he had hired as his Chief of Security had become so much more over the last few weeks. He considered the man a friend. Something he'd never had before.

"You can have a life here, Afon. You wanted a fresh start. Why not give our world a chance?" RITA2 gently suggested.

He scowled when his thoughts were so easily discerned, even by a super computer. "I have nothing here," he said.

RITA2 gave him a tender smile. "On the contrary, I think you have everything that is worth having," she countered.

He looked down when Marcelo moved, and placed his hand on his friend's shoulder to keep him from trying to sit up. Marcelo opened his eyes, blinked, and gave him a half-drunken smile.

"Are's… we going… home? To the ship?" Marcelo slurred.

Afon squeezed Marcelo's shoulder. "Yes, my friend. We're going back," he quietly promised.

∽

Derik landed the Juangan fighter nearly a mile from where his ship was hidden. He felt it would be safer to walk the rest of the way and give himself time to cool down. Imagining the Juangans torturing her had driven him close to the breaking point. When he realized how close he had come to killing her himself, he felt physically ill.

He jogged most of the way, slowing only when he reached the upper level of the canyon and needed to make his way down. By the time he reached the bottom, he was calm again. It was amazing what a little time—carefully trying not to kill yourself—could do to help put things into perspective.

*I'm glad you are feeling better,* she observed with dry humor.

*How much of my thoughts did you listen to?* he asked with a wince.

*Mm, pretty much all of them. I thought your plans to tie me up were particularly interesting. I have to warn you that there were a few who tried that in the past and it never worked out well for them,* she teased.

*Yes, but did they bind you with love?* he quipped in return.

*No, and that is why you are the most creative of them all,* she laughed.

Derik could see the ship under the overhang. The smile on his face grew when he saw Amelia sitting on a rock with her knees drawn up and her chin resting on her arms. She slowly stood up when she saw him.

He opened his arms to her when he was ten feet away. She walked forward, speeding up when she was a couple feet from him. He caught her as she jumped, sliding one arm around her back while cupping her buttocks with the other. She wrapped her legs around his waist and hugged him, burying her face against his neck with a muffled sniff.

They didn't speak. After several minutes, he gently lowered her feet to the ground. He tenderly tucked a strand of her hair behind her ear.

"How is Marcelo?" she asked, lifting her hand to touch his when he cupped her cheek.

"He'll be fine. I gave Afon a healing injector. Using the training bots was a smart idea," he commented.

She huffed out a short laugh. "It was RITA2's idea to use the bots, but you know I'm a whiz at cyberwar. We did it together. I asked RITA2 to program the bots to attack only the Juangans. Then I saw a couple of the lizards loading some women and children into the transport, so I slipped into their midst and joined them. I couldn't let those monsters take them, Derik, not after you told me what would happen to them." She swallowed. "I shot the lizards," she quietly said.

She stared at his chest as she said the last words. He trailed his fingers down her cheek to her chin, and she looked up at him, her eyes glistening with tears.

"The Juangans do not deserve your tears, Amelia. They would have slaughtered the women and children without a second thought," he comforted.

She sniffed and nodded. "I know. DAR said the same thing. He helped me fly the transport. It wasn't as difficult as I thought it would be," she said.

He laughed when her eyes brightened in wonder. "I still plan on teaching you how to fly a shuttle. My idea of taking you away for a few days did not work out very well. We will need to return to Baade so that I can make proper repairs to our ship and brief the Council on what has happened here," he said with a deep sigh.

"The journey here was fun, and last night was pretty exciting," she reminded him.

He reached down and clasped her fingers where she was caressing his skin through the gap in his shirt. Lifting them to his lips, he pressed a kissed to the tips. He raised an eyebrow and gave her an inviting look.

"We could still make it exciting," he suggested.

"Now you're talking," she breathed.

She gave him a tender kiss. He closed his eyes, embracing the tidal wave of sensations that washed through him. He could see the shimmering delicate silver threads that tied them together, wrapping the two of them in their beauty.

Fragmented memories swept through his mind. He wasn't sure if they were his memories or hers. In the end, it didn't matter. He remembered her beautiful, defiant eyes gazing back at him through the narrow opening through the wall the night they met, her quirky smile when she looked at him, her tender touch when he had been wounded, and her wonder when he had taken her the first time. These wonderful memories filled him with a sense of peace.

He opened his eyes when she ended the kiss and touched his cheek. He could see the silver threads in her eyes and knew that she was remembering the same moments. She was defiant in the face of danger, and she was stubborn, strong, smart, and beautiful. He wouldn't have her any other way.

"I love you, Amelia," he murmured, his voice raw with emotion.

She gave him a watery smile and tilted her head. "I know," she softly replied.

"Today—I've almost lost you so many times. My heart hurts with the fear of never seeing your beautiful smile again, or never feeling the warm touch of your hands on me again. The two years that I waited...." He shook his head as raw emotion took his voice away.

"I'm not the one who got shot," she playfully reminded him before her expression became serious. "The timing wasn't right. I wasn't ready to accept you. Things always work out for the best, even when it doesn't seem like it at the time. My mom told me that a long time ago. Sometimes it is hard to believe, but things happen for a reason. We have a lot to live for," she quietly reflected.

"Yes, we do," he agreed.

"If the guys aren't going to be back for a while, I'd just like to spend time with you," she said, biting her lip.

"Are you asking me out on a date?" he asked with a raised eyebrow.

She tilted her head and studied his face for a second before she slowly nodded. "Yeah, I guess I am," she said in a thoughtful voice.

He bent his head down and brushed a kiss across her lips. "I would love to," he murmured.

She slipped her hand into his and turned around. He looked around the canyon. It might not have been what he planned, but did it really matter where they were as long as they were there together?

"So, I've never actually asked anyone to go on a date before. What exactly are we supposed to do?" she suddenly asked.

"I have no idea. I guess whatever we want," he laughed.

Walking backwards, she looked up at him and grinned. "Do you want to take a look at RITA2 and DAR's programming? I found this thread of code that will blow your mind," she suggested with a hopeful expression.

"I can't wait," he chuckled.

Studying the AIs' computer code wasn't exactly what he had in mind, though. He wrapped his arm around her and turned her back toward the ship. Her excited monologue about the code captured his attention and made him realize that one thing was for certain—life would never be boring with his little computer hacker.

∽

Nearly a mile away, a lone figure staggered to the Juangan fighter— a glowing sword gripped in his bloody claw. Colonel Tusk approached the fighter with care. He gazed out at the vast landscape, searching for the occupant who had abandoned the spacecraft.

He knelt on one knee in the sand and ran a claw over the outline of a boot. He looked up and sneered in triumph. His rumbling snarl was swept away on the wind. He painfully ran his hand over his face to clear his blurred vision. His skin had been scrubbed raw by the blowing sand. Dark blue blood from the gash on his head dripped down his face, mixing with the sand and coating his hand with a sticky ooze.

Rising to his feet, he ignored the pain pulsing through his body. He had survived the crash, only to come close to dying in the sandstorm. His thirst for revenge was what had kept him going. He gazed at the sky where the flashes of burning debris were still visible.

It was time for a change. The Juangans needed a leader who would unite them against a common enemy. His rage hardened into cold determination. It was time for a new regime to control the galaxies. A war was coming, and he was going to lead it. It was time to show the Prime that they were no longer the strongest species in the galaxy.

Staggering over to the fighter, he climbed inside. Sealing the door, he grabbed a medical kit on his way to the cockpit. Minutes later, he was leaving the atmosphere, his ship passing through the floating graveyard of his father's Command ship.

"I will personally rip the heart out of Teriff 'Tag Krell Manok's chest and eat it, but not before I kill every one of his offspring and their mates," he snarled.

He looked at the screen when the sensor alerted him to the approach of several large warships. Programming his destination into the computer, he made the jump to light speed as they appeared on the far side of the planet. Soon it would be his warship moving freely through the galaxy, he silently vowed as the ship's velocity forced him back against the seat.

# EPILOGUE

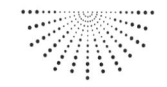

**Two weeks later:**
**Baade Council Room**

"Quiet down! We have a lot to discuss today, not the least of which are the dangers presented by the Juangans," Teriff shouted above the roar of voices.

The room became ominously quiet. Derik sat beside Amelia. He could feel her hands trembling. He knew she wasn't afraid. If anything, she was furious enough to compete with his father at the moment.

"It's not funny," she hissed under her breath.

He looked at her with an innocent expression. "I'm not laughing," he defended.

She scowled at him before turning to face the front again when Teriff slapped his hand on the table. Derik squeezed her hand under the table in comfort. It was true, he wasn't laughing—out loud.

In the two weeks since they had returned to Baade, all hell had broken loose—if you knew what he meant, as Bert would say. Amelia's mother had proved more resilient and enterprising than the Council had expected. She had somehow managed to open a Gateway and slip through it. Unfortunately, the doorway had not been to Earth. Rav had found out, and instead of telling the other Council members what had happened, he'd taken it upon himself to go after Anne.

If that wasn't enough, Hendrik had vanished as well. Now, RITA2 and DAR sat next to their young replications, Darian and Rena, who currently resembled the epitome of two bored, and slightly mutinous, teenagers. Turning his attention to RITA2, Derik found it hard to imagine any parent looking more cross and nervous at the same time as the elegantly dressed AI computer sitting at the far end of the table.

"Where is my mother?" Runt demanded.

Teriff shot her a pained expression. "We are working on that," he grunted in a low voice.

"Work harder," she snapped.

"I'm so sorry, Amelia. Darian and Rena were just trying to help," RITA2 began.

"Don't blame me!" Darian interjected. "This was all Rena's fault. She was the one playing with the Gateway software."

Rena angrily turned to her brother. "Yeah, well, who opened it the second time?" she retorted.

"Hey, don't blame me. I'm still in the adaptive learning mode. If Dad hadn't posted that glowing code with the keywords 'Stay Out!', I never would have messed with it. That is like trying to keep Aunty Tink's vidcom that tells the warriors what a blow..." Darian defended

"Enough or I'll dismantle you two myself!" Teriff threatened with a warning look.

Rena rolled her green eyes. "I'd like to see you try," she mumbled.

"Rena," DAR sternly admonished.

She looked at her father with glistening eyes. "What? You always blame us! It isn't our fault that we're inquisitive. It's the way we were replicated," she sniffed before she disappeared.

Darian raised his hands. "I'm just a product of my programming," he said before he vanished as well.

RITA2 looked at Teriff with an apologetic expression. "DAR and I are going through their memory storage. Even if anything was deleted, we should still be able to access it. It may take a while. Both are having growing issues. I think they need more space," she said.

Teriff threaded his fingers through his hair. "You work on finding out where Rav and Anne are, and shut down access to the Gateway for those two kids of yours. I don't want anything else happening," he ordered.

"Already done," she said with a relieved smile.

Teriff turned to DAR. "I want you to find out what in the hell the Juangans are up to. There are reports from some of the fleet that a new leader has taken over the Juangan forces. I want to know who it is and what they are up to. They are becoming more brazen in their attacks, and I want it stopped now," he instructed.

"Yes, sir," DAR said.

RITA2 and DAR looked at each other with a relieved expression before they faded away to complete their assignments. Derik waited for his father to continue. The other members of the Council appeared to be waiting as well.

"What about Hendrik?" Brawn asked.

Teriff sank down into his chair. "He'll recover. At least we know where he is. Cosmos woke me this morning yelling about how he wanted some kind of warning before we sent any warriors through. It seems that the human woman called Trudy shoots first and asks who it is later," he replied with a grin.

"Serves Hendrik right," Brawn snickered.

Teriff grudgingly nodded. "I've ordered support for the residents on the planet side of Quadrule Five. Reports indicate the moon itself was not attacked; the Juangans were focused on destroying the communication satellites first. Quadrule Five is a strategic location due to its position near the edge of where we know the Juangans roam. The Juangans have always avoided attacking such an ambitious target in the past, but under this new leadership, that has clearly changed. I suggest that we move to yellow alert until we confirm that this is an isolated incident," he finished.

"I agree. The attack felt different from previous ones," Derik said, looking around the table.

"It was my understanding that the Command ship and all of the Juangan crew were eliminated," Brawn said.

Derik nodded. "They were, but I'm telling you, there was something different about this attack. As Father stated, the Juangans don't attack settlements. They usually focus on smaller, easier targets like merchant and cargo freighters," he argued.

Brawn nodded. "I agree, then. Yellow alert until we have more information," he conceded.

"What about my uncle—and Marcelo? Have you decided what you are going to do to them? They helped us, you know," Runt suddenly asked.

Teriff waved his hand. "They are to be returned to Earth under strict supervision," he stated.

"What kind of supervision?" Runt asked suspiciously.

"RITA and FRED are handling it," Teriff gruffly asserted. "If there isn't anything else, this meeting is adjourned. I'll inform your brothers of what was discussed. It is Tilly and Angus' anniversary, and there will be a party for them. Tresa warned me that I better not be late," Teriff added, standing up.

∽

"Do you really think that she is okay?" Runt wondered as they walked along the corridor back to their quarters.

Derik knew Amelia was asking about her mother.

He gripped her hand. "Yes. She knows how to take care of herself. She has proven that many times. Plus, Rav went after her. If nothing else, trying to keep him from getting himself killed will keep her on her toes," he joked in a light-hearted voice.

She nodded. "That's true. You guys seem to have a knack for getting shot. Look at Hendrik," she agreed.

He stopped and pulled her around until she faced him. In the last two weeks, there had been one distraction after another. Last night, he'd finally had a chance to contact Angus Bell. He had wanted a human male's perspective on what he should do next. Angus had suggested that since Amelia wasn't interested in a big wedding and they were technically already married according to his people, Derik might want to take her on a special trip called a Honeymoon.

"I was thinking that we could try to go away again—this time someplace a little closer," he said.

"Hmm. I'm not so sure. *Is* there a place where we won't be shot at?" she asked.

He chuckled. "Yes, I know the perfect place. Do you like the beach?" he asked.

She looked at him in surprise, then her expression became thoughtful. "You know, I don't know. I've never been," she confessed.

"I think you'll love it," he said, squeezing her hand. "I'll even show you how to fly the shuttle on the way there."

Her eyes lit up with delight before she bit her lip. "I don't know how to swim. I don't even have a bathing suit," she fretted.

"I'll teach you—and where we're going, you won't need to wear anything," he promised.

"Oh—okay. When do we leave?" she asked with a growing smile.

"Right now," he chuckled.

Still holding hands, they took off running down the corridor. Several warriors stepped to the side, giving them plenty of room when they saw them. Derik understood their envious expressions and could sympathize with them now that he knew what he had almost missed.

He had never expected to be gifted with a bond mate. At seventeen, he'd thought his life was about to end. Instead, a beautiful goddess wielding a hammer had given him a chance to reap the rewards of the ultimate gift from the Goddess—a mate with a brilliant spirit who made his life an amazing adventure every day.

"Derik, I forgot to tell you something," she breathlessly laughed as they neared the exit.

He slowed down and paused at the door. "Yes?" he asked.

She took in a deep breath, shook her head, and stepped closer to him. Rising up on her toes, she held his shoulders and looked him in the eye. He touched her cheek when he saw the slight sheen of tears in her eyes.

"What is it?" he worried.

"I wanted… I just wanted to tell you that I love you," she murmured before she brushed a soft kiss across his lips.

He looked at her with a tender expression and brushed his hand along her flushed cheek. "I know," he softly replied. "I've always known, my beautiful Amelia."

To Be Continued… **Rav's Warrior Woman:**
Cosmos' Gateway Book 8

Can two souls from different worlds maintain a temporary truce long enough to discover where they have unwittingly been sent through the Gateway? Their very survival may depend on it!

*Coming soon.*

In the meantime, there are other series!
S.E. Smith recommends this standalone romance
from the Dragon Lords of Valdier series:

**Twin Dragons' Destiny**
*USA Today Bestseller!*

Twin dragons have been feared above all other dragon-shifters because of Barrack and Brogan, the original twin dragons, who became murderously insane. Their new story begins with their death.

. . .

Delilah Rosewater is haunted by dreams of her death. They feel so real, and her waking life is plagued by the feeling that time is running out for her. As she searches for the one person she thinks could understand, she is shocked to instead come face-to-face with two irritating men who claim to be from another world!

Check out the full book here: books2read.com/twindragonsdestiny

# ADDITIONAL BOOKS

If you loved this story by me (S.E. Smith) please leave a review! You can discover additional books at: http://sesmithfl.com and http://sesmithya.com or find your favorite way to keep in touch here: https://sesmithfl.com/contact-me/ Be sure to sign up for my newsletter to hear about new releases!

**Recommended Reading Order Lists:**
http://sesmithfl.com/reading-list-by-events/
http://sesmithfl.com/reading-list-by-series/

**The Series**

**Science Fiction / Romance**

Dragon Lords of Valdier Series
*It all started with a king who crashed on Earth, desperately hurt. He inadvertently discovered a species that would save his own.*

Curizan Warrior Series
*The Curizans have a secret, kept even from their closest allies, but even they*

are not immune to the draw of a little known species from an isolated planet called Earth.

## Marastin Dow Warriors Series
*The Marastin Dow are reviled and feared for their ruthlessness, but not all want to live a life of murder. Some wait for just the right time to escape....*

## Sarafin Warriors Series
*A hilariously ridiculous human family who happen to be quite formidable... and a secret hidden on Earth. The origin of the Sarafin species is more than it seems. Those cat-shifting aliens won't know what hit them!*

## Dragonlings of Valdier Novellas
*The Valdier, Sarafin, and Curizan Lords had children who just cannot stop getting into trouble! There is nothing as cute or funny as magical, shapeshifting kids, and nothing as heartwarming as family.*

## Cosmos' Gateway Series
*Cosmos created a portal between his lab and the warriors of Prime. Discover new worlds, new species, and outrageous adventures as secrets are unravelled and bridges are crossed.*

## The Alliance Series
*When Earth received its first visitors from space, the planet was thrown into a panicked chaos. The Trivators came to bring Earth into the Alliance of Star Systems, but now they must take control to prevent the humans from destroying themselves. No one was prepared for how the humans will affect the Trivators, though, starting with a family of three sisters....*

## Lords of Kassis Series
*It began with a random abduction and a stowaway, and yet, somehow, the Kassisans knew the humans were coming long before now. The fate of more than one world hangs in the balance, and time is not always linear....*

## Zion Warriors Series

*Time travel, epic heroics, and love beyond measure. Sci-fi adventures with heart and soul, laughter, and awe-inspiring discovery...*

**Paranormal / Fantasy / Romance**

Magic, New Mexico Series
*Within New Mexico is a small town named Magic, an... unusual town, to say the least. With no beginning and no end, spanning genres, authors, and universes, hilarity and drama combine to keep you on the edge of your seat!*

Spirit Pass Series
*There is a physical connection between two times. Follow the stories of those who travel back and forth. These westerns are as wild as they come!*

Second Chance Series
*Stand-alone worlds featuring a woman who remembers her own death. Fiery and mysterious, these books will steal your heart.*

More Than Human Series
*Long ago there was a war on Earth between shifters and humans. Humans lost, and today they know they will become extinct if something is not done....*

The Fairy Tale Series
*A twist on your favorite fairy tales!*

A Seven Kingdoms Tale
*Long ago, a strange entity came to the Seven Kingdoms to conquer and feed on their life force. It found a host, and she battled it within her body for centuries while destruction and devastation surrounded her. Our story begins when the end is near, and a portal is opened....*

**Epic Science Fiction / Action Adventure**

Project Gliese 581G Series
*An international team leave Earth to investigate a mysterious object in our*

solar system that was clearly made by <u>someone</u>, someone who isn't from Earth. Discover new worlds and conflicts in a sci-fi adventure sure to become your favorite!

**New Adult / Young Adult**

<u>Breaking Free Series</u>
*A journey that will challenge everything she has ever believed about herself as danger reveals itself in sudden, heart-stopping moments.*

<u>The Dust Series</u>
*Fragments of a comet hit Earth, and Dust wakes to discover the world as he knew it is gone. It isn't the only thing that has changed, though, so has Dust...*

# ABOUT THE AUTHOR

S.E. Smith is an *internationally acclaimed*, *New York Times* **and** *USA TODAY Bestselling* author of science fiction, romance, fantasy, paranormal, and contemporary works for adults, young adults, and children. She enjoys writing a wide variety of genres that pull her readers into worlds that take them away.

Printed in Great Britain
by Amazon